DAW Books presents
the novels of Rachel Atwood

WALK THE WILD WITH ME
OUTCASTS OF THE WILDWOOD

Outcasts
of the
Wildwood

Rachel Atwood

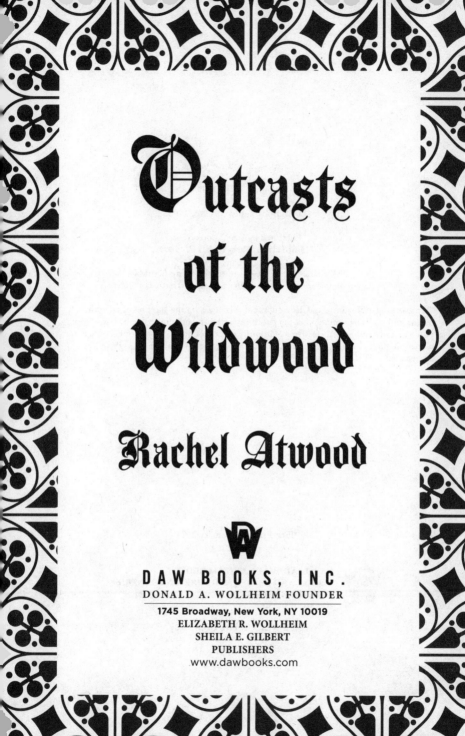

DAW BOOKS, INC.
DONALD A. WOLLHEIM FOUNDER

1745 Broadway, New York, NY 10019
ELIZABETH R. WOLLHEIM
SHEILA E. GILBERT
PUBLISHERS
www.dawbooks.com

First Printing, January 2021
1st Printing

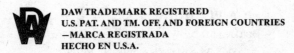

DAW TRADEMARK REGISTERED
U.S. PAT. AND TM. OFF. AND FOREIGN COUNTRIES
—MARCA REGISTRADA
HECHO EN U.S.A.

PRINTED IN THE U.S.A.

To all of the foresters and fire fighters who put their lives on the line to protect our forests and the homes of all the wildlife.

Acknowledgments

Over the many years, and several pen names, of my career, the one constant has been Sheila Gilbert, my editor and publisher at DAW Books. Thank you for being my friend as well as colleague.

Prologue

Anno Domini 1208 in the Royal Forest of Sherwood, ninth year of the reign of King John. The autumnal equinox.

 "The time has come for me to pass the authority of the Green Man to the heir of *my* choosing," Little John announced, making certain his voice carried to the circle of human and fae friends who had come to observe this rare ritual.

He took his place at the center of the triad of standing stones. Dawn had just begun to brighten the day on the autumnal equinox. The gravestone where the first Earl of Locksley had been buried seven generations before had become their altar. It stood between John and two of his sons.

They faced him, each strong and resolute. Both sons had his oak-brown hair and beard. Their eyes took on hints of red or yellow, depending upon their surroundings and the direction of the sun.

Derwyn, the eldest of all his offspring, near reached John in height, but not yet his breadth. He still had some growing to do over the next three hundred years. He also needed to learn to restrain his temper and spread his tolerance to include the humans and the fae who shared the forest with the animal life that found shelter and sustenance here.

That temper had worsened over the past few years. And his patience had diminished.

Verne, only a decade younger than Derwyn, promised to overreach John's height and breadth. He had demonstrated both compassion and diplomacy among the denizens of the forest. Listening to both sides of an argument among the Wild Folk was a natural talent for him, rather than learned wisdom. He seemed to have grown into a useful mediator. His oldest brother had not.

Unlike many of the Wild Folk, Little John had included his children in his daily life within the forest. There was too much at stake to neglect them.

Both sons stepped forward, expectation written on their faces and in their posture.

Tradition dictated that the eldest son should succeed the father. Not so different from the human laws.

However. . . .

Human politics had showed how sometimes the eldest son was not always the best candidate to lead. The old way among the Saxon tribes had few inheritance laws. The Jarls, or noblemen, elected the best candidate rather than the oldest son of their previous leader.

King John had seized his crown based upon a similar theory. At the time, John, an adult who had sired children, seemed a better candidate than his stripling nephew, Arthur, who had never lived in England and was easily led by the

French king. Prince Arthur, like his uncle, King Richard the Lionhearted, loved war too much and women too little.

Ten years into John's reign, he had alienated half his nobles, nearly all of the reigning kings across the Channel, and the head of their Church.

"Once our ritual is complete," Little John continued, even though all he wanted to do was retreat to his tree for a few months, "my heir must return to his tree form for a minimum of a year, four full seasons. On this autumnal equinox, today, the year of spreading roots through every furlong of Sherwood Forest will begin. Only when that process is complete, may you emerge from your tree form to walk among your subjects."

During that year, John would continue as the Green Man, with ever-decreasing magic, and gradually withdraw his involvement in the everyday life of the forest to spend his time loving Jane, and perhaps fathering human children with her.

Little John paused, stretching his stiff fingers that had curled in on themselves. Jane, his beloved Jane, had soothed his nervousness with her gentle words and encouragement. His eyes found her in the crowd of onlookers. Never one to draw attention to herself, she half-hid behind his old friend Father Tuck and his protégé Nick. One tiny smile from Jane gave him the courage to do what he must.

"The dryad who replaces me must have the skills of both a diplomat and a warrior, of a priest and a judge. The word of the Green Man is the law of the forest. The lives of all those who find shelter and sustenance within the bounds of this wood are subject to the Green Man's law."

Derwyn's eyes opened wide, and his mouth turned down

in a frown. Twigs began forming within his hair and beard in preparation for returning to his tree form, a tall sturdy oak.

A shadow of sadness overlay John's determination. He loved all of his children. Why had Derwyn grown away from the traits required of the next Green Man?

"The son I must deny the right to become the Green Man will lose his dryad affinity for the forest. He must henceforth walk among men as a man without the comfort of his tree form. He must dwell with humans outside Sherwood Forest."

Derwyn took another step forward, a deep frown drawing his face into a thickening mask of furrows.

Robin Goodfellow bounded into the circle and kicked Derwyn in the shins. His shrunken, gnomelike fae persona could hardly penetrate Derwyn's hide any more than an annoying gnat on a hot summer's day.

Derwyn ignored him.

But he stepped away from Blaidd, the fae father and protector of all the wolves of the forest. He bared his fangs briefly, then continued to circle the area, keeping everyone in their designated place.

Robin drew one of his arrows from a bark quiver and jabbed Derwyn with the broad flint point.

Derwyn jerked, losing all vestiges of his tree.

Little John turned his attention to Verne. "The demands placed upon the Green Man require more than size or power. My second son, Llwyf, a gentle, straightforward man, is half elm and therefore ineligible to become the Green Man. I choose instead, Verne, my third son, as the one most likely to succeed. Step forward, Verne of the Greenwood."

Derwyn took three steps forward to Verne's two shorter strides. "You can't!" he said, loudly enough to be heard at distant Locksley Abbey.

"The Green Man does not roar except in grief when the king's foresters cut down a tree prematurely," Robin Good-fellow sneered even as he stretched into his normal body of a handsome lordling wearing Lincoln green with a strung bow and an arrow already nocked. "I have an iron broadpoint on this barb, Derwyn. I will pierce your hide with it and watch you writhe in agony as you burn beneath your skin." Robin raised his aim toward his target's heart. With only a few feet separating them, the arrow, one crafted and blessed by Little John himself, would penetrate deeply enough to cause serious harm. Perhaps death.

Derwyn backed off, an ugly snarl on his normally hand-some face.

Blaidd the wolf-king, sprawled on the ground between Derwyn and his brother, looking more like a bored dog than a fierce protector.

Verne took another step forward and knelt at the altar stone.

John placed his hands on his youngest son's head. His mind turned inward toward the store of ancient lore that resided in his heart.

With a deep breath and closed eyes, he willed that treasure to flow upward and out of his mouth in an ancient language so old and little understood that even he never used it.

The words came slowly at first, then faster and faster as everything John had learned, the knowledge of his father, his grandfather, and fifteen grandfathers before flooded out of him and filled Verne.

The boy gulped, his throat apple bobbing nervously. Then he looked up with eyes glazed in wonder. He stumbled to his feet, never dislodging his father's grip. When he stood tall and strong with his balance firm, his hands reached up to grasp John's temples.

He took over the task of reciting the lore in an enchanting rhythm that took on the cadence of a hymn of glory and awe.

His feet stretched and sprouted roots. Branches and leaves twisted through his hair and beard. His skin took on the texture of thick bark.

Other voices joined him: Herne the Huntsman, Ardenia the water sprite, Will Scarlett the red bird messenger, the dryads and sylphs, nymphs and trolls, and all the others, lifted their voices in a song as old as time. Only the humans remained silent, not being a part of the forest magic.

But Father Tuck and Nick mouthed the words in a half-remembered litany of joy. Forest blood ran thin in them but surged upward with the ritual.

The magic of the moment spread to include them and Jane, but left Derwyn and the other humans in a pocket of normality.

The knowledge and awareness of the lands of Sherwood withdrew from John.

A bubble of panic pressed on his throat. He was losing the best part of himself.

Easy, silly boy, Elena, the goddess of crossroads, cemeteries, and sorcery, giggled at him. She lived in a little three-faced cup that young Nick carried in his sleeve. *Rest easy. You are more than the Green Man. So very much more. And now you can fully live the other parts of your life with Jane. Let go of the Green Man and live fully as John.*

John breathed deeply, filling his body with precious air. A second breath and he knew that Elena had the right of it.

The far reaches of Sherwood Forest faded first from his awareness, then more and more pulled away from all directions. His rootlets shriveled. And then they exposed a subterranean void he had not observed before; a void that should not be beneath a knoll that overlooked ruined Locksley Castle. He made note of it and continued to pull his roots closer and closer to him.

Vacant numbness filled his head. He fell to his knees and his hands dropped to his sides, his position with Verne fully reversed.

The land rippled and shook, knocking the watching people to their knees. The smallest of the triad of standing stones tilted and then righted again. A tremendous groan reverberated around the clearing, deafening John. But he couldn't move his hands to cover his ears.

Blackness encroached upon his peripheral vision. "Such emptiness," he gasped. His entire being had shrunk to just his physical body, devoid of the forest. "I'm alone. So utterly alone."

Verne staggered backward, hands clutching his own temples as he tried to contain and absorb the new knowledge. Unknowingly, he rooted himself to the center of the clearing, the heart of the forest. As he stretched and grew into a stalwart

oak of middling height and breadth, all those around him
grew silent with respectful awe.

Blaidd shifted until he sat attentively by the feet of his new
master.

Only Derwyn frowned and sneered.

John remembered that same moment in his own life almost four hundred years ago. And now he was empty and
alone.

"You are not alone, my beloved. I am with you always,"
Jane whispered, kneeling beside him. "You are mortal now.
We are together for the rest of our lives."

You have given much to the forest, my boy, Elena said. *The time
has come to allow the forest to give back to you. Love your Jane. Cher-
ish her as you cherished Sherwood.*

One

Anno Domini 1209,
the tenth year of King John's reign. Late March.

ick deftly wielded his belt knife to carefully cut a withered turnip into two neat halves. Satisfied with the equality of the pieces, he handed one piece to Hilde, the girl from the convent who'd rescued herself from cruel punishments. They both wore monastic robes, his dark gray, hers closer to black, the only garments they owned. She'd kept hers when she left Our Lady of Sorrows. His had been new from Locksley Abbey at Yule.

Nick edged a little closer to her on the thick branch of a sprawling maple tree just coming into leaf. The warmth of her thigh so close to his own sent tingles up and down his body, settling in his mid-region.

"Does anyone travel the Royal Road anymore?" he asked, peering down to the right and left along the dirt track that needed grading before a noble carriage could pass without breaking an axle.

"Not unless they are on royal business," Hilde replied. She cocked her head as if listening to distant thunder.

"People on royal business either carry a fat purse that needs lightening, or they carry a royal warrant for the arrest of the leaders of the Woodwose." Nick touched the little silver cup hidden within his sleeve, hoping that Elena, the goddess of crossroads, cemeteries, and sorcery, would awaken and guide him. She'd slept all winter but had not deserted him. Her presence comforted him that she'd be with him when he needed her. For now.

"Do you have any more food with you?" Hilde asked, returning her attention to him.

"I found two hunks of bread in the abbey larder." He reached into his sleeve to retrieve them. His fingertips brushed Elena's three-faced cup again.

He felt her stir, as if she rolled over in her sleep and dismissed the disturbance. She'd been like that most of the winter, and it worried him. Maybe he was no longer worthy of her attention, and he should replace her behind the ancient pagan altar in the abbey crypt.

Normally, he'd gobble all of the provisions he'd purloined from the abbey kitchen. However, sharing the food as well as the watch duty with Hilde made it all taste better. On this fine spring day, with a gentle breeze and no rain, he wanted for nothing more.

Except he'd left illuminating a capital C on a manuscript less than half done. How to finish the twining vines and flowers eluded him. A piece of his mind chewed on the problem while he shared the watch and his meal with Hilde.

She examined the dry bread for evidence of mold. Finding none, she closed her eyes and bit off a small corner of the hunk. Nick watched with fascination as she chewed the bread carefully and eventually swallowed it. She sighed deeply with satisfaction and took another bite, making the bread last a long time.

"I haven't had so much bread to call my own in . . . I don't remember how long." She drew in a long breath of satisfaction and dropped her head to Nick's shoulder in easy camaraderie.

The intimacy of her gesture startled Nick so much he nearly fell from their perch. He had to grab a skinny branch that jutted out from an adjacent stout limb for balance. Smiling to himself, he let his free arm creep around Hilde's waist. She didn't jerk away or slap his hand as she should.

"What happened last equinox, Nick?" she asked. "The forest hasn't felt the same since. It's quieter. The birds do not sing as brightly, nor do the frogs croak so loudly. Even the wind does not talk to the tree canopy as it should."

"Were you there, by the standing stones during the ritual?" He hadn't noticed anything but the ceremony whereby his friend Little John passed his authority to one of his sons.

"In the back. Behind a smaller oak. The Church says we aren't supposed to think of trees as living beings, but the one who hid me felt feminine and happy."

Nick sorted through the folklore he'd heard and read during his time in the Locksley Abbey scriptorium. Two years he'd been allowed to draw flowing designs around the enlarged first letter of a chapter. Two years in which he read every word of every scroll he could find.

"She's a dryad, perhaps Verne's mother. I guess she was very proud of her boy, though dryads rarely interact with their offspring. Little John's sons are special because he took the time and trouble to nurture them and bring them into the human community when he could. He took his duty as the Green Man very seriously and wanted to train his successor."

"That's sad," Hilde said, sitting up straighter. "To have a mother and know who she is but not have her care about you."

Cold invaded Nick on that side. He didn't dare pull her back. Her own mother had sold her and her twin brother to the Church because, when widowed, she had no way of supporting her five children. The man willing to marry her could only afford to take on the three youngest children and apprentice them. Hilde knew how to find her mother in Nottingham, but also knew she would not be welcome, especially since she now brought the taint of outlawry with her.

"So, what really happened in the clearing, aside from singing strange hymns in a foreign language?" Hilde asked, breaking away from her inner sadness. "I couldn't hear everything Little John said, but it must have been important for the ceremony to take place by the standing stones. The Wild Folk consider them like a church. An important cathedral."

"It was a ritual few mortals witness. Father Tuck said he never thought he'd live long enough to see the passing of power from one great forest lord to his heir. Tuck's an old man and Little John is considered young among his kind. He should be strong and vigorous for another century or two before he begins a long and slow decline. You and I are not likely to live that long, let alone Father Tuck. He's in his seventies, at least."

"But Little John fell in love with a mortal and his need to stay with her overwhelmed his duty to the forest," Hilde sighed. She held his gaze for a long moment, then looked away toward the road.

Nick had spent far too much time this last winter thinking about Hilde, the sister of his deceased best friend, Dom. She hid in the forest with the Woodwose, those who lived illegally within the royal preserve. Sometimes he thought that living wild was more comfortable than his dormitory room in the abbey. Stone walls sheltered him against wind and rain, but confined him to the same strictly defined and cramped space. The wild gave him broad vistas and infinite possibilities.

He often wondered if he could make a match with her. More important, should he? His body thought they would deal well together—and then guilt flooded him because he was destined to be a monk or a priest and would never know a woman. But he could think of no better way to honor Dom than to marry and thus protect Hilde from a harsh world. He also had a duty and love for the abbey and his life there illuminating manuscripts with tiny drawings of the forest creatures peeking out from entwined vines and other flourishes. And learning new things. The abbey library offered him glimpses of other lands and peoples. In the abbey, he could learn the answers to many of his questions or dream of other ways to satisfy his immense curiosity.

He wavered between his choices every night.

Making a decision must wait for both of them. Thirteen winters had brought both of them to the brink of adulthood; the brink only.

"Little John has heirs. He ruled for over three hundred years and guided the Wild Folk through many changes and dangers. He has earned his rest and his right to mortality," Nick said, envying his friend.

"Father Tuck has forest blood within him. Did you know that, Nick?"

"Yes."

A long moment passed between them.

"How do you know?" Hilde pressed for an answer—as he knew she would.

"He is my great-grandsire."

The distance between them grew, more than just the inches between his shoulder and hers.

"Tuck is as far removed from Herne the Huntsman as I am from him. The forest runs thin in us. It has granted us good health, and he has lived longer than most men. Even men who have good food, shelter, and healers close by."

"But . . . but he's just a mendicant priest wandering the wildwood. He sleeps on the ground every night and eats the poor rations we Woodwose can cobble together."

"He is more. Much, much more, but he cannot go home to the abbey while King John and the Holy Father refuse to compromise."

"Only the senior clergy were exiled by King John!" Hilde gasped.

Nick remained silent. Not everyone could keep a secret as well as he did. Hilde might whisper a small truth to a friend. The friend would want to feel important and thus pass that special bit of knowledge to the blacksmith or the miller. He would then whisper the secret to a resident of Nottingham in return for an advantage in a trade. That person must tell the guard at the gate in order to slip in or out of the city after hours, and thus the guard would report to the sheriff. "Father Tuck is no safer in his own abbey than he is with the Wood-wose."

"When I lived at the convent, the sisters spoke of an Abbot Mæson who had escorted the Reverend Mother to Paris." She looked at him with wide eyes and a pout of innocence.

"A man with forest blood cannot leave England for long. The foreign land would kill him." Nick wanted to trust Hilde with this secret. Their friendship had begun with trust. But trust was a fragile thing that had to be constantly renewed to stay strong.

She was bright. She'd figure it out.

"He may have forest blood, but he is still human, an old man, and he felt the cold and damp more than usual this past winter," Hilde said. "Spring warms the land; the days grow longer and the sun brighter. The Woodwose left their winter cave weeks ago. He lingers in his hermitage cavern with his warm fire and protection from the wind. He needs to return to the abbey before the elements rob him of strength and judgment."

Nick's mouth watered at the thought of his next meal in

the refectory come sunset: hot soup, a piece of dried fruit, a slice of bread, and a cup of watered ale.

"I miss him at the abbey, Hilde. Prefect Andrew and Father Blaine do not have his experience and wisdom. They act like they are only pretending to lead us until he comes home."

"Could Father Tuck return in disguise and whisper advice to them from the shadows?" Hilde asked.

"I'm afraid that will not happen soon. Prefect Andrew knows how to find him in time of need. Father Blaine will not look for him even if he knows that he needs to."

"If you suggest to him to seek shelter within the abbey, he might come." Nick urged Hilde to speak for him. "I know his joints ache, and he stumbles more often in the cold than during summer. I have Brother Luke's notes on healing herbs. I can try different salves and infusions to help him. Brother Daffyd knows more about healing than I do. He'll help." Nick's enthusiasm for the plan grew.

"Can you hide him so that those who do not need to know who he is and where he is will keep the secret?"

"If you convince him to dress as a mendicant friar with a vow of silence between dawn and dusk, he could remain unnoticed. I'll hide him in the orphans' dormitory." He had to pause and gulp before speaking again. "Dom . . . Dom's cot is still empty."

She turned her head away, mourning again the loss of her brother, her twin.

"Mourning is normal, Hilde. We've both lost too many people in our short lives." Nick dashed away a single tear, hoping Hilde wouldn't notice. "You are my friend now. I'd never have met you if Dom had lived."

"Aye, there's that."

"You said the forest does not seem the same since the ritual," Nick had to change the subject before they both ended up sobbing uncontrollably, and not keeping watch over the crossroads as they must.

He noticed Blaidd and his wolf lieutenants prowling the fringes of the crossroads, much more diligent than he.

"Perhaps Sherwood feels the loss of one Green Man and the new one hasn't had time yet to make contact with all of his subjects, or fully establish his awareness of every life, each blade of grass, and grain of dirt. The land knows its loss. Maybe the forest is holding its breath waiting," Nick said. He took a moment to savor another tiny bite of the hard bread.

"Magic?" Hilde asked. She clutched her dark robe at the throat where she wore a hand-carved talisman of protection. "I saw Faery magic last summer, but it was . . . isolated, didn't touch normal people."

"Magic is all about us if we only look and believe," Nick tried to explain. He touched Elena's pitcher again and felt it warm to his touch. "The Church teaches that magic doesn't exist, but we have to be on guard against traps of evil that look like magic. The Church is gone from England now. For a time. There is no one to tell us not to look for dryads and gnomes and water sprites and all the other Wild Folk. They have always been here. We just couldn't see them even when we did see them."

"I know. It's . . . it's just hard to believe what I see every day after a lifetime of being told otherwise."

Nick swallowed his own excitement for finally having met the strangers in the forest who had become friends. It had started last May Day and grew every time he visited the forest. "For the next half year, until Verne can emerge from his tree, the forest will not be safe for anyone. Father Tuck is even more vulnerable because of his age. Please, can you convince him to come back to the abbey?"

"I'll do my best when he comes among us again. I will urge him to return home before the first frost shrivels the oak leaves and sends the badgers to sleep in their dens. I'll remind him that the abbey is the only place where he can warm his bones."

A hunting horn broke the silence of the forest. All within, birds and badgers, deer and mice, paused in silence, deciding how best to protect themselves from invaders.

Blaidd lifted his snout and sniffed. He laid back his ears and scuttled into the undergrowth. His pack followed suit. But Nick knew they observed silently hidden amongst the foliage.

"'Tis late in the day for the sheriff's men to begin a hunt," Nick muttered. "'Tis almost Sext." The abbey bells no longer rang the changes of the day, but Nick's growing body knew how long since he'd broken his nighttime fast, at Prime, and how many more hours he'd have to endure before he could eat again. The purloined turnip and bread would not fill him for long.

"Why blow a hunting horn if not hunting?" She leaned

forward to get a better look, keeping one hand on the tree trunk and the other on Nick's shoulder.

"That horn does not sound like the hunt is on. It is more a warning that important people travel the Royal Road through Sherwood," Nick said. He pulled up his feet and hugged his knees to make himself less visible from below.

Hilde sniffed, then wrinkled her nose in distaste. "I do not like this incursion."

Nick grabbed a branch for balance and leaned forward, peering through the new leaves.

"They're stopping at the crossroads and dismounting," Hilde whispered.

"Who?" Nick asked on equally hushed tones.

"Sir Philip Marc and three others dressed too fine to be anything but barons or knights. Battle swords ride their hips."

Nothing ceremonial about the men, Nick noted. The French mercenaries who had befriended and remained loyal to King John wore leather and chain mail as if prepared for a skirmish. Peasants didn't have that luxury.

Robin Goodfellow often led the outlaws in ambushes, without even leather armor, to free the sheriff and his guests of their silver pennies.

"Anyone else?" Hilde squinted, then she too drew up her dangling legs, making her silhouette smaller.

"A hunched man, rudely dressed, follows them on foot. He carries an ax. A woodsman's ax, too heavy and long-handled for battle." Nick's heart beat faster, and his breaths came short and shallow. "I think we have a problem."

"I do not like this." Hilde clung to the tree trunk. "Time for you to go home to the abbey. I must warn the others." She shimmied down the tree trunk to the ground on the opposite side from the road. She quickly disappeared into the greenery, one shadow among many, as she hurried toward the Wood-wose encampment.

Two

uck stretched and yawned as he shrugged off the last of the winter sleepiness. Only then did he step outside the entrance to his snug cave. With a little fire beside his bedroll and a fresh spring bubbling up from a secluded niche, he had endured the cold winter better than previous years when he slept rough with the Woodwose.

This winter, his outlawed friends had found a cave adjacent to his own for their winter sojourn. That cave was now empty and his informant, Blaidd, the father of the wolves, told him that last autumn's enclave near Ardenia's pond was fully occupied.

Sheltered by the cave, he had slept longer and deeper than during the decades of monastic life when the bells summoned him to Mass seven times a day.

He missed the bells.

He didn't miss having his sleep interrupted at midnight for

Vespers and then in the deepest darkest hours of the night for Lauds, only to rise for the day at dawn, Prime. He had a duty then to attend or preside over seven Masses a day. He shared that duty with one other priest at Locksley Abbey, serving twenty monks and ten orphan boys.

Sleep, as a younger man, paled in comparison to the deep sense of communion with God at each celebration and the broad connection to all the world when he lifted the chalice for the sacrament of the Eucharist.

"I'm an old man now," he muttered to himself. "I haven't many years left to . . ."

He no longer knew what he needed to do, except keep vigil and wait for King John and the Holy Father to find a political compromise to end the exile of the Church in England.

Before he did anything else, he knelt before his makeshift altar—a flattened boulder growing out of the cave floor—and began the time-honored ritual of prayers and psalms, a taste of bread, and a sip of wine. Peace settled on his mind like a warm and soothing blanket.

Faith satisfied, he set about replenishing his body.

He made short work of his morning ablutions, stoking the fire, and finding food in the larder—a wooden box with a rope and peg latch to keep rodents out—the villagers and Woodwose kept it filled for him.

Then he donned the thick woolen monk's robe of his Order and sat in the sunlight at the opening of his hermitage with his face bared and his feet tucked beneath him. His prayer beads slipped effortlessly through his fingers while he recited his daily petitions.

"Excuse me, Holy One," a deep voice interrupted Tuck's meditation.

He opened one eye a slit to see who came to seek his wisdom.

Another monk stood between him and the sun, wearing a pale gray robe, cowl up to shadow his face. A nameless and faceless messenger from abroad.

Thus, the magnificent Church Tuck adored was reduced to passing information along secret channels, hiding from the world where once they were openly welcomed.

"Yes, my son. How may I serve you this day?" Tuck asked.

"A missive from the archbishop." The anonymous courier held out a small fold of parchment bearing a dark red wax seal.

Tuck took the packet and slid it up his sleeve. He nodded to the younger man—he had to be young to brave the rigors of secret travel.

"Sir. I was told the message is important and requires your immediate attention. I am to await a reply to His Grace the archbishop."

"The archbishop, yes," Tuck muttered.

By long English tradition, Stephan Langdon was not yet the Archbishop of Canterbury, highest prelate in all of England—surpassing even the Archbishop of York. King John must accept Langdon, the compromise candidate chosen by the Pope. John wanted his trusted chancellor and adviser to assume the role. The brothers of Canterbury wanted one of their own. Pope Innocent III offered Stephan Langdon as a compromise, an Englishman who had been educated and taken Orders on the continent. He hadn't set foot in England since childhood and was now middle-aged.

"Take your ease inside," Tuck said. "My crude hermitage has little to offer, but you may break your fast and ease your thirst while I read and compose a reply." He bowed his head in prayer until the messenger slipped inside the cave. Tuck waited for his footsteps to grow softer as he put distance between them.

At last, when assured of privacy, Tuck took out the much-folded, scraped, and reused parchment, not much longer than his hand, broke the seal, and read the missive.

Not important. Just a request for a routine report on the state of the land and how the people fared without the guidance of Holy Mother Church. But written beneath the obvious message, in tiny letters of a secret code, Tuck read a message that King John must increase taxes again to pay for a new military campaign in France. The Archbishop feared the Sheriff of Nottingham would seize the Abbey's silver chalice and plate, declaring that since the Church no longer served England, what they left behind when the senior clergy fled now belonged to the king.

"Oh, dear." He sighed heavily and wondered which messenger he could trust to send to his abbey and have Prefect Andrew hide the valuables in the crypt, behind the skeletal remains of an early abbot.

Young Nick was the only one who moved freely between the Woodwose and the abbey. Tuck needed ready access to the boy.

The time had come to move back to the encampment. His days of peaceful solitude had come to an end.

But what to write to the archbishop?

"I can't very well tell him that without the Church, the people can now see and interact with the Wild Folk of the forest, and that according to my spies, the nobles and men-at-arms spend the time they should be attending Mass in hunting, cavorting, and gambling. They don't seem to care that they are being deprived of soul-saving rituals," he muttered to himself.

His fingers cramped with the bone disease at the idea of taking up a quill to write.

Then he turned to the courier. "Tell your master he must be patient a while longer. He needs for John to curb the authority and rights the barons presumed were theirs while King Richard was absent from England for most of ten years. When they rebel, Bishop Langdon can negotiate a compromise, a peace treaty between them and the king. Then and only then may the Church return to England."

Tuck filled his water jug and returned to his post by the entrance. He needed to absorb more sunlight before he moved back to the secret enclave.

Robin of Locksley stood strong and tall, his bowstring pulled taut, back to his ear. His shoulders tensed with the strength necessary to hold the weapon steady. The bow itself bent into a half circle. He knew his arrow, formed of a single straight branch without a knot or twist in its grain, would fly true. Only the flint tip he'd knapped last night bothered him.

Was it sharp enough to penetrate to a boar's heart? Was the stone strong enough at its core not to shatter if it struck bone instead?

While his mind fought with itself, a seasoned boar with long tusks that curved back nearly to his ears rooted about the base of a tree, seeking succulent growths at the base of a gnarled root. It grunted with alternate pleasure and disappointment, its little eyes constantly moving and wary of intruders, ears twitching with every tiny sound that reached them.

Robin waited for the massive beast to extend its search for food around the tree and come into his line of sight. His upper arm trembled with the tension of holding his bow taut for longer than he planned.

He dared not relax the string and thus spoil his aim; or miss the shot entirely as the boar moved cautiously in and out of range.

A sharp crackle of tusk breaking through a tangle of twigs and branches echoed from one tree trunk to another. Then Robin noted the plop of dirt clods impacting soft moss behind the boar.

Robin took a half step to his left. The foliage was thicker here, but the boar dipped his head just so . . .

He loosed the arrow. The thwap of his line sang against his ear. The feathers of the fletching grazed his cheek. The tension in his arms recoiled, bringing knots to his forearms.

His instincts demanded he shrink into his Robin Good-fellow body. Gnomes didn't develop sore muscles.

He fought the urge, preparing to climb the nearest tree, out of reach of the now bellowing and enraged boar.

"Knew I should have brought a poleax," he muttered.

The boar narrowed its tiny eyes and ran forward. The arrow embedded in its neck bobbed with each galloping step. Blood spurted in long arcs from the wound.

Robin calculated how much farther the wounded boar could run, and how fast.

He jumped and grabbed a branch above his head, swinging his long human legs up to cross his ankles around the limb.

The boar charged directly beneath him, swinging its lethal tusks right and left, up and down, seeking the source of its pain. With one long squealing screech of agony, it crashed tusks first into the turf. Broken fern fronds sagged to cover it in a green shroud.

Robin dropped to the ground, jarring his joints, the urge to change nearly overwhelming him. He'd been tall for too long.

Gnomes couldn't sling a boar on a pole and carry it back to camp.

His curse demanded he prance around as the giggling Puck for half of each day. But he'd learned that he didn't have to spend those hours all at once.

Carefully, he stowed his bow and quiver beneath a fern and shrank to half his normal height, feeling his nose stretch into a sharp point as it curved and dipped to meet his now jutting chin.

Two young men crept out of the brush to help him butcher the beast and haul it back to camp. This was young Gabe's first hunt. He clenched his jaw shut and grimly produced his knife to gut the boar.

The other boy . . .

"Nick? Aren't you supposed to be holed up in the abbey scriptorium until spring?" he asked the gangling youth in a dark woolen robe that no longer reached his ankles. He'd grown over the course of the winter; his height and the length of his feet had outstripped the breadth of his shoulders and fullness of his chest.

"Soon enough, sir. I've come to warn you of a troublesome sighting at the crossroads. Thought I might help while I'm here."

Robin Goodfellow unsheathed his own long knife and straddled the boar. Nick shied away as Robin and the Wood-wose boy bled and gutted the boar in swift and deft strokes. Butchering animals was not part of Nick's protected life at the abbey. He'd have to learn something of the harsh realities of living wild if his budding romance with Hilde overwhelmed his thirst for knowledge within the abbey.

One look at the paleness of Nick's face told Robin this was not the time to initiate him into the rituals of the hunt.

"What did you observe?" he asked as he slit the throat of his kill.

"The sheriff's men brought a newcomer to the forest; a man hunched over so that he appears to have no neck at all, and his head leads his entire body," Nick said with his back turned toward Robin.

"People born with deformities are often exiled from their fellow humans." He clamped down on his disgust both at the practice and the legend of evil that surrounded such persons. He currently resembled a misshapen hunchback.

Only the Wild Folk and the Woodwose understood his curse.

"This man was not escorted into exile. He was brought here with a purpose. He carried a woodsman's ax."

"A forester for the sheriff?" Robin asked, not wanting to hear the answer he knew must come.

"Foresters work in teams. This man was left alone."

Chills ran up and down Robin's spine. "An ax is a useful tool for survival. The Woodwose have stolen several over the years."

"You had to steal your tools and the weapons you cannot make yourself. This man carried it proudly as if it belonged to him and him alone. The sheriff's men did not question his right to carry it."

Robin straightened from his grisly task. "Which direction did he take?"

If Little John were still the Green Man, he'd have the ability and the authority to find the man and judge if his task was worthy and beneficial to the health of the forest.

Little John currently lived as a mortal man with a new bride whose belly swelled with their first child. He'd relinquished his authority and magic. His son and successor, Verne, still held vigil in the sacred clearing. He couldn't step forth from his tree for another half year. Until then his knowledge of the forest and his rule over it all would be incomplete and ineffectual.

It was up to Robin and some of the others to discover the nature of the stranger's quest.

"From the main crossroad, he traveled southwest on foot by the trail that parallels Ardenia's creek," Nick said. "The sheriff's men turned around and rode off in the direction of Nottingham."

"Nothing of importance to the southwest. No settlements that we know of, no hermitages, not even ancient sacred sites."

"What about Elena's Crossing?" Nick asked. He fingered something inside his sleeve, the place where he carried Elena's silver, three-faced cup.

The little goddess had been remarkably silent all winter. Robin missed her delicate chuckle like tiny silver bells blowing in the wind.

"The cross carved from a single standing stone at that crossroad is too close to the abbey and the village. A man escorted to the depths of Sherwood would not backtrack to a market road. Whatever his purpose here, he needs privacy."

"He needs watching," Nick insisted.

"Aye, he needs watching. I'll send Will Scarlett to see what he's up to. Will can fly around the forest and no one will notice another red bird singing for a mate."

"Will Scarlett can make the angels weep with his songs. He can't remember what day it is for more than three heartbeats."

"Taking messages hither, thither, and yon is why we nurture Will Scarlett," Robin affirmed. "As long as we keep it simple, Will does fine. Just remember to write down the message for the recipient if it's complicated, or you need to keep the details correct."

Nick knew that Will Scarlett was forgetful and easily distracted. Everyone who dealt with him knew that.

Robin snorted his agreement. "Now, Hilde's turn at watching the crossroad is over. You need to hie yourself back to the protection of your abbey. I'll deal with the stranger."

Nick skipped away, all too eagerly.

Three

ilde approached the Woodwose encampment cautiously. Living rough with them through three seasons and more had taught her wariness. She'd lived in a convent for the year before that, where avoiding contact with a particular sister—who could only relieve her own mental anguish by inflicting pain on others—had become a survival skill. She'd learned early on to look, listen, and sniff every walkway in every direction to make certain no one followed her, and that no one who shouldn't watch the outlaws, didn't. They were only outlaws because they had no home. Not having a place to live, under the protection and control of a lord, was illegal. So, they lived outside the law in the forbidden Royal Forest.

She'd tolerated the convent for the same reason.

The life of an outlaw seemed almost a luxury in comparison—

even living in the damp cave for the winter with only rocks for a bed had been easier than life in the convent.

When she'd circled the cluster of cooking fires and rude lean-to shelters three times, she entered the clearing from the side opposite her first approach.

"Catryn." Hilde spoke loudly and touched the arm of the old woman who sat in front of the fire dicing turnips from the winter storage. As each chunk plopped into the simmering stewpot, she smiled and hummed to herself.

Hilde remembered the tune from her childhood. Mam sang it to each of her new babes while she nursed them. Happier times. Simpler times.

"Catryn, have you seen Tuck? Has he come out of his winter hermitage yet?" Hilde tried again to gain the old woman's attention.

"Tuck? You mean the priest that hides from the king and the Church? He dresses like a peasant now. No rich robes or gilded shepherd's crook for the likes of our Tuck."

Catryn wasn't known to be overly smart, but she was wonderful at tending the fire and minding fussy babes. She was a widow without children. Like the rest of them, she had nowhere else to go. Sometimes her mind lived in other times and places.

"Aye, Father Tuck. I need to talk to him."

"Have to wait a bit. He's gone off with Robin and Will and Little John. Left just after dawn. Said they had business in Nottingham." Catryn returned to her humming and chopping vegetables. She'd finished with the turnips and taken up a few wild onions.

"Nottingham?" That didn't sound right. If the men traveled to the sheriff's home, they'd be gone the entire day. Maybe well into the next if they decided not to travel at night—dangerous for even the fae leaders of the Wild Folk. They would also discuss their plans with the entire community the night before leaving.

On another thought . . . the community would have a welcome for Tuck when he came out of hiding from the worst of the cold weather.

Venturing into the lair of the enemy, the city of Nottingham, was serious business that put them all at risk.

Catryn must be remembering a different conversation from a different day. Hilde was never certain.

She rose from her crouch beside the old woman and wandered toward a round, wattle-and-daub hut with a turf roof, set aside from the other shelters. Little John had built it for Jane, making sure that the walls of woven reeds covered in river clay were weathertight *and* blended into the woodland. He had used no magic to hide it. Still, one had to know it was there to find it.

"Hoi, the house," Hilde called softly. Raised voices were another thing to avoid while living as an outlaw. Sound carried through the green in unpredictable ways, attracting the attention of outsiders. The winter cave had bent and channeled sound oddly, making no conversation truly private. Was that why Tuck had chosen a cave separate from the Woodwose? A very narrow, wet, and twisted tunnel that only a child could negotiate connected the two dwellings. The separation gave Tuck

a modicum of privacy for his political machinations and un-
announced visitors.

Jane peeked out from behind the leather door covering of
the hut. When she recognized Hilde, she pushed aside the boar
hides she'd stitched together in such a way that some air and
light entered her home while keeping annoying insects, peep-
ers, and strong winds out.

"I'm looking for Tuck," Hilde explained as she moved
closer, so she wouldn't have to speak too loudly. "Is he still in
winter hiding?"

"I haven't seen him since we came home, a full moon ago."
Jane stepped free of the house and sank onto a smooth boulder
that caught the early spring sunlight. She sank onto her favored seat and lifted her face to the strong light, like a cat
basking in a puddle of sunshine. Her hands rubbed gently
along the sides of her swelling belly. She and John hadn't
waited long to recite their vows before Father Tuck and the
assembled population after her rescue from enslavement by a
band of wicked faeries. Within weeks, they'd started their
family. Any day now. . . .

"What about John or Robin?" Hilde pressed. She had information that required action.

"Robin went hunting. Will flew off about the same time.
John should return from his daily conversation with Verne
any time now. He rarely stays much beyond noon. Though I
can't call it a conversation. John talks. I presume Verne listens. It's hard to tell how a tree communicates. John says it's
important that he keep Verne's mind awake and working

during this year. And to make sure their old friend Blaidd
stands guard. He even tromped through two feet of snow to
go to Verne every day during the winter. Those were days
when I feared he'd freeze to death." She paused and stared
into the distance, all the while rubbing her belly. "I hope John
finds some fresh pigweed on his way home. I've a hankering
for it."

With Jane so close to her time, John was not likely to linger
long or stray far from the direct path to the sacred clearing.

Strange. Hilde felt more like she was attending Mass whilst
among the three standing stones than in the big church with
stained glass windows at the convent. And she no longer felt
guilty for such blasphemous thoughts. Father Tuck had said
that God watched over each of them, no matter where they
were or how they honored Him.

"My mam always wanted pigweed the day before she went
into labor," Hilde dragged her mind back to Jane. "She said it
was too bitter any other time."

Jane stilled in contemplation. But her hand continued to
stroke her belly. Was she soothing the baby or marking small
contractions?

Hilde decided to wait for John to return before searching
further for someone to talk to about the hunched man and his
ax. She didn't want to leave Jane alone. "Can I help you with
anything, fetch a bucket of water?"

"That would be very helpful." Jane sighed with relief and
tilted her head toward the empty wooden bucket on the other
side of the doorway. "I just do not have the will to walk as far
as the creek today."

Oh, dear, Jane thought. She now had another reason to stay close. The Woodwose camp was likely to add another life to their numbers tonight. Tomorrow at the latest.

Nick dropped from the overhanging branch of an apple tree into the walled courtyard of the infirmary. Last summer he'd tended the herb garden here under the direction of Brother Luke. The old man could remember every cutting and seed he'd brought from abroad during his rambling youth. Age had finally taken him, leaving Nick with sheaves of parchment filled with notes and drawings about how and when to use which plant.

Over the course of the winter, whenever he had a few free moments, and enough light to work by, he'd organized the notes and copied them out with a fair hand. Now that spring was upon them, he hoped to finish the drawings, working with the living plants for accuracy. Brother Daffyd, the healer, encouraged him, and was anxious for him to finish. The Welsh brother had no talent to either copy script or draw. But once given a few leaves of St. John's wort, or marigold, he knew how to use them to best advantage with his patients.

Nick remained crouched low beside the outer wall of the courtyard while he waited to see if anyone had noted his clandestine return to the abbey.

"Not so long a drop from yon branch as last summer, eh, Nick?" Brother Thom, the abbey blacksmith asked. He sprawled upon a stone bench, cradling a badly burned left hand. This was the first day since his accident at the Epiphany that he had cast off the protective sling.

Nick blushed, then straightened to his full height, surprised that he could reach up and grasp the branch—an old friend since early childhood—without jumping, or rising to tiptoe.

"Aye, yer going to be a tall one," Brother Thom chuckled. "Still got some growing to do. Don't know that we've any spare postulant robes to fit you now. You cast aside student robes a year ago when they only reached your knees."

Nick tugged his robe downward from the restriction of his rope belt. At the solstice he'd needed to tuck folds of the coarse wool above the belt. Now that the equinox had passed, three days ago, he couldn't get any more length no matter how hard he tried to cover his ankles.

"Ye'll need new sandals as well, boy. Yer toes be hanging over the ends and getting mighty dirty."

"I'd rather go barefoot," Nick murmured in embarrassment. Little John and Robin Goodfellow had taught him the value of feeling the earth against his soles and examining the quality of the dirt with his toes. Vibrations from passing game or people told him much and helped him find ways around dangerous footing or hiding places from predators.

"Why haven't you called Brother Daffyd to report my truancy?" he asked.

"Boys been climbing in and out of the abbey by yon branch for many a long year. It be necessary for young'ns to explore and think up new ways to defy the rules. Teaches them to use their noggins for more than reciting prayers in Latin that they don't understand. What good are rules and prayers if you don't understand what they're fer? Besides, Father Blaine don't like boys what can think. He knows they's smarter than he and that scares him."

"How's your hand?" Nick asked, stepping closer and peering at the scars and unnatural bend of the fingers. The grotesque condition of the hand was easier to bear than a discussion of Father Blaine's shortcomings.

"Better. Got more movement of me fingers than I thought I'd have when that pot of molten copper split and spilled all over m' hand. Strength still missing."

"Good that you can wiggle the fingers. Movement will restore however much strength you can regain." Nick took the cupped hand and gently massaged the fingers. He felt the bones beneath the skin. Not a lot of muscle anymore. Maybe with time and gentle working Brother Thom would regain some use of it.

"Good you returned when you did. Father Blaine is on a tear today, wanting to bash heads and send the boys to bed without supper for no reason," Brother Thom whispered. He relaxed his shoulders and his breathing came easier as Nick worked the stiffness from his hand.

Nick looked over his shoulder to see if the red poppies in the northwestern corner of the courtyard were close to blooming yet. Brother Luke had taught him how to "milk" them for a powerful medicine that eased the worst pains imaginable. He and Brother Daffyd had doled out the juice drop by drop to Brother Thom for three months. They'd used all of the precious store and were not likely to have more for another week or two.

Willow bark tea would help, but not enough, unless a miracle visited Brother Thom.

Nick whispered a little prayer that no one else broke a bone or came down with the coughing sickness before they had more of the poppy juice.

A tiny tabby kitten peeked out from beneath the frothy poppy leaves. It blinked and scuttled backward into hiding.

Ah! He knew how to finish the illumination he'd left this morning.

"Where's Prefect Andrew? I need to talk to him." The business of the hunched laborer with an ax needed addressing more urgently than finishing his drawings in the scriptorium. If anyone could find Tuck and start an investigation, it was the prefect.

"Ain't seen Andrew all day, not since we broke our fast at dawn. You disappeared right after, my boy."

"I had errands for Prefect Andrew in the village. Now I need to report to him."

Brother Thom shrugged his shoulders and yawned. Then he dropped his chin to his chest as if in deep prayer but more likely the beginnings of a nap.

"The sun has moved, my friend. Time to return you to your bed."

Brother Thom murmured a slight protest as Nick got his hands beneath the big man's shoulders and guided him to his feet. "You've lost some girth over the winter, Brother. I doubt I could have budged you before the accident. You need to eat more, keep up your strength."

More mumbles.

Nick eased Brother Thom through the wide door to the infirmary only to meet the stern and disapproving gaze of Father Blaine. "Where have you been?" He raised his rod of discipline over his shoulder preparing to strike Nick across his back.

Robin Goodfellow peered at the top of a tall and gangling maple tree. His gnomish eyes didn't like the glare of late afternoon sunlight bathing new leaves and reflecting downward. His skin itched as well. Time to grow big and human again. And still he waited, wanting to save his tall form until he gathered others around him.

What was keeping Will Scarlett from returning with news? Robin had sent him flying as soon as Nick told him about the stranger with a long and lethal ax.

He heard the flutter of wings before he saw a red splotch land on a topmost branch and set it swaying.

Breathing deeply in relief, Robin let himself stretch upward, bringing his nose and chin back into alignment, and banishing his hairy warts. He welcomed the painful crunch and grind of his joints as a sign that soon he could breathe deeply and normally, that his heart would beat strong and true, and that his words would not be marred by a lisp. By the time he reached his full height and could manipulate a bow again, Will had fluttered to the ground and transformed from bird to man. His change was natural and happened more quickly than Robin's. Will Scarlett had no limitations on how long he could or must stay in one form or another.

Long ago, a sorcerer had cursed Robin to his half-fae existence. The same sorcerer had taken Robin's love, Marian, and hidden her while she slept the decades away, neither aging nor living, unaware of the passage of time. Robin had to break her curse and his own at the same time, or both would die and crumble to dust.

But first he had to find her.

His heart ached with emptiness that his beloved lady could not rise from her bier and share a life with him.

"Did you find the stranger?" Robin asked, shrugging and twisting his shoulders to banish the last vestiges of his hump, and thoughts of Marian.

"The man with the bloody long ax that bites into trees and dryads alike?"

"Aye, that one."

"He's building a shelter atop a knoll in the direction of midsummer morning sunrise." Will's words lilted as if he needed to sing them. One day he'd likely turn the story of his flight and discovery into a ballad.

"Why?"

Will lifted one shoulder and turned his attention to his fingertips. His nails were always sharp and clean, unlike most men who lived rough and dug in the dirt without shovels as did most of the Woodwose.

"Did you hear any conversations among the sheriff's men as to why they escorted him here and turned him loose?" If the man were an outlaw, he'd have been running ahead of the knights and he'd have sought the other outlaws for shelter, food, and protection.

"Something about a kill."

"Kill what, or who?"

"Kill wood. I guess. Burning. The sheriff will be warm next winter."

"A kiln! He's a charcoal burner. And he has a license to clear the forest. That man will kill a full acre of trees before the moon changes. By the winter solstice, he'll take down one hundred acres. Or more. We have to tell Tuck. He has contacts in the city who can stop the man."

"Why not tell Little John?" Will looked up as if scouting his flight path toward the cave where the old priest lingered, waiting for warmer weather to rejoin the Woodwose.

"Little John gave up his magic and his authority in order to live as a man. He can do nothing to save the forest. And Verne is still dreaming in his tree. He won't be free to walk among us for another half year."

"Little John is still a big man with strong fists. He can intimidate any one man," Will answered.

"Aye, there's that. But if the sheriff's men brought the burner to the forest, then he must have a royal license to produce charcoal. Only Tuck knows the people who can revoke that license and put a stop to the tyranny against the forest."

"You fetch Little John to do what he must to frighten the man away. I'll find Tuck and bring him to camp."

"Maybe Hilde will have some ideas," Robin mused. "She talks to Nick. Between them, they'll come up with a plan."

"Hilde? The girl who ran away from the convent? She's still a child." Will dismissed the idea before he forgot it. Maybe dismissing Hilde and her plans meant he'd remember. One never knew what kind of twists Will's mind took.

"Our people listen to her. She's a good girl, strong of will as well as body. She's the one who moved us to a cave for the winter. We were warmer than the previous winters and fewer among us died from chill and coughs. She's the one who organizes work parties and regular watchers. I'd not have thought to hunt boar today if she hadn't prodded me out of camp and sent boys to help bring the beast back to the cookfire. Without her, we wouldn't have firm escape plans should the sheriff and his men come calling. Last time that happened, we scattered willy-nilly, and half of our number were caught and taken to Nottingham for trial and hanging." He snorted a rude laugh. "Hilde, barely a woman, is already our leader, though none will say so."

Will raised an eyebrow while he thought about it.

Robin counted the moments passing as the idea penetrated the birdman's mind, took root, and made sense to him.

"After I send Tuck home, I'll summon Nick from his abbey. Hilde thinks better with him at her side."

"We'll make plans over roasted boar tonight. The charcoal burner will have to settle for cold rations and sleep in his unfinished hut. He hasn't had time to weave a wind-tight frame and daub it with muddy clay and let it dry before tonight's rain."

"There's a beaver lodge on the stream near his hut. I'll ask them to steal the twigs from his frame. They'll welcome the new building material and fresh bark." Will chuckled as he stretched his arms wide, sprouting bright red feathers until the bird took over his body and he flew off on his errands.

Robin settled in for a long walk toward camp, grateful that his human legs covered the distance in half the time as his gnome form.

Four

 knew I slept. Dark clouds filled with beings I could not recognize pressed upon my mind, blocking out my daytime life. They screamed and howled at me to relieve their pain. Nameless things from deep within the abyss.

Absently, I rubbed the raw crystal I kept with me always. The nameless creatures took their agony elsewhere.

I drifted to another time and place. Not the happiest of times, but the day I first met my Robin. Robin of Locksley, second son of the earl.

My own father, Baron of Wentworth, had died a few weeks earlier. I mourned him deeply, feeling a great hole in my middle. I was familiar with Death's dark tread on the stairs of Papa's small castle. He came frequently during winter. But summer was supposed to be bright and carefree, filled with warmth and freshly harvested food, and free of the diseases that made us all vulnerable to Death.

But summer was also the time of battles and war that took our men away. So many did not return. Like my father.

Since I had no brothers left alive, King Henry decreed that my mother must marry a landless knight who was a boon companion of His Grace and her dower lands would become his. I must go to the Earl of Locksley for wardship. He would hold and administer my lands until I was old enough to marry. Then my husband would hold my dower for our children.

I knew from the moment the letter came from Henry, the second of that name, King of England by the Grace of God, and duke of more French lands than owned by the king of France, that I would marry the earl's eldest son, also named Henry.

But I was only eight summers old. Marriage would have to wait.

And so I traveled the twenty miles from Wentworth to Locksley astride my sturdy but placid pony, with my childhood nurse, two hunting dogs, and a cart carrying my one small trunk of clothes and personal possessions. The rest of the cart was filled with crates of plate and jewels that formed part of my dowry.

The gatehouse tower of Locksley Castle loomed above us. The passage through the walls stretched on and on. I dared not look up, knowing that the tunnel was riddled with traps to quell potential attackers of this strategic point to the south of Sherwood Forest.

We burst into the open bailey bustling with the activity of dozens of soldiers and craftsmen, women, children, fractious horses, bleating sheep, and lowing cattle. A normal day at the earl's home on a sunny summer day when he was not at war.

Three men waited at the top of the stairs leading from the bailey to the tower. The central figure was old, a little older than my father had been, wearing ordinary woolen robes over his shirt. Only the crest embroidered on his sleeveless jerkin betrayed him as the earl. His auburn hair and ginger beard faded toward gray. He engaged in heated debate with a much younger man to his right. This person wore chain mail armor with a tabard also emblazoned with the Locksley crest, and cradled a helm beneath his arm. His right hand gripped his long sword, fingers clenching and releasing frequently in agitation. He shouted something I could not comprehend, drowned out by the normal activity around them.

On the older man's left stood another young man, a teenager, judging by his gangly arms and oversized feet. His plain doublet and hose looked strained, as if they fit him well not too long ago, but he'd grown faster than his tailor could make new clothes for him. He, too, sported the auburn hair of the earl and his ginger beard wasn't much more than a vague shadow on his chin. He stood apart from the other two, slightly turned away from their argument.

They all looked enough alike to be family. The earl and two sons. A slender heir barely as tall as his father, who looked shrunken within his armor, and another boy destined to be tall with a broad chest and determined chin, probably destined for a career in the church.

The second son's eyes widened and brightened when he caught sight of me approaching the family stronghold. He blithely ran down the steps and fetched up right in front of where my pony stopped.

"Robin of Locksley at your service, Lady Marian." He bowed politely as he steadied the pony with a grip on her bridle and a soothing touch on her neck. "May I help you down?"

"I can manage." I slid downward, facing my mount on my own. When I turned, Robin stood close enough to assist me, should I lose my balance, but far enough away not to intrude. I had just a few heartbeats to study the boy, perhaps sixteen years, old enough to go to battle or take priestly vows.

His light brown eyes, not so different in color from his hair, engaged mine in equal appraisal. His mouth quirked up in a smile. The sun chose that moment to burst free of a small cloud and shone on his face.

I saw then the handsome man he would become, strong and decisive, an able lord or, more likely, a prelate of the church who would rise to the highest levels and advise great lords, possibly the king himself.

Without a moment's hesitation, I knew that I was safe with him.

Derwyn paused in the shadow of the tall wall of Nottingham. He pressed his back against the dressed stones for balance while he tugged on his boots. He'd had to pay the tanner extra to make them wide enough for his broad feet. Still, they pinched his toes into numbness.

Stamping his feet to make the boots fit better, he straightened and scouted the open but guarded gate.

Two men wearing leather-and-mail armor with helms

pulled down to protect their pates stood side-by-side. Each held a long pike, butt end anchored close to their feet, arms stretched to the side so that their weapons formed a crossed barrier. Two more guards slouched more casually near the inner opening. The tunnel through the massive wall was nearly twenty feet long. In his tree form, Derwyn could have put his roots at the gate and his top branches would burst into the city above the wall.

But he no longer had a tree form. His *father* had robbed him of it. And so he must walk among men and wear itchy clothing and too-tight boots. But he still slept on the ground, sheltered by a rocky overhang and warmed by animal furs. He would not dwell indoors, in a rude hut, or the luxurious rooms the sheriff had offered him. The finely woven linen and wool that the sheriff had given him when he made his first petition gave him little ease. He wanted the comfort of bark and sap.

He'd never get them again.

And neither would his brother Verne, or any of the other dryad kin if all went as planned.

So, for the dozenth time, Derwyn presented himself to the guards at the gate. "His lordship summoned me," he said plainly, without preamble. He left comfortable chats to lesser men than he.

The nameless guard on the left recognized him and brought his pike close to his body, giving Derwyn scant room to pass. The other man was slower to open the pathway.

Derwyn glared down at him, a full head and a half taller than the armed man.

The guard swallowed deeply, lowered his gaze from Derwyn's unspoken challenge, and pulled his pike out of the way.

Head high, Derwyn stalked inward through the stony darkness. He made note of the shadowy cracks above him, places where a defender in the tower could drop blades or boiling oil upon an invader's head. Those traps made Derwyn nervous. He did not like confined places. And he did not like dealing with men.

Robin Goodfellow and Herne the Huntsmen, fae who could take human form (enemies though they were), were more his kin than the people who lived too closely in the city.

"Follow me," one of the interior guards said, heaving himself away from the arch support as if it took greater strength than he possessed to shift upright.

Derwyn wondered if the man had forest blood in his ancestry and was more comfortable walking on all fours. His arms did seem unusually long.

"Heard you killed the hunchback," the guard said around a lazy yawn.

Derwyn smiled inwardly. He hoped that bit of news meant his plan had fallen into place. "I have never met a hunchback and certainly have not laid hands upon him."

"Hmph. You might not have killed him, but your whispered words into the sheriff's ear led to his exile into the forest. That's as good as dead for an honest Christian. No Church to protect us. No wonder we get more and more people coming here for shelter. The fae's running wild, they are." The guard made the sign of the cross.

Derwyn edged a step to the side. Not that he put much stock in the superstitions of men. He did note that the guard wore a carved wooden talisman on a leather thong about his neck. The

Woodwose wore similar symbols as they faced daily challenges to their health and welfare. Of late, he'd noticed more and more of the pendants on city folk. Some itinerant priest carved and blessed them in the absence of Church authority.

"I know the way to the castle keep," Derwyn said, growing weary of the guard's gossip.

"Got my orders, sir. You aren't allowed to wander the city alone. His lordship said so, specific to me this morning."

Derwyn growled, an angry retort upon his lips. He swallowed the words and scowled at a wayward child running through the crowd without heed of toes and knees he banged with a stick pony.

The boy child screamed and ran back to his mother, neatly leaping the midden in the center of the cobbles.

"See, that's why his lordship don't want you loose among his people. You're bigger 'n most of 'em, and you scare them, and then they complain to him that he ain't protectin' 'em like 'e should."

Derwyn schooled his expression to blankness. He still needed the sheriff to complete his planned vengeance.

Hilde settled the water bucket just inside the little hut. Jane still sat on her flat rock, but no longer basked with the spring sun on her face. She hunched forward with a puzzled look on her face. Her hands rubbed her belly in a new rhythm.

"Jane, I think you need to retire inside while I fetch Pippa."

"I don't need a midwife yet," Jane insisted. She sat up

straighter, pushing against her lower back with one hand while cupping her belly with the other.

"I helped my mam birth the last two of her babes. I think you need Pippa, sooner than you think." Hilde hiked up her robe enough to run back to the central fire. This time of day most of the women had scattered to various chores of digging wild roots, gathering firewood, fetching water, all the little things that kept the camp working.

Old Catryn still cut turnips and onions into tiny pieces, letting them drop into the stewpot. She might have been a midwife once, but no longer. She couldn't remember why she was in a certain place for more than a few heartbeats before wandering off to do something else.

Hilde drew a deep breath and listened to the forest. A soft murmur of voices, that might have been mistaken for the babbling of a creek, came to her from the direction of Ardenia's pond.

She directed her feet to follow that path. Pippa was there, talking to the water sprite—who stood in the shallows combing her long silvery blonde hair. Pippa scrubbed her spare shift with sand while they discussed the warmth of the day after a near-freezing night.

"Pippa, I think Jane is in labor," Hilde whispered with some urgency. She always had to remember to keep her words quiet near water that carried sound where trees absorbed it.

"It's her first. She'll be at it for hours before she needs me," Pippa replied. She held up the shift to the sunlight, seeking any lingering stains.

"That's just it. She's been rubbing her belly for most of the morning, and last evening as well. She may be further along than she thinks. My mam was like that with her last one, barely felt the pains for a full day and then two long cramps and the babe was crowning."

"Oh." Pippa paused, biting her lip. "OH!" She took the time to spread her clean shift flat on the grass before hastening back toward camp and Jane's hut. "I'll need the shift when we're done!" she called over her shoulder.

Hilde followed on her heels, knowing in her heart that Jane might need extra hands for a big babe and no experience in birthing.

They passed Herne in his human form rather than the eight-point stag, on his way to visit with Ardenia, his mate. He looked amiable enough at the moment and not in need of an arbiter. With those two, one never knew. Their quarrels were legend, often requiring Little John to separate them and force promises of peace and compromise that lasted a few days, a week at most.

"Why the haste?" Herne asked, grasping Hilde's arm to force her to pause. "On such a fine day, one should walk slowly, appreciating the gift of the sun and warm air."

Briefly Hilde explained her errand. "Find Little John," she said and dashed off.

"Of course. A momentous day for him. I know where to find him." He turned and headed in a different direction, Ardenia forgotten for now.

By the time Hilde ducked through the doorway into the dark hut, Pippa had built up the fire, stripped Jane and settled her onto her pallet. She squatted, clinging to the central ridge pole. The skin of her belly rippled with a new contraction. She grasped the pole with both hands, panting through the pain. Another push from her belly muscles followed it closely. Barely two heartbeats between the two.

The babe was coming fast.

"What do you need?" Hilde asked, checking for the neat pile of rags and big leaves to mop up the messy process of bringing a child into the world.

"You and two others to hold her up while she pushes the baby out. It's a big one, likely going to be as big as its father."

"Jane!" John bellowed. He sounded as if he stood just outside the door. When Hilde looked, she saw him thrashing along the path two dozen yards or more away.

"And keep him outside," Pippa insisted.

Hilde grabbed the spare bucket and stepped outside. The moment John stepped into the clearing before the hut, she thrust it at him. "We'll need water. From the pond, not the creek. Ardenia will grant it healing powers."

He stood there, clutching the bucket to his chest as a talisman. "But . . . but . . ." His mouth worked, but no other words escaped him.

"'Tis women's work this day. You may fetch and carry, but you cannot yet step inside."

John gawped a few moments more, then dashed off in the direction of the pond.

When Hilde returned to Pippa's side, the midwife had a short, but very sharp flint knife in her hand.

"Holy Mother Mary, I hope we don't have to cut the babe out of her."

"We're going to need the help of more than just the blessed mother. Nick's goddess Elena will be a bigger help."

But Nick had gone home to the abbey. By the time someone ran to fetch him and the goddess who resided in the little silver cup, Jane might be dead.

Five

urry, hurry, hurry! Elena prodded Nick with a stab of pain behind his eyes.

He blinked rapidly and sat up straight. Without thinking, he wiped his quill with a rag and set it aside in its specially carved holder, protecting the nib and keeping it from dripping on clean parchment.

The little tabby cat he'd drawn within the decorative leaves and fronds seemed to blink back at him as she appeared and disappeared with the shift of each glance.

As his eyes cleared from his meditative trance, he realized he'd drawn the face of a green man in the floral design around a Capital F at the beginning of the page of his illuminated manuscript. The cat he'd drawn deliberately.

Stop your idle musing and get over the wall. I need to be with Jane. Right Now!

"Oh."

Brother Theo, the master of the scriptorium, paced the far

side of the big, airy room, careful to never block the light from the tall windows.

Nick pushed back his bench and stood carefully. He kept his legs close together as if a different urgent matter pressed upon him.

"You should know how to hold it by now," the older monk said with a frown.

"Sorry," Nick ground out from between clenched teeth. "This morning's ale was a bit off." Then he dashed out the door without further apology or explanation.

No one stopped him as he pelted along the cloister corridor toward the infirmary at the far end of the building.

Brother Daffyd dozed beside the cot of an old man from the village who had no family left to tend his final illness. Nick took advantage of the absence of people who might stop him and aimed for the friendly branch that allowed him to climb the wall.

Apple blossoms had begun to swell the buds near the tips of each twig. He did his best to keep from damaging any of them.

Once atop the wall, he crouched, took off his sandals, and tied them to his rope belt. Then he listened for intruders. Prefect Andrew, the priest who presided over the abbey while Father Tuck—or Abbot Mæson as he was known among the clergy—remained in exile, paced the orderly rows between the orchard trees. He seemed deep in thought with his head lowered and his hands clasped behind his back.

Drop to the ground now. Elena instructed Nick.

He saw that the prefect had reached the end of the row farthest from the wall and still had his back toward Nick.

The tree gave him enough support to break his descent. His bare feet gripped the land to further soften any sound he might make.

Hold your breath.

Nick obeyed the goddess. He'd done this before.

As long as he did not breathe, she cloaked him with a twist of light that humans could not penetrate with their gaze.

Then he ran, barely touching the ground with his toes until blackness pressed against the sides of his vision and his chest ached.

A moment later, he opened his mouth to gasp for air and found himself at the base of the stone cross at the crossroad.

"Halfway there," he crowed.

As much as his heaving chest urged him to sit still a few moments longer, he scrambled to his feet and leaped across the western road to a game trail that led him deep into Sherwood Forest.

Robin slid into his gnome form, crossed his weary legs, and dropped to the ground in a comfortable sit. From this vantage point, atop a grassy knoll, he surveyed the lands around him. This had been his favorite spot since childhood when he needed to be alone. The place where he'd brought Marian when she needed fresh air away from the gossiping women in the stillroom, or the solar where they spun and wove new cloth.

He had no place in the Woodwose camp right now. The women bustled back and forth from the cookfire to Jane's and John's hut, being useful. The men—including John—paced, accomplishing nothing other than occasionally fetching another bucket of water.

Robin decided to be elsewhere for the rest of the day. And so he sat where he had always sat, short legs stretched out before him, back resting against a fallen tree trunk, and his bow and quiver close to hand. Strange how his favorite weapon shrank or grew with his form. It had become as much a part of his identity as his Lincoln-green jerkin and hose.

At the bottom of his hill, a slow and meandering creek wound around the next rocky cliff and hillside. Long ago, that trickle of water had been an impressive motte defending the castle atop the cliff. No longer. The mighty walls had begun to crumble. Ambitious villagers and knights had stolen blocks from the ramparts to become foundation stones for newer homes and fortifications. The fields and pastures stretching out from the base of the castle crag lay neglected.

The land belonged to King John now, and he had no use for it other than another useless place to hoard. He found value in keeping others from claiming it.

Robin's heart grew heavy with regret. If only he'd come home from the Second Crusade when the battles ended, he'd have been here when his father fell ill and died, and his brother jumped—or was pushed—from the top of the keep onto the cobblestoned courtyard and died. He could have claimed the title and honors and Marian before the cursed sorcerer tainted all that Robin loved.

A flash of movement and a noise off to his right grabbed his attention. He reached for his bow and considered growing tall again.

But he'd only been gnomish a short time after extending his time as a man to the edge of his limits. If he stretched out again so soon, he'd only be able to hold his tall form a short time.

Maybe he should just run away.

While he considered his options, a bent figure moved away from the tree line and became more real than a shadow. Peering through rheumy eyes, Robin made out the hunchback dragging stout branches behind him, and his ax over one shoulder. The charcoal burner with material to build his kiln.

He was strong to carry that load alone, without breathing hard.

Robin sat his ground, not willing to run away from a man as ugly as himself. Though without the hump, he might be considered roughly handsome, his nose was a normal length and breadth, but a bit crooked from an old break. A child with a deformity couldn't grow up without bullies beating on him. Robin had seen it often enough both among the Crusaders and the cities of Europe where he'd wandered for too many years.

He found it hard to discern a chin amongst the man's

scanty beard and the twigs he carried. It could be strongly determined, or weak and receding. One would make him good looking, the other would merely confirm his deformity.

"Hoi, stranger!" Robin called.

The hunchback lifted his head in startlement, dropping his bundle, and bringing his ax to bear, straight forward, head lifted to strike a killing blow.

Robin pulled in a sharp breath and fitted an arrow to the string, ready to flee or transform as needed.

The hunchback narrowed his eyes and peered at Robin as if unsure what to make of the ugly gnome with fae features. He didn't relax his grip on his ax.

"I wish you no ill," Robin said. He casually loosened his bowstring and placed the arrow with its broad boar tip back into the bark quiver.

"Where'd you spring from?"

At least that's what Robin thought the man said. Hard to tell around his heavy lisp with a crude accent. He halted between words as if he had to think about each one or struggled to get them out. Then he noticed the sideways angle of the chin hiding behind the scant beard.

Someone had broken that jaw, probably with a heavy blow from a cudgel, and it had not been set or healed properly.

Life—no, *people*—had not been kind to this man.

"Join me in watching the land melt into spring," Robin invited, gesturing to a clear space on the other side of his stump.

"Can't. Got work." The man gathered up his bundle of twigs and sticks and hauled them up to the crown of the hill, only feet from where Robin sat.

"What kind of work?" Robin asked, as if he didn't know.

"Paying work."

"Who pays you?"

"Sheriff."

Robin snorted a derisive laugh. "Ye'll nevah see a coin from tha' man." Damnation, he hated how his tongue swelled and made him lisp when he was in short form.

The hunchback shrugged, if you could call that uncomfortable twist and ripple of his spine a shrug.

"Got a name, Stranger?"

"William." He made it sound like "Gquillum."

"Well, Liam, sit a spell and rest from your labors. If Sir Philip Marc parts with a coin in your direction, it won't happen until you're done, and he's had three seasons or more to think about it."

"You know the sheriff?"

Robin wished he'd never met the ruthless French mercenary who was now the king's favorite. They'd encountered each other at an archery contest last spring, and a few other times since King John had appointed him Sheriff of Nottingham.

Liam paused in lining up the strongest branches in straight lines. As he worked, his nimble fingers sorted the lesser twigs by thickness and length. A bit of planning now would make weaving the framework for the kiln easier.

Too efficient for Robin's liking.

"Folks call me Puck," Robin said. He pulled a long blade of grass from a tuft and began chewing sweet moisture from the base.

"Robin Goodfellow, more like." Liam settled himself against

the stump and sighed deeply. He stretched out his legs as well, easing his back by letting something else support it. Remaining upright must be uncomfortable for him at the best of times.

"That, too. I've never figured out if 'Puck' is affectionate or derisive."

"Depends upon what you just did."

Robin let loose a belly laugh, throwing back his head and knocking his green cap askew against the log. He rubbed his nearly bald pate and found a bit of a lump rising. *Oh, well!* It would heal when he grew tall again.

"So, what is this important work you are doing for the sheriff that you won't be paid for?"

Liam closed his mouth and turned his face away. His breathing quickly became labored; the broken jaw and nose probably interfered with his normal passage of air. Still he said nothing.

"An ax like that means you will be felling some trees. Can't cut trees in Sherwood Forest, a Royal Forest, without a royal warrant."

"Sheriff's man says Sir Philip has a warrant for a charcoal kiln. He chose me." Liam heaved himself to his feet, using the ax as a crutch.

Robin wished he had something sturdier than his bow to leverage himself upward.

According to the position of the sun, he'd only been gone from camp three hours. Likely nothing had happened on the baby front yet. He should stay here a bit longer.

"How much charcoal does Sir Philip need?" he called after Liam.

"Two tons 'afore winter solstice. Need to build the kiln

and get it working in two days." Of course, that speech took as long as the shadow cast by the fallen tree trunk to lengthen half a hand's width.

Or so it seemed.

"You know that the river sand dries unevenly in mortar. Not enough lime in it. I don't suppose the sheriff gave you any lime in that bundle of food his men left for you?"

Liam dropped his ax and sat heavily on the rough ground. "Kiln won't work without mortar."

"There's river clay, same's the villagers use to build their wattle-and-daub huts."

Liam looked up, his brow smoother. "Where?"

"Two days' walk upriver."

Liam's face fell again in disappointment.

"I'll cut my wattle today. Tomorrow, early, I'll set off for the clay to make my daub. Will you stay and break bread with me tonight and point the way in the morning?" A very long speech by the hunchback. But he managed to work his mouth around all the words.

Robin checked the sun again. He had time. "Real bread?" His mouth watered.

"Baked yesterday in Nottingham."

Nick stumbled to a halt. A stitch grabbed his right side, sharp, penetrating, breath-robbing.

Don't stop. Not now. I need to be with Jane and John, now.

"Sorry. I . . . can't . . . run . . . anymore," Nick gasped.

Too many turns of the hourglass sitting in the scriptorium this winter, Elena said flatly.

Nick heard a sneer in her mental voice.

Let me go to them. You can follow on your own. She stabbed his mind as sharply as the stitch in his side.

"No. The last time you did that I got lost, lured away by a malevolent tree and trapped by a very hungry Mamoch, the mother of all pigs."

You know the paths from this direction. You've walked them often enough to know the landmarks. Now Elena sounded petulant.

"I missed Brother Luke's passing," Nick protested. "I was his scribe . . . and his friend. I had a right to be there!"

Granted.

"Just give me one moment more to recover my breath."

One moment only. Then Elena began chanting in that ancient, liquid sounding language that Nick swore he must learn before another summer passed.

Gentle warmth filled his body and sent new energy to his limbs. The pain in his side vanished.

"Thank you, Elena." Sorcery might be a sin, as defined by the Church, but at this moment Nick welcomed the healing spirit behind the magic. Maybe the only sin was the Church not understanding the blessings in some magic.

He didn't want to think on that. So he took off running again, along a familiar path that took him to the Woodwose camp in less time than he thought necessary.

I need to be inside Jane's hut.

Nick nodded, knowing Elena would understand his agreement without words.

None of those gathered in the clearing seemed to notice him. He searched for Hilde, not seeing her lithe form among the women.

Quietly, he trod the narrow path toward the creek. When he could hear the chuckling water, but not yet see it, he turned onto a side path no wider than his feet.

The hut looked more like a moss-covered boulder than construct.

Put me inside the door and then leave. Elena seemed distant, focused elsewhere than on him.

Separating himself from her little vessel was always hard. He knew from experience that she only demanded it when necessary, like when she had to accompany Ardenia to Nottingham and carry water from the water sprite's pond to help her escape through the rivulets, or when she'd had to open the gateway to the Faery enclave beneath a hill in order to rescue Jane.

Nick drew the three-faced pitcher from his sleeve, kissed the shiny silver that never tarnished, and placed it just beyond the leather flap that separated him from the interior. "I've brought Elena," he called to the women he sensed were within.

"Just in time!" Hilde called back to him.

Relief washed through him. Between them, Elena and Hilde would make certain all would be well with Jane and the babe.

He walked away with light heels and a lighter heart, to join the men pacing around and around the central hearth.

Six

*ome!*

Tuck hadn't heard that voice on the wind in a long, long time. Not since the night he kept vigil before taking his first vows as a postulant monk at Locksley Abbey.

"Elena?" He thought about shifting his butt to a more comfortable position, but he knew the urgency behind her voice. He'd responded to it often enough when he was Nick's age. Sometimes she'd summoned him to the village to baptize an infant destined to take its last breath within hours of birth. The parents deemed it important that the child have a name and blessing before dying, and so Tuck had complied.

Another time Elena had sent him running to the Woodwose to warn them of the sheriff's men approaching with sword and fire.

Best he creak himself upward rather than seek comfort. "What do I need to take?"

You will not return.

"That sounds ominous."

You are needed.

Silence.

His innards felt like they collapsed with emptiness. Long ago, he'd tucked Elena back into her niche beside the pagan altar in the crypt of the abbey to await the next student who needed her. He'd missed the completeness she granted him in all those long years.

Their communion was not necessarily better than the one he felt with God every time he celebrated Mass and the sacrament of the Eucharist. Elena gave him a *different* sense of accomplishment and usefulness.

He replenished himself with a deep breath as he gathered his few belongings—a spare robe and shirt, battered sandals, and his priestly gear. Since Pope Innocent III had excommunicated King John and placed all of England under interdict, no priest was allowed to celebrate any of the sacraments except baptism and funeral rites. If Elena wanted him to bring his kit, then something dire portended.

"I have felt at home here," he muttered to himself as he surveyed the cave to make sure he'd forgotten nothing. "But I am not meant to have a home. This hermitage will suit another better than it does me."

He gathered the last measure of oats and partial wheel of old cheese. He had a long walk ahead of him.

A sudden weight in his sleeve startled him out of his reverie.

Cautiously, he felt inside the voluminous folds of wool. "Just like days of old," he marveled. Elena had returned to him.

Hold your breath. I will take you where you need to go.

He obeyed, visualizing the three-way crossroad with the tall stone cross marker. As a youth, Elena had always returned him there when he held his breath so long that he lost consciousness.

Not today.

When he opened his eyes, he found himself at the edge of Ardenia's pond, within shouting distance of the Woodwose camp. The sun was just an hour shy of setting.

"About time you came home," Nick grumbled and took the pack from Tuck. "This way. The babe is just birthed and having trouble breathing."

Hilde stepped outside Jane's hut, carrying the mewling newborn wrapped in one of Little John's old shirts.

"Do I dare do this?" she asked the sky, no longer certain who she prayed to anymore.

You must.

"I guess that you are Elena," she said in wonder. "You've never spoken to me before today." Elena had nudged her with images in her mind, showing her how to free the cord from around the baby's neck and how to guide her out butt first. Somehow, Pippa had been given directions where to cut Jane to widen the child's exit. Better a clean cut that could be stitched correctly afterward, than a ragged tear that would never heal straight and strong.

And I can't speak to anyone but Nick until needed. You know what to do. Save the child.

"The priests say it is God's will. . . ."

God helps those who help themselves! God gave you the knowledge for a reason. DO IT!

Hilde took a deep breath to fortify herself. Then she stuck her littlest finger inside the babe's mouth and twisted it within the gob of mucus that made breathing difficult for the helpless girl child. Gently, turning her finger this way and that until completely engulfed in the sticky mess, she pulled her finger free of the slackening mouth.

And pulled.

And pulled.

A long string of the ugly yellowish stuff came free.

The babe gagged and then . . .

Miracle of miracles, she cried at the indignity of birth and life and hunger and needing her mama.

Hilde kissed the child's forehead and carried her back inside the hut. Jane opened her tired arms and brought her baby to her breast where she latched on and suckled greedily.

"She lives and breathes?" Pippa sat back on her haunches, almost as tired from the birthing process as the exhausted mother and babe.

"Aye. A miracle with a little help." Hilde glanced at the tiny three-faced pitcher beside the door. The silver had looked dull and empty all day. Now it glowed softly in the waning light.

She bleeds too much, Elena said.

Pippa must have heard her, for she wrapped a heated stone

from the hearth in her apron and placed it upon Jane's now slack belly. Then she took a handful of moss from her basket and stuffed it inside the birth canal. Finally, she unraveled a thread from the shirt wrapping the child and used it with her delicate silver needle to stitch Jane closed.

By the time they'd finished cleaning up after themselves, Jane and her child slept.

"We can let John see them, but he needs to stay away," Pippa ordered.

"Not much chance of that," Hilde replied as she stepped outside again.

The men must have heard the baby cry, for they gathered at the tree line. They stood silently with shoulders hunched, fists clenched, and beards quivering.

John looked up with hope and worry in his eyes.

"A big healthy girl," Hilde told him, loudly enough for the rest to hear.

The men cheered and slapped each other on the back.

John took one step forward and stopped. "May I. . . ?"

"Yes, go see her. Hold her hand, given her a sip of water when she wakes, but let them both sleep as long as they need."

Little John dashed past her without a sidelong glance. Pippa barred the door. John removed her slight barrier by picking her up at the waist, planting a resounding kiss on her mouth, and setting her aside.

Pippa blushed, then scurried back toward camp. The men followed her with calls for ale to celebrate.

"Is it okay if I retrieve Elena?" Nick asked staring at the hut in wonder.

"If you are quiet and do not disturb them," Hilde replied.

"And me?" Tuck asked hesitantly. "Why was I summoned if the babe thrives and does not need baptism right now?"

"For that, you must ask Elena," Nick laughed and slapped the old man's back.

"You were summoned because you are needed as a leader and adviser for all of us," Hilde replied.

Seven

he last rays of daylight slanted above the horizon, turning the rolling hills of the forest canopy a soft pink. Robin Goodfellow leaned against his stump, watching a fire within a small circle of rocks. The red-and-gold flames with a strong white heart robbed the sky of color and brilliance.

Robin's eyes drooped in a quest for sleep. Liam snored, already lost in slumber. The man worked hard, Robin had to admit. He suspected that the charcoal burner was never truly comfortable with his crooked spine—even in his current pose on his side, with knees curled up nearly to his nose and a soft pack with a change of clothes inside for a pillow—and had to exhaust himself each day in order to find any sleep at all.

The need to grow tall pulled at Robin's joints and dragged sleep from his mind.

Oh, well. With Liam asleep, he could transform now and

not worry about the man knowing his fae nature. That long and very sharp ax rested close to the charcoal burner's hand. He'd use it to defend himself. Anything fae frightened most people who did not live within the forest.

Slowly, so as not to disturb his companion, Robin rolled to his side and struggled to his feet. His knees didn't like the shift of position, so he paused to rub the kinks out. Even this nearly immortal body aged and suffered in the cool damp weather. His joints told him there would be rain by morning even before his nose detected the shift in the breeze.

He hobbled toward a tall stand of concealing shrubbery and let the forces of his curse take over. As his limbs lengthened and his nose and chin shortened, he welcomed the shift from the aches and pains of aging to the mere twisting in transformation. Within moments he was tall, strong, and young again. He didn't care that he could no longer hear or smell so keenly. He had his youthful eyes and body back.

In his peripheral vision, he detected a swaying motion in the middle of a nearby tree. There was just enough light left in the sky to see that the center of the movement was red. A bird chirped a joyful song as it took wing and landed at his feet. Within moments, Will Scarlett stood before him, a big grin on his face, and his cocked hat tilted at a jauntier angle that usual.

"It's a girl!" he crowed. "A big healthy girl who will thrive now that Hilde has worked a miracle and kept her from choking on her first breath."

There was only one new child in the Woodwose camp that Will would be excited about.

"Little John and Jane?" Robin asked, a bubble of joy building in his middle.

"Who else?" Will turned his attention to the snoring figure a few yards to his right. He jerked his chin at Liam and raised his tufted eyebrows in question.

"An interesting man. We're becoming friends," Robin admitted. "He works where and when he can. Even if the sheriff reneges on promised payment, he'll have food and shelter, and a new change of clothes."

"Tuck has returned to the camp," Will said, apparently satisfied with Robin's explanation of the stranger's presence.

"Good. You must tell him and the others of the sheriff's latest plan to drive us from the forest."

Will looked puzzled, eyes narrowed and brows drawn inward to nearly meet across the top of his nose.

"The charcoal burner," Robin reminded him. "Unchecked, he'll clear hundreds of acres of woodland."

Will nodded as if he understood. With his bird brain, one could never tell.

"Maybe I should return to camp tomorrow."

Will's face brightened without the burden of remembering what he was supposed to do.

"Why not now?" Will looked up to the sky that rapidly lost its connection to the sun.

"You may fly at night if you wish. I do not desire to walk that far in the dark." He knew all too well the creatures that prowled the shadows. Young Nick had been trapped by an insane tree and in a pit dug by Mamoch, the mother of all the wild pigs, with tusks as long as Robin's forearm. Only Nick's wits had freed him from the dangers.

Robin dismissed his friend, and returned to the fire where he could sleep with a degree of warmth and comfort. He had no fear of being discovered in his tall form. The curse would change him back to a gnome before dawn whether he willed it or no.

Will dropped into his bird form and flew off before he'd finished transforming.

Nick timed his return to the abbey so that he could lift his cowl and fold his hands in prayer as he processed into the Lady Chapel for silent meditation before the evening meal in the refectory. He'd rather have stayed with the Woodwose and feasted on roast boar and fresh ale, but the men had sent him home.

"I sense the time is coming when we will need your ears and your voice among the abbey folk and the city dwellers," Father Tuck had said. "They won't respect you if you spend too much time in the wild."

And so Nick knelt on the cold stone floor and fingered his beads. The familiar ritual relaxed his shoulders and his mind. He quickly fell into a meditative trance where he forgot Elena and his forest friends, and let the peace of the ordered abbey life wash over him. Deep in his heart, he knew that this was where he belonged. For now.

After a short hour on his knees, Prefect Andrew touched a small silver bell and chanted a three-fold Amen to signal the end of the meditation that replaced the Mass at None—sunset.

Nick's stomach growled in response, jumping awake after nearly a full day of emptiness. Perhaps the scant winter rations would give way to something fresh and more filling than diluted turnip soup, hard bread, and stale cheese. His mouth watered at the thought of the broth enriched by a few eggs, or maybe even a chicken. The old hens were growing lazy about laying and younger birds needed to replace them.

The abbey orphans and the monks continued their silence while Father Blaine read the lessons for the day from the podium.

Sleep began to tug at Nick's eyes. He'd had a long and active day running back and forth to the forest camp and completing the illumination in the scriptorium.

He aimed his steps toward the dormitory when he led the boys into the cloister. From the stumbling shuffle of some of the youngest ones, he knew that they, too, longed for rest.

The clanging of the bell at the front gate jarred him awake. His body stiffened with alarm. The portal should be closed and barred for the night. Only something very important or someone quite desperate would seek entrance this late.

"Take the boys to their cots," Nick whispered to Henry, his friend and the next eldest among the orphans.

He wheeled to return to the refectory and out the other door into the forecourt. The ancient porter slid the viewing port aside and peered out into the dark night.

"Sanctuary! I beg sanctuary," a man's tenor voice cried

through the grille. "Please. You must grant me protection from the king's men."

Derwyn studied the dregs in his cup. Wretched stuff. He didn't understand why Sir Philip Marc, Sheriff of Nottingham devoted so much time and effort in maintaining his stock of wine.

"Have some more," Sir Philip said, holding a silver pitcher out to him.

They lounged in the sheriff's private quarters. Derwyn didn't know if there was a noble wife or not. None seemed in residence, but there was a constant parade of nubile women who helped Sir Philip warm his bed.

"I've had enough drink for now," Derwyn replied. He needed to seek his own bed and sleep off the three cups he'd already drunk. He could swill ale from morning to night without ill effect, but the wine went straight to his head.

"You'll sleep in the hall with the rest of my men. You needn't worry about walking home in the dark. Where is your home by the way?"

"In the forest."

"Tsk, tsk, tsk. Sherwood is a Royal Forest. No one may dwell there." Sir Philip slurred his words a little, not enough to indicate that he couldn't think straight.

"You don't have enough men to clear the forest of all those who dwell, pasture, and hunt there with or without license."

"The day will come, soon, when none of the Woodwose or the poachers can stay hidden. Thanks to you."

"I didn't get you the royal license to hire a charcoal burner to clear the forest. You did that all by yourself." Others would seek to blame Derwyn, but his name was nowhere on any of the correspondence between Sir Philip and the king.

"That is true. In clearing the forest, we will drive out the Woodwose and make them face the punishment they deserve."

"That is all I ask."

"At the same time, you will have no home to return to either. You will need shelter. I offer it to you."

"I cannot sleep indoors or with others. They snore and they smell."

"You will sleep when you've had enough sleepless nights. Spread your pallet across my threshold, away from the others. An assassin will have to trip over you to get to me."

"I did not know that your life has been threatened." Derwyn sat up straighter, feet flat on the stone floor rather than stretched out before the fire. Damnit, these stone castles held the cold against all attempts to warm them.

He didn't used to feel the cold. He could always retreat into his tree to ward off the worst frost. His father had robbed him of that small privilege. Not even the thought of Little John suffering the same fate as the rest of his merry little band warmed Derwyn's feet, even if it did bring a fiery glow to his heart.

"The cost of the license for the charcoal burner means I will have to raise taxes again to cover it. There are always ungrateful wretches who will seek my death rather than pay taxes."

Derwyn grunted in response, not understanding the concept of taxes.

"Most people don't think far enough ahead to try to do something about my need to raise taxes."

Derwyn sort of understood that. Most of the humans he'd dealt with would rather run away than think or do something about their desperate circumstances.

"But there is one man in the city who stirs up trouble with his songs," the sheriff continued without pause, other than to pour more wine into Derwyn's cup.

He'd placed the plain pottery vessel on the table between them rather than continue drinking—or smelling—the vile liquid. It had gone sour and acidic, but it came from France—wherever that was—and therefore, must be better than anything produced locally.

"This songsmith, some call him a bard, but I do not like his music well enough to grant him that honor, calls himself Alain a'Dale and claims to be the illegitimate son of King John."

Illegitimacy was another concept Derwyn had yet to investigate. City dwellers and nobles seemed to value legitimate offspring and cast off the others. In the wild, all children were cherished. A healthy child was more important than naming the sire.

"If King John is the man's sire, then he has a claim to the crown along with Prince Henry. . . ."

"No, no, he doesn't. King John does not own to him. He has no claim at all."

"Then he has been cast aside." As Derwyn had been. He

had a sense of kindred with this Alain a'Dale without having met him.

"The important thing is that this wandering minstrel is singing rousing songs against the king, against me, and denouncing the charcoal burner in Sherwood Forest."

"Who listens to him?" Listening and heeding were two different things. He'd never have revenge on Little John and his brother Verne unless the charcoal burner continued his work uninterrupted for at least a year.

"The man sings in every tavern in the city. Many listen to him. Some of them mutter against me and the charcoal burner. They can do nothing about the king and the many beds he sleeps in. But they think they can do something about taxes and charcoal burners and *me*. That is why I need you to sleep across my doorway. My life is in danger because of this minstrel."

"Why not just arrest this Alain a'Dale and throw him in one of your dungeons?"

"He can still sing in the dungeon. I need him silenced before he flees to the wildwood and disappears from my jurisdiction."

"Oh." That was a concept Derwyn understood. Sherwood Forest should have been his jurisdiction, the lands within his authority.

Instead, Verne had inherited the authority and the power. Derwyn had only another six moon passages before his brother emerged from his tree and exerted that authority and power to keep out the charcoal burner.

"A man as tall and strong as you could intimidate Alain a'Dale into silence."

"You want me to kill him?" The very idea of murdering a kindred spirit, a fellow cast off, panged Derwyn's heart.

"Yes. And quickly. I'll send a dozen men-at-arms with you. But his voice has to be silenced, once and for all."

Eight

ick shifted anxiously from foot to foot while he waited in the shadows between the guesthouse and the main gate. He'd never encountered someone needing sanctuary. What crime could this man have committed that the *king's* men pursued him?

Prefect Andrew hastened to the gate before Father Blaine. He waved aside Brother Porter and peered through the grille at the offender. "Your name and why do you require sanctuary?" he hissed at the stranger.

"They call me Alain a'Dale. I'm a minstrel. The king and the sheriff object to my songs of satire." His voice faded and came back stronger as he looked over his shoulder for signs of pursuit and then back again.

The sounds of horse hooves drilling against the packed dirt of the road came from a near distance. They'd easily ford the millstream below the falls and the marsh between the abbey and the bridge.

"Quickly. Please," Alain a'Dale pleaded.

Prefect Andrew gestured to Brother Porter to remove the crossbar from the pedestrian portal within the large double gate.

Nick dashed forward and pushed the sticking bar into its slot just as Father Blaine scurried up beside them.

"We can't let him in!" the young priest protested. "Since the interdict, we can offer no sanctuary. Only priests may enter the church and then only by the side door."

"We have a duty to those in distress that is not bound by Church law, or Civil law. We have only God's law," Prefect Andrew pronounced, sounding a lot like the exiled Abbot Mæson, or Father Tuck as most knew him these days.

Father Blaine crossed himself and muttered a prayer that clearly included the word *blasphemy*.

Nick continued holding the bar in place while Brother Porter latched it.

"I . . . I shall have to report this to. . . ." Father Blaine said, pulling himself up to his full height that barely reached Prefect Andrew's chin.

"Who can you report to? All of the senior clergy are in exile," Prefect Andrew spat. "A letter to the Pope will be confiscated at the port."

"I shall report to the sheriff."

"He has no authority over an abbey, or a church."

Nick tugged the portal open far enough to allow a slender young man, not much older than himself, to limp in. He doubled over and clutched his side.

"You'll need to go into the church and place a hand on the high altar," Nick whispered to him.

The minstrel looked around in confusion. Locksley was a small abbey with only a few buildings, all made of the same dressed stone. Only the width of the double door differentiated the church from the cloister and the guesthouse. Barns and storage sheds were beyond the wall, closer to the gardens and orchards.

Nick got his shoulder under the stranger's arm and dragged him toward the cloister so they could enter the church from other than the main doors. His brief glance outside had revealed a troop of horsemen with torches approaching from the northeast, the direction of Nottingham.

Prefect Andrew slammed the crossbar back into place with a loud thump. "I am senior to you, Blaine. Abbot Mæson left me in charge. I grant this man sanctuary. Now get out of our way while I tend to him. He's bleeding and in need of our care." He stomped up beside Nick and the refugee, taking part of the burden of the now stumbling man.

Nick hadn't noticed the blood streaming from a cut at the man's temple. It stained his free-flowing blond hair. Another darkness at his side marred his light-colored shirt. "I'll fetch Brother Daffyd and his kit," he whispered to Prefect Andrew as he hastened into the cloister and thence to the infirmary in the opposite corner.

In his mind, he ran an inventory of their stores. The poppy

juice was gone. Would an infusion of willow bark be enough to ease Alain a'Dale's pain?

"Why so restless, Robin?" Father Tuck asked. He had to shift from his customary stump to the ground and still could not ease his back and legs. "You leave me unsettled."

Robin the Archer paused in his circular movement. "The forest seems amiss," he replied.

"I am too far removed from my wild ancestors to sense the mood of the woods," Tuck grumbled. But now that Robin had spoken, he wondered if whatever was amiss also left him unsettled and unable to find comfort, even with the fire warming his feet and good friends warming his heart.

They both looked in the direction of Little John's and Jane's hut. "Is he too far removed from the Green Man to sense what we sense?" Tuck asked.

"Tonight, he is preoccupied with his wife and newborn child," Robin replied. "I don't know that he has any other human children. He is enamored of the babe."

"The sun has set. Will Scarlett does not like flying after dark to spy out the cause," Tuck grumbled. A part of him missed young Nick's comments—some of them echoes of Elena's observations. He rolled to his feet and joined Robin in his meandering path around and through the camp.

"We need to find out if the charcoal burner's presence upsets the balance of life within the forest." Robin did not falter in his progress.

"Of course, it does." Tuck snapped his fingers with realization. "The question remains; what can we do about him?"

"I've delayed him a few days by sending him in search of lime to mortar his kiln." A brief grin flashed across Robin's face, then dissolved. "But he is dogged in his determination to do his work and do it well. He will not give the sheriff any reason to exile or kill him, just because his humpback incites superstitious fear among the city dwellers."

"You say he might be handsome without the twist in his spine and his lisping speech."

"Perhaps. I am not one to judge beauty." Robin marched ahead of Tuck, presenting only his back for observation.

"Has the hunchback made you think more deeply about your curse?" Tuck called after his friend.

Robin grumbled something unintelligible.

Vibrations through the ground stopped their pacing. They both turned to face the intruder, knees bent, fists balled, eyes searching, ready to fight or flee.

A magnificent eight-point stag, big-bodied, as tall at the shoulder as a normal man, rusty fur rippling with nervous twitches. An instant later, Herne the Huntsman emerged from his fae persona. The huge antler rack lingered longer than the rest of his body. He had to close his eyes and shake his head to rid himself of the last vestiges of the king of the forest.

"What brings you, friend?" Tuck asked, approaching the man, flat hand raised in peaceful greeting.

"The road," Herne gasped, not yet recovered from his long run and hasty transformation.

"The Royal Road?" Robin asked, stepping closer, also hand up, signaling no violent intentions.

Herne shook his head again and swallowed deeply, his throat apple bobbing. "From Nottingham to Locksley Abbey. Men on horseback, riding fast, torches and swords and . . . horns."

Message given, he whirled to face the forest once more and fled two rapid steps as he shape-changed once more. The deer disappeared into the gloom in the blink of an eye.

"Herne doesn't usually concern himself with people outside Sherwood," Robin said, continuing to stare at the spot where the Huntsman had vanished.

"The road from Nottingham goes nowhere but the abbey in these parts." Concern began as an uncomfortable wiggle in Tuck's belly.

"They have hunting horns. The hue and cry!" Robin cried as he started toward the exit from the camp toward the Royal Road—the fastest and surest way toward the abbey. He stopped abruptly and began the shrinking process to transform into his gnome figure.

"Robin," Tuck said in the voice he usually reserved for recalcitrant students.

The archer froze with only his nose extended and his ears protruding.

Tuck gasped, never having seen him only partially in both forms. "Even Robin Goodfellow cannot see in the dark. We have to wait for morning."

"I worry about Nick." Robin resumed his manly face.

"Nick is smart. And resourceful. He's not been near Nottingham in many months. The hue and cry cannot be for him," Tuck reassured himself as well as his companion. But he did worry for the abbey and for all of the men who'd found a home and a calling there. They were all his responsibility.

"Can your monks hold off men-at-arms with swords and torches?" Robin asked. "The Church no longer has a presence in England. Will soldiers with their bloodlust roused pause to consider their immortal souls if they burn the place down in search of their quarry?" he shuddered.

Tuck had heard his confession often enough to know a few of his hideous deeds during the Crusades and later as a mercenary for the Holy Roman Emperor—all in the name of the peaceful and beneficent Church that Tuck loved.

Another Frenchman rose up from the tangled mass of dead and dying soldiers, pike aimed at Robin's head.

He ducked and rammed his bloody sword deep into the man's gut. Then he rolled out of the way of the spraying blood and guts only to encounter a knight with a sword raised above his head. Robin yanked his own weapon free of the pikeman and brought it to bear just in time to block the downward thrust from the unknown knight.

"Do ye yield?" bellowed the Frenchman in a southern accent that spoke more of Spain than France.

Robin couldn't remember who he was supposed to be fighting in this battle. Or who he was fighting for.

The last he remembered, the Holy Roman Emperor had paid him and his band of mercenaries. Next month, whoever was King of France these·days, would pay him more to fight on the other side.

"I'll die first," he shouted back to his opponent as he rolled, tangling his feet with the other man and bringing him down to ground level, his sword flailing dangerously as did his arms.

Robin called upon his exhausted body to keep moving, putting enough distance between himself and the knight to come back to his feet and position himself for battle once more.

All around him, the sounds of other men fighting for their lives—weapons clashing, throats groaning as they suffered wounds or died—faded from his awareness. His concentration focused on the French knight.

He, too, fought to rise and face Robin. But he collapsed to his knees, clutching his helm. His sword dropped from nerveless fingers.

Blood trickled beneath his helm, down his neck.

He swayed and didn't try to catch his balance.

Robin raised his sword to give the man a killing blow. The *coup de grace*.

But he couldn't. He couldn't kill an unarmed man who was half dead already.

He looked around to see who he had to defend himself against next.

Only a few men continued to fight. Their blows slowed as exhaustion claimed them. Long shadows stretched across the field, the last of the sunlight glinting off dulled and dented armor.

"I think it's time I went home," he whispered. Inside his head his words sounded like the toll of a bronze bell.

Home!

Marian!

He had to go now. He'd waited too long for his beloved Marian to grow up. If he didn't claim her now, he never would. Not waiting to report to his commander or check on the welfare of his men, he limped toward the rear lines, grabbed the bridle of the nearest horse, and mounted. Too tired to think, he kicked the unfamiliar animal into a trot, checked his bearing by the sun, and rode west toward the Channel and a port.

Home and Marian beckoned him like a holy vision. His life as a Crusader and a mercenary was done. Finished.

He had more than enough money stashed with the Templar Order to buy back Marian's dower lands. He had no more valid reasons for staying away from home and Marian.

Nick sprinted up the bell tower ladder of the abbey church. More squat than tall, and with room for only one small bronze bell, the bell ringer's loft still had a better view of the forecourt and the fields to the west than any other place in the abbey.

He leaned out, hoping his dark robe would help hide him if the leader of the men-at-arms chanced to look up. The man rode a tall black horse, and a jewel in the pommel of his sword winked in the torchlight. A minor noble whom Nick had never seen before, though he'd seen the sheriff and his cronies many times as they traveled the Royal Road or visited the local village for one reason or another.

The abbey sat on a side road south and west of the Royal Road on a lane that went nowhere else. The troop of armed men would not come here by mistake or seeking shelter for the night.

The conversation between Father Blaine and the noble came to him in brief snatches as the men shifted about the forecourt.

"A warrant from the king."

"We are isolated and offer no concern to His Highness."

"The sheriff begs to differ. You offer sanctuary even though the Church no longer has authority in England."

"The laws of sanctuary predate the Church in England," Brother Theo replied. He presided over the scriptorium and was probably the most learned man in the abbey. Only Abbot Mæson had wider knowledge. But the abbot had taken himself into exile. As far as the sheriff and king knew, he'd gone to Paris.

Is that true? Nick asked Elena.

Of course. That is why the Christian monks have never desecrated my pagan altar in the crypt.

"Lay people may not enter the Church." Father Blaine took up a place bracing his feet and folding his arms into his sleeves. For once in his life, he stood firm. "The Holy Father has decreed that under the interdict, only priests may pass within the church and they may not use the front door."

Nick had known that and instinctively led the man seeking sanctuary through a side door that led to the vestry and the

Lady Chapel. He thought he'd read that sanctuary could only be granted at the high altar, behind the rood screen, a place forbidden to lay people now.

A conundrum.

The noble dismounted. "I recognize no authority here. Not even God's." He shoved Father Blaine's slight form aside. His heavy boots echoed against the stone steps leading to the church.

"You may not enter, for fear of your immortal soul!" Brother Theo affirmed, loud enough to be heard inside and all around the forecourt.

The mounted men shifted nervously in their saddles. Only two of the dozen dismounted and joined their leader. They kept one hand on the pommels of their swords, ready to draw and engage in battle against unarmed monks.

You must hide Alain a'Dale. Take him to Father Tuck.

Nick didn't question the little goddess. He hastened down the ladder to the spiral staircase of the tower and along the nave to the rood screen. "Can he travel?" he whispered to Brother Daffyd, where he knelt beside the refugee, applying pressure to the wound on his side.

"He shouldn't," the physician hissed back at him.

"The king's men approach."

"I heard." Brother Daffyd bit his lip as he searched the shadowed space for a hiding place.

"I will hold them back," Brother Thom, the blacksmith, said. He clenched his good hand into a tight fist and settled his broad shoulders beneath his robes.

"You can't. You are not well," Brother Daffyd protested.

"I may not have my full strength back yet. But I can make these men think twice about proceeding further, delay them a bit while you get yon minstrel over the orchard wall. Nick knows where to go from there." He took a stance at the base of the dais. His grim frown and lowered brow reminded Nick of Little John when he took offense at some puny human.

Nick bent and draped Alain a'Dale's arm over his shoulder and heaved upward. Brother Daffyd grabbed the man around the waist and led them both out the postern door into the cloister as someone outside pounded on the front door with the pommel of his sword demanding entry. The latch was flimsy and would not keep them out for long.

Nine

"nly priests are allowed to enter the church, and then they must use a portal other than the regular, public one," Brother Daffyd reminded Nick. He checked the cloister for any sign of watchers, armed or not.

"So if the men-at-arms have actually read the Proclamation of Interdict, they do not have to honor this man's sanctuary claim because he should not have entered the church at all." Nick shook his head at the puzzle as he adjusted his grip on Alain a'Dale. The minstrel had lost too much blood and hung heavily between them. "But then, the soldiers should not be allowed to enter the sacred space to find this man."

"Unless they use their swords, and that defilement will cost them their immortal souls unless they confess and do penance."

"Do we dare cover him in a monk's robe and hide him in your infirmary?" Nick thought through the problem of getting Alain a'Dale over the orchard wall and into Sherwood Forest. He could, of course, use Elena to take him to the crossroad in the blink of an eye. That might be far enough. They could hide in the underbrush behind the stone cross that marked the spot where three roads met and diverged again.

The sanctity of crossroads is not protected by any but me. The soldiers can violate the space without a second thought to your Church laws, Elena reminded Nick.

Ancient custom and superstition might slow them down, Nick chuckled back to the little goddess.

Then aloud he asked, "Will the soldiers think to look for Alain at the crossroad?"

"Can you get him that far?" Brother Daffyd asked. "He's dead weight right now." He looked Nick up and down, assessing his strength.

"I'll try . . ." Alain whispered through a split lip that oozed blood with each word.

"A cup of ale laced with poppy juice," Nick said. He knew precisely how much poppy juice they had left . . . three drops. Would that ease Alain's pain enough to get him over the wall?

Nick dared not disappear within the abbey. He had to keep Elena a secret, that was part of his bargain with her. He also had to avoid an accusation of witchcraft. He didn't fancy burning at the stake for that crime against God.

"Worth a try, boy. I'd go with you, but when yon baron searches the precincts, he will expect to find an infirmarian."

Brother Daffyd helped Nick settle the minstrel beneath the overhanging apple tree, then hastened back into the infirmary.

"Rest easy a few moments," Nick placed his hand on Alain's chest, urging him to cease twitching and trying to get his legs beneath him. At least he breathed steadily, if a little shallow. Brother Daffyd had bound his ribs tightly to contain the slashing wound along his side. That had to make drawing a deep breath difficult.

After what felt like hours, Brother Daffyd returned with a wooden mug frothing with fresh small beer. Nick's mouth watered, craving the moisture.

The infirmarian knelt beside his patient and coaxed some of the drugged beer between his lips. After a first, difficult swallow, Alain drank deeply, eagerly.

As Nick watched by the feeble light showing through the infirmary windows, Alain's eyes cleared of the pain glaze and he took a deeper breath.

"Let's go," Nick said. He stood and surveyed the wall and the stoutness of the overhanging branch.

Behind him, he heard shouts and stomping feet. He didn't have long before the men-at-arms would find them.

"I'll climb up. Then you push and I'll pull him to the top."

"Easy on his shoulders. His ribs are hurting."

"I don't think there's a way to do this without hurting him. Master Minstrel, do your best to keep from crying out your pain."

Alain nodded and clenched his jaw. Brother Daffyd got his hands into Alain's armpits and lifted him upward.

Alain moaned but kept his mouth closed. He took two deep breaths, then nodded that he was ready for the next move.

Brother Daffyd guided his hands upward. The patient had to stretch to grasp the branch. Nick had to reset his balance and reach farther down than he liked to grab hold of his other hand. He wasn't a tall man, probably an inch or two shorter than Nick himself.

Brother Daffyd shifted to push Alain upward from his knees.

Slowly, with at least three pauses for both Nick and Alain to regain their breath, they got him perched atop the wall.

"He looks mighty pale," Nick whispered back to Brother Daffyd.

"Give him as many breaks as possible. Try to keep him from bleeding more."

Nick girded himself and dropped to the ground on the other side. "Just let yourself fall. I'll catch you."

"Heard that one before." Before either of them could think better of this adventure, Alain turned around so that he faced Nick and let go.

Nick broke his fall more than caught him. He lay sprawled on the ground, Alain's weight heavy on his chest. A quick check to the bandages revealed no new blood to Nick's fingertips.

Hold your breath! Elena broke her silence.

The sounds of angry men shouting on the other side of the wall alerted Nick a heartbeat later.

He obeyed.

I don't like this part, he informed the little goddess.

Necessary.

Before Nick could think about it, his mind grew fuzzy. The world enveloped him in darkness.

Hilde waited until false dawn lessened the shadows along the canopy of tall trees. She hadn't slept much since she'd overheard Herne warn Robin and Tuck about riders bearing swords and torches. She worried for Nick.

But if he managed to flee Locksley Abbey, she knew where he would go first.

Blaidd, the father of the wolves, paced the fringe of the camp. Somehow, she knew that he'd follow her and keep her safe.

As soon as dawn had brightened the sky enough that most forest predators would seek their burrows and lairs, she crept forth. Blaidd might protect her from another wolf, or even a bear, but he'd be no match against Mamoch or one of her tusked consorts.

Hilde grabbed a water skin, a handful of tubers and the last of the cooked grains, now cold, placing the food into a bowl. At the last moment she turned back and grabbed her kit of clean bandages and healing potions. With Nick and the forest wild, she never knew in advance what she'd need.

In the low dawn light, she made good time, even as she paused frequently to find landmarks near lush berry bushes just coming into flower, fiddlehead ferns, and stray apple trees amongst the maples. Soon the forest would feed the Wood-wose more lavishly than the villagers who relied on over-worked gardens and the occasional bounty from the abbey or the sheriff.

The sun had risen a full length above the horizon when she came near the tangled oak tree where she'd taken shelter from Mamoch, the mother of all wild pigs, perpetually pregnant and raveningly hungry.

Sherwood Forest ended just beyond that tree at the market road.

Hilde let the tree shade and shadow her while she looked and sniffed for intruders. Three days before the market in the village, few used the road that connected outlying dwellings with the mill and the village grown up around it.

She listened for the sounds of riders or marching soldiers. Only the occasional bird chirp, the rustle of mice seeking a meal among the grasses, and the swish of tree branches stirring in the morning breeze. A chill brushed her cheek. Rain soon. By midafternoon, at the latest. She needed to hurry.

Off to the south of her, the mostly hidden shape of Blaidd raised his muzzle and seemingly nodded to her. She felt as if she could trust him. All was safe.

A flash of red appeared in her peripheral vision, and she pressed her back tightly against the oak while her eyes sought the unnatural color.

A red bird landed on a low branch, setting it aflutter.

"Will," she called softly. "Will Scarlett." Another protector?

Blaidd faded into the broad meadow grasses.

Instantly, the bird dropped to the ground, transforming into a slight man with a jaunty cap sporting a red feather. "Tuck says I must find you and help with whatever you find."

Leave it to Tuck to know where she headed and why.

"To the crossroad, then." She gestured along the road, little more than two ruts, the width of wagon wheels, with new grass sprouting along the center hump and the deep verges.

Will whistled a spritely tune that set a somewhat faster pace than Hilde thought wise. Three full seasons with the Woodwose had taught her caution. Will rarely thought farther ahead than his next three steps. She followed him toward the crossroad two steps behind, keeping a wary lookout. Blaidd had disappeared and offered no help.

Then Will stopped short and held out his arms to keep Hilde from moving forward. "I smell blood," he whispered.

Hilde crouched behind a flowering clump of berry vines.

"Human blood," Will added, dropping down beside her.

She expected him to shrink into his bird form and fly off. He remained at her side. At her inquisitive gaze, he shrugged. "Tuck said I must stay with you until you send me back to bring help."

"Good enough." She peered between the leafy vines in search of something out of place.

The tall stone cross at the crossroad dominated the triangle of land at the junction of three roads. Two wayward goats nibbled at the grass and encroaching weeds, keeping them from overwhelming the sacred space.

She saw no one standing or sitting.

"Where are you, Nick?" she asked the wind.

An annoying bird whistled into Nick's ear.

Groggily he swatted at the noise.

The bird called again, just as loudly, and just as intrusive.

In self-defense Nick cracked open one heavy eyelid. "Where am I?" he whispered, more a thought directed to Elena.

Where do you expect to be?

With that thought came a tingling jolt from the top of Nick's head to his toes and back again.

His eyes opened, and his mind began working. "A tangle

of ferns and vines covering me. Us." He noted the weight of Alain a'Dale stretched out beside him, his head on Nick's shoulder.

Memory flooded through him. The banging on the abbey gate, shuffling through the postern into the church that had been sealed for nigh on a year, helping Brother Daffyd clean and bandage Alain's wounds, then the dragging of him to the infirmary herb garden and up onto the orchard wall.

"I held my breath until I passed out and you brought us to the crossroad."

Then you crawled beneath the shrubbery at the tree line and fell asleep.

Nick lifted a branch, trying not to disturb Alain. He winced and blinked rapidly at the brightness of the sun. "Why did you let me sleep so long? We should have been moving before dawn. Now the sun has been up at least an hour." He shifted to dislodge Alain from his shoulder.

The minstrel groaned and rolled over, flinging an arm across Nick's middle, pinning him in place.

Nick gingerly lifted that arm by the minstrel's fine linen sleeve. Judging by the texture of his shirt, Alain a'Dale had lived a privileged life before he ran afoul of the law.

"Angelique, *mon amour,*" Alain mumbled and held Nick tighter.

"Um . . . I'm not Angelique," Nick replied, trying for his most masculine voice and hoping it didn't crack and reach into a small boy's range.

Alain opened one eye a slit. "Don't care, you'll do." He lifted his face, lips pursed.

Appalled, Nick rolled to the other side and to his knees. Then he wondered at the tightness in his groin.

He'd heard whispers among the monks and the older orphans a few years back. Some men preferred other men to women. They were not liked, but tolerated as long as they confessed and did penance. Some men didn't care about men or women as long as they were young, too young to know what predators did to them. They were not tolerated. Some men didn't care as long as their partners were human. Godly men walked away.

"We'd best move on," he said. "If you are recovered enough for . . . *that*, you can walk."

"Any food?" Alain asked testing his ribs and shoulder for injury and fresh bleeding, not at all embarrassed.

Elena chuckled.

Nick scowled. *It's not funny.*

"Nick?" A soft feminine voice called from beyond the screening bush.

"Hilde? How'd you find me?"

She sighed. "Where else would I look for you when there's trouble? I see a trail of blood. Are you hurt?" Concern clouded her voice even as her shadow blocked the light drifting through the branches.

"Not me. Our guest has wounds that need tending again," he said, crawling out from the rough shelter.

"Guest?" she squeaked as he stood up.

"Aye. Alain a'Dale, minstrel, angered the sheriff with his songs. Apparently, the king has little use for him, either." He straightened his robe and shuffled his feet, trying to center himself.

A heartbeat later, Alain also crawled from beneath the shielding branches. His tawny jerkin, the same color as his hair, did little to hide the bloodstains across his middle, and under the light of the sun, his face had more swollen bruises than natural color.

Hilde, bless her, did not gasp in dismay. Like the good, practical girl she was, she assessed him, looked to the pack on her back, then turned to face the man behind her.

Nick kicked himself mentally for not noticing another intruder. He needed to be more observant. He'd confess to Father Tuck when they reached the Woodwose camp.

"Will, go fetch Robin and John. We'll need help getting him home and sheltered."

Will Scarlett's clothes began to glow a deeper red.

"Not here," Nick warned him with a heavy hand on his shoulder.

Will needed a moment to figure out what was being asked of him. Then he looked keenly at Alain, a stranger, and nodded. He turned and ran across one of the three roads into the trees before shifting into his bird form.

"What was that about?" Alain asked.

Nick shrugged and pulled his own pack from the burrow behind the stone cross. "I doubt you'll walk far without food and water," he said. "We have some time before the others join us." He made to sit, cross-legged on the grass at the front of the cross.

"Not here," Hilde insisted, hands on hips and chin thrust out in stubbornness.

Nick knew enough not to cross her when she took on that posture.

"There's a creek just beyond yon oak. There's shadow there to hide within. Shelter from the next rain shower as well." She looked to the skies, and a single fat drop fell upon her face.

"Can you walk, Alain?" Nick asked, juggling to get one arm through the strap of his pack and the other beneath Alain's arm.

"Won't know until I try. Do you have my lute?" He paused looking into all the dark shadows.

"You didn't have one with you when you banged on the abbey gate demanding sanctuary," Nick replied.

"Satan take them all!" He clenched his fist and bunched his shoulders as if preparing to hit someone. Then he gasped and clutched his middle instead. "The only thing of value I owned, and that self-important knight smashed it." A tear leaked from the corner of his eye. "My father gifted me that lute when my mum died."

Hilde had the grace to look away. Then she pushed her own shoulder beneath his arm and led them toward the tree line across the road.

The silence among them was a palpable thing, almost an impish thing from the Dark Lord putting up barriers among them.

Ten

uck shivered beneath the shelter of a crude lean-to. The morning had promised warmth and sunlight, then betrayed him with this heavy downpour of rain. Thick malicious drops that sought out, and found, every threadbare spot of his leather jerkin and hose. His leg coverings had been fine and warm when he set out from the abbey a year ago in his royal-imposed exile. Now they were thin and bared as much skin as they covered.

His knees and hands ached with the joint disease.

This shower presaged a more vicious storm. Already, the sky thickened and lowered, changing the uncertain light to near twilight.

"If I could leave England, I'd be in Rome where they barely notice winter and summer dominates the weather three-quarters of the year's turning."

He dragged a deer hide blanket over him.

Ah, a modicum of warmth.

He glared out at the old woman who sat by the fire mindlessly cutting up turnips, wild onions, and wild carrots into the stewpot. She didn't seem to notice, let alone mind, the rain. She had her duty and she fulfilled it, every day, all day, as long as the youngsters brought her more vegetables to cut into the pot.

Nearby, Robin Goodfellow skinned a brace of hares he'd snared earlier. The Woodwose would dine well tonight. Tuck refused to think about the graciousness of the abbot's table before his exile. He didn't always fare better than the brother monks and orphan boys. But if a villager graced them with a partridge or a haunch of wild boar, he was granted first cut.

"I need to puzzle out what to do about the charcoal burner," he told himself quite firmly. "What will the sheriff gain from the very expensive royal license to clear the forest? Why has he come now?"

"Perhaps you should ask who prods the sheriff into action," Little John said. He dropped cross-legged at the opening of the lean-to. None of the stacked and woven branches covered the big man. He, too, seemed oblivious to the intense rain.

But then Little John had spent as much time in his tree, soaking up the rain, as he had in skin, until last autumn.

"What have you heard?" Tuck asked his friend.

"I've just spent the morning communing with Verne." He sniffed the stew with relish as Robin added chunks of meat to the cauldron. The rabbit bones went in as well, to add flavor to the mix.

"And Verne tells you what?"

"That there is much bustle at the edges of our forest. Nottingham expands beyond its walls, and a new village has begun near the fishing pond."

"King John would not grant those privileges cheaply," Tuck said. His mind began to swirl around a myriad of ideas, seeking a chain of logic between them. "Is the king raising money to go to war again?"

"That I do not know. But unless King John and the Holy Father come to terms soon, other countries may find themselves willing to invade from across the sea."

For Little John to speculate on politics beyond Sherwood Forest, the situation must be dire.

"The last time King John went to war, he collected a lot of silver pennies in scutage from his barons and then dismissed them. Then he used the money to hire foreign mercenaries. When the battles in France were over, His Highness turned the mercenaries loose here in England rather than send them home, Sir Philip Marc among them. They pillaged and burned their way across England. Sherwood suffered mightily. And continues to suffer now that Sir Philip is sheriff. The man has no honor, and fewer scruples." Tuck struggled to sit up before continuing his tirade. He coughed and rubbed his knuckles while he gathered his thoughts.

"Nick's parents, their entire village, died at the hand of those mercenaries. He was the only survivor." Tuck remembered vividly how he'd found the toddler digging in the ashes for his mother. He'd only been three or four at the time. Old enough to speak and feed himself from the bowl placed before him, but barely out of nappies.

"How does Verne know about the new building? Isn't he stuck in his tree in the clearing by the standing stones?"

"Aye. But trees talk to each other, letting the breeze carry their thoughts."

Little John would know that.

"The trees and shrubs, even the grasses, shout alarms to the creatures of the wood. Yon hares were easily snared because they fled from the verge of the forest where village gardens offer easy pickings." Little John lapsed into a long, still silence.

"Do you miss your tree, my friend?"

"Sometimes. Less so with each day. Especially now that I have a human daughter who needs me much more than any of my dryad offspring ever did." He heaved himself upward. "I've been gone too long. I need to check on Jane, see if she and the babe need anything." In three long strides he had disappeared into the shelter of the wood.

A loud flutter of wings masked the sound of Little John's footsteps.

Will Scarlett appeared even as the bird's feet touched ground. The red feather in his cap looked wet and bedraggled.

"What brings you with such urgency?" Tuck asked the birdman.

"Hilde requires assistance. She has found Nick and a wounded man who flees the sheriff's men. She waits by the crossroad." Without warning, he spread his arms and sprouted feathers again, a vivid red, more brilliant than usual. Two strides and three flaps and he rose again to the tree canopy.

He must be agitated. His words had been strong, without hesitation or wondering why he'd been sent.

"I'll go." Robin grabbed his bow and quiver even as he grew tall and long-legged.

"I should join you . . ." Tuck made to cast off his comforting blanket.

"You'll only slow me down. Stay here and keep warm. We don't want you coming down with the lung sickness." And then he, too, was gone, running lightly along a barely seen path.

Tuck settled back beneath his blanket, mind too anxious to fall into the rhythms of sleep, his body not restless enough to make him move.

"What are the king and sheriff up to?" he asked the wind.

It answered with a fresh spate of rain.

Tuck longed for the shelter of his cave where he could hunker by the fire without fear of burning down his leaking roof. At the cave, messengers from his fellow clergymen could find him.

But old Catryn by the stewpot fed him much better than his own cooking of offerings from the villagers.

⁕

Nick pulled up the cowl of his robe so that it covered his head and shadowed his face. Then he climbed the twisted branches of the old oak tree. From up here he had a better view of three different game trails through the underbrush. He scanned them for signs of rescue or pursuit.

He could also more easily ignore Alain a'Dale taking every opportunity to fondle Hilde in places Nick barely dared think about let alone touch.

"Keep your hands to yourself, treacherous bastard!" Hilde admonished the minstrel. Her words were followed by a resounding slap.

"What will you do if I don't?" Alain replied with a sneer in his voice.

"I'll haul you back to the middle of the road and leave you to be found by the sheriff's men."

Nick watched her walk along the path that led most directly to the Woodwose camp. She, too, had drawn up her cowl to cover her dark hair. He chuckled to himself. He needn't worry about Hilde. She could take care of herself.

"How long must we wait?" Alain called up to Nick. He'd lowered his voice to a discreet level, obviously aware of the strange echoes and enhancements of sound within the wildwood.

"An hour, if someone comes directly. No telling if they are all out hunting and foraging." Nick settled into a broad fork of the tree, continuing his vigil.

"I could use some ale to wet my throat."

"None left."

Blessed silence between them for several long moments.

"I'm not used to being alone unless I'm composing and then I have my lute for company. My lovely lute. A gift from my father. He left it with my mother before disappearing on the battlefields of France."

"I liked you better when you were unconscious."

"If I had some ale, I could sing to pass the time."

"You'd attract attention."

"That is an art I must practice as a minstrel. What good are my songs if people ignore me?"

"What good are your songs if they get you killed?"

Another long silence that made Nick feel heavy.

The sight of Hilde running back toward them lightened his gloom.

She waited until she reached the tree before speaking, keeping her voice low so that *she* wouldn't attract attention from the nearby road. "Robin comes with Llwyf."

"That didn't take long," Alain said.

Nick did not enlighten him that Llwyf was a dryad, son of the Green Man, and had ways of moving through the forest with great strides that ate up the distance in moments instead of hours. Robin, too, had some form of magic that Nick had not witnessed to travel quickly when needed.

No sense in frightening Alain with knowledge of the Wild Folk. He might easily decide that the gaol in Nottingham Castle would be safer than living in Sherwood Forest.

Riding on Llwyf's back wasn't much different for Robin than having Little John carry him. The son of an elm had grown almost as tall as his father, but his stride was definitely shorter.

Still they progressed through Sherwood Forest much faster than Robin could have run the distance on his own.

He'd just caught a glimpse of the top of the old oak where Will had said Nick and Hilde awaited them, rising above the canopy when the red bird flitted about his head, chittering and flapping in agitation. Will was upset enough that he couldn't, or wouldn't, take his mannish form long enough to impart understandable words.

"Smell that?" Llwyf asked, wriggling his nose.

"Fire," Robin exclaimed as his nose caught the drift of smoke through the rain. "Must be a big one for it to penetrate the gloom."

"The only thing that will burn in this muck is a sheltered blaze fed by men." Llwyf began to shake even as he lengthened his stride.

"The charcoal burner," Robin reassured Llwyf. "No need to fear the spread of the flames."

"Smells strange. Not a natural fire."

Robin sniffed again. Sharp. Acrid. "He's burning limestone to make his plaster for lining the kiln inside and out."

Llwyf shook his great head, shedding rain all over Robin. "I do not like this. Not at all, at all."

"Keep going. We'll deal with Nick's and Hilde's refugee, and then I'll go to Liam afterward. If he's just now burning limestone, he'll need another two days at least before the kiln is ready."

"A man can clear a lot of forest in two days while waiting to burn," Llwyf grumbled.

"Aye, but he can't stray far from the lime. And he has to feed that fire often to keep it hot enough." Robin had learned that much from the masons his father hired to repair the ramparts of Locksley Castle when he was but a child.

A few more long strides and Robin saw Hilde jump up and down, waving her arms in silent signal that she awaited them.

"Once we get the stranger settled, may I request assistance in reaching the charcoal burner's camp?" he asked Llwyf.

"Gladly. I want the man gone. Quickly. He's a menace to all that grows in or near our home."

"That is not all that threatens us." Robin turned his head to catch the source of the new sound that threatened them. "Horses. A dozen of them. Well shod. Traveling light, slowing often. A search. But are they seeking a fresh game trail for hunters or something else?"

"Someone else," Llwyf grunted. "Yon oak is too close to the road for our friends to hide long."

"Then hurry. We have only moments to get them and their injured refugee well hidden."

Eleven

erwyn did not like the way his mount paced unevenly, obviously trying to dislodge him from its bony back. Neither of the two knights or the nine men-at-arms seemed to have as much discomfort from riding as he did. He could have run beside the mounted men without trouble. He was used to striding about the entire forest daily.

But now, the forest as well as his horse made his skin prickle all over. He was not wanted here. As long as he kept to the road, the spirits of the woods could not reject him.

Soon, though, they'd reach the crossroad. From there, the knight—he couldn't remember the man's name, nor did he want to—could spot the gnarled old oak that Derwyn knew had given shelter to humans before. That tree stood just within the natural boundary of Sherwood Forest—a dividing line determined by wildwood, not by any human markings or deeds or decision.

Derwyn would not be able to cross that line. His gut boiled at the idea that he'd never be able to go home again, never find solace in his tree again.

How did he explain that to the knights without them burning him for a witch?

"There, sir," the leading man pointed to his right as he came abreast of the oak. "Just as he described it, a twisted oak with a broad branch growing low to the ground, not but two hundred paces from the road."

"We are too late," Derwyn muttered. He knew it without even approaching the massive old oak. "They have fled."

"Then we must follow them," the lead knight said. Sir Eustace, that was his name.

"Once inside Sherwood, you'll not find the criminals. If you ride the Royal Road, they might find you, if they choose. And you will not fare well when they do." Derwyn clicked his tongue at his mount and tugged on the reins, as he'd been taught. The beast plodded around to face the other direction. It needed a stern kick from the rider's heels to get it moving again.

The only mount the sheriff could find strong enough to carry Derwyn's size was more suited to pulling a plow or a cart than carrying a man. But once turned, with its nose headed toward home where its food trough resided, it decided to move with a bit more brightness in its step.

Derwyn settled into the saddle as best he could and let the horse do the work of returning to Nottingham.

He'd rather walk.

Llwyf carried Alain into the forest. Hilde didn't even try to keep up. She didn't like the deep bruising across the man's ribs,

nor the whistling edge to his breathing. Most likely, whoever
had beat him had cracked a bone in there. She sincerely hoped
a bit of rib did not bend out of place and puncture his lung.

The only cure for either condition was time. And rest. And
quiet.

She'd only spent a brief part of the morning with him and
already she wished he would cease the constant flow of words.
Granted, he had a lovely voice and spoke with musical phras-
ing, a lot like Will Scarlett, as if his next word would be the
beginning of a song. But she'd heard too many words and not
enough music.

Will flitted about above her head, staying close as if worried about her. The farther ahead Llwyf strode the tighter
circles Will flew. Robin had harried off to the south. Nick
had stayed at the crossroad. She was truly alone in the wildwood, as she had not been since she first fled the convent.

Something felt amiss. The quiet. The only sounds she heard
were the plop of raindrops on broad leaves, the "shushing"
sound of a rivulet seeking a creek, and the squish of her own
footsteps in the thickening mud along the trail. Where was the
breeze dancing among the treetops? Why had all the birds
gone quiet?

"You need to quicken your steps," Will said anxiously
from right beside her. He'd dropped to the ground and as-
sumed his man form while she listened for the normal sounds
of the forest.

"What is out there?" She lengthened her stride even as she
spoke. She knew that Mamoch, the monstrous mother of all

the wild pigs, perpetually pregnant or nursing, and never sated, still lived and roamed freely.

Little John's magic, when he'd been the Green Man, had kept her at bay from humans.

Little John's magic faded as Verne stretched his roots to all the far-flung lands of Sherwood. In less than half a year's turning Verne would emerge from his tree and John would be a mere mortal.

Would Verne hold to his father's wish to protect John's friends?

"The sheriff's men ride the Royal Road. Derwyn is no longer with them."

Hilde resisted the urge to snort in derision. The Wood-wose and the Wild Folk had no fear of the sheriff's men as long as they remained on the road.

"Where is Derwyn?" a new thought struck her. The tree man had left Sherwood with a great deal of anger in him. He reminded Hilde of Sister Marie Josef, back at the convent. The only way she could cope with her own inner pain was to lash out at all those around her, usually Hilde.

Will shrugged, half-flapping his arms in a very birdlike gesture.

"Then what disturbs you?" Prying words out of Will required all of Hilde's patience. Unless he sang. With a lute or drum in his hands, his thoughts came out strong and coherent as well as lovely, memorable because they were set to music.

She hadn't heard Alain sing to know if his spoken words were just babble and his music communicated his true thoughts.

Will's mouth opened and closed twice before he thought to bring a lute out of his satchel. The pack was as much a part of his costume as the red feather in his cap, always there, rarely noticed. But the flat and thin satchel produced whatever instrument Will needed, when he needed it the most.

He strummed a chord, quick and slightly off tone.

Hilde increased her pace in response to the anxiety there.

"John is not here." Will sang. "John cannot speak for us. Those who wish us harm step forth."

"Who wishes us harm?"

Will produced a new red feather from his satchel and tucked it behind her ear.

Suddenly her feet felt lighter even as her need to run faster weighed heavy on her mind.

She began running. Will kept pace beside her. Feathers sprouted on his arms, but he remained mostly human.

Then she heard it, the snuffling grunt of Mamoch. Chills ran through Hilde. She had to get back to camp where Little John's influence still reigned.

The path ahead grew narrower, the trees closer, close enough to block the rain from falling. More dead skeleton trees stripped of bark stretched their naked arms toward her, twigs grasping like hands.

"Will?"

"I'm here. I will not leave you."

Mist descended upon them like a blanket, dampening sound, making the air too heavy to breathe. She couldn't see more than a single step ahead of her.

"Where are we?" she gasped as she ran faster.

"Near the sacred circle."

"What? The standing stones are on the other side of the forest."

"No longer. The evil tree shifts things about to suit his needs."

She remembered Nick speaking of the malevolent spirit dwelling inside a gnarled old tree of indeterminant kind that had tried to absorb him and Henry. They had invoked Little John's name and the tree released them from his spell. But they'd fallen into Mamoch's trap instead.

The forest was not always a kind and gentle place for the unwary. Gloomy darkness descended upon them though she knew the sun had risen only halfway to noon.

She had Will beside her and his feather in her hair to hasten her steps. She hadn't realized why he'd given it to her at the time. Now she knew.

Then he took her hand and led her to the left, along a trail she could barely see for the encroaching ground cover.

Ground cover! Low growing plants meant there was light penetrating the canopy.

The air moved more freely when she breathed. The rain faded to a drizzle. Trees looked healthier, greener. Safer.

And then they burst into the clearing around the triad of standing stones; an outer barrier of boulders did not impede them. But the darkness that had followed them stopped short as they stepped between two low stones.

Will kept her hand in his as they found shelter and ease at the foot of the largest standing stone.

"Thank you." She took the feather out of her hair and handed it back to him.

"Keep it. If you hold it in your hand and think of me, I will know and come to your aid. Besides, it looks more beautiful on you than on me."

Prefect Andrew awaited Nick in the walled garden outside the infirmary. He seemed most interested in the row of budding poppy plants along the north wall where they caught the most sunlight and the stonework trapped heat for them.

Nick saw him as soon as he climbed the old apple tree that overhung the eastern wall. He paused a moment to think about what to say to the man who ran the abbey in Abbot Mæson's absence.

"You can come down now, Nick," Prefect Andrew said quietly.

"I have seen Alain a'Dale to safety, sir," Nick said, bowing with hands folded into his sleeves, out of habit as well as respect.

"Good. I trust Father Tuck will see to his welfare, both physical and spiritual."

Nick had suspected for some time that Prefect Andrew knew how to contact the abbot in exile. He didn't know how frequently they communicated.

"Father Tuck's representatives met us partway to their hiding place. I trust them to take the refugee to the reverend father." Was that vague enough to keep them out of trouble if anyone listened? Nick wouldn't be surprised to find one of the sheriff's men hiding just inside the infirmary, ear pressed to the door.

"Very good." Prefect Andrew nodded and turned to go back into the building.

"Um . . . sir . . . um . . . I've been thinking."

"Is there danger in your thoughts?"

"Perhaps."

The prefect sighed and turned to face Nick. His gaze met Nick's and held. An old trick meant to encourage truth in the coming conversation.

"I think that since Father Tuck may not return home, perhaps I need to stay with him. He ages and the joint disease hinders his ability to write missives. Some days he needs to be reminded to eat as the perplexities of current politics engage all of his attention." Nick lowered his gaze and drooped his shoulders in a posture of humility, though he wanted to stand tall and straight and dispute any argument forthcoming.

"You are needed in the scriptorium."

"Not so much, sir. Since the interdict we have no new commissions to illuminate manuscripts." He didn't mention how his fingers and mind itched to complete the book of herb lore Brother Luke had dictated to him before his passing last summer.

"Let me think on this. I see the wisdom of sending you as scribe and assistant to our beloved abbot in exile." Prefect Andrew rubbed his chin in thought. "We also need to keep you safe here while you finish your training. You cannot take your first vows as a postulant until the Holy Father lifts the interdict. That could be next week or a year from now."

"I obey your wisdom and authority, sir."

"*If* I grant you permission to leave, it will be with the

understanding that you will return when Father Tuck sends you, or if you determine he needs the physician. And when this interdict is lifted, you will make this abbey your home for at least one year before you make a final decision to take Orders or not."

Nick gulped. More than he could hope for. If the prefect granted him leave.

But he knew, permission or not, he'd fill a pack with his spare smallclothes and whatever food he could liberate from the kitchen before Sext. He needed to be with Father Tuck right now.

Hilde needed him, too.

Twelve

obin engaged the magic inherent in his gnome form to hasten his passage through Sherwood. The procedure of *willing* himself elsewhere always left him limp with exhaustion. If he'd been born a gnome, it might be easier to move himself from place to place when urgency required.

But he'd been born human. Any time magic proved difficult to the point of exhaustion, he ignored it and walked, even if the distance was long and arduous. What good was moving a full league or two away in an eye-blink if he arrived unable to move a muscle for an hour or more?

He landed in a crumpled heap beside the log that had offered him seating beside the charcoal burner.

"I thought gnomes had magic," Liam said grumpily. He sat at the other end of the fallen tree, using it as a backrest while he munched some hard bread and cheese. A flask of ale rested beside him.

Robin's mouth was dry. The ale would help him recover.

"Here." Liam thrust the flask at him, as if he'd read Robin's mind.

Half the flask went down Robin's throat before he thought to conserve any of the precious brew for his new friend.

"Go ahead and finish it. I have another with the promise of more later in the day. The sheriff thinks I must need more than a normal man with the lavish supplies written into our agreement."

"You can read and write?" Robin knew those were skills reserved for men of the Church and a few nobles. As second son, he'd grown up expecting to take Orders and therefore had been taught literary skills. His brother expected to inherit titles and lands and would hire others to deal with written words for him.

But Robin had fallen in love and found the profits of a Crusader and mercenary to support a wife more to his liking than the celibate life of a priest.

"Aye, my mother sent me to the priory five leagues south of here as soon as she knew I'd never grow a straight back." Liam shrugged acceptance of his lot in life.

"Why'd you leave?" Life in a priory might have been safer than living daily with the superstition and revilement of village or city folk.

"The barley crop was blighted the third year I was there. They blamed me; said I was cursed by Satan. They drove me out with stout sticks and heavy stones."

Robin shuddered along with his new friend. A bad world

they had both inherited, when even men of the Church showed no mercy or compassion to such as he and Liam.

But some clergymen prayed for and with him, men like Father Tuck. "Your mother should have sent you to Locksley Abbey, where compassion is part of their daily life."

"Mam didn't want me close by, didn't want to ever see me again," Liam said flatly.

"She lives near here, then?" Robin pushed himself upward, letting the log support his recovering body.

"Aye, in the abbey village."

"Have you seen her?"

"No." Liam ended the conversation by heaving himself to his feet. "Another day of burning limestone and I should have enough to make my mortar for the kiln."

"Will you build a hut for shelter?" Robin asked, eyeing the sky for signs of rain-laden clouds. He also sought excuses to delay Liam's felling trees to turn into charcoal for the sheriff.

Liam turned his face up to the sky as well. "Might be for the best. If you help, we can make it big enough for both of us. You look like you are in need of a place away from the weather as much as I."

"Aye," Robin agreed. "Come autumn, I feel the cold wind in my joints." He wiggled his bottom, trying to dig himself a little deeper into the turf to guard against the weather.

A tingle of magic, like the echo of a giant's footsteps in the distance, worked its way up his spine and outward through his arms and fingers.

What?

This required investigation. Another reason to remain with Liam and keep him from felling the forest.

Liam jerked his head down once in agreement to Robin's previous statement. "Kiln first. Then a hut."

He marched off toward the embers of the hot fire within a ring of stones that continued to burn limestone.

The smoke near choked Robin. All he wanted to do was dig. Would Liam object? Or ask too many questions?

He loosed a string of curses in his mind, wishing he had Little John's wisdom to rely upon.

My fingers ached within my dream. I knew it had to be a dream, for spring had come again and warmth filled the castle bailey once more, while my body chilled and I breathed the stale air of a winter that would never end. The dark beings of my half-death lingered and howled around the edges of my awareness.

Absently, I rubbed the crystal, stroking the rough rock that surrounded the clear bits that winked at me in the sunshine.

Once again, I was in an earlier time and place, different from the darkness of my current life.

In that long-ago sunshine, I lifted my face to the sun. My tears turned the light within the crystal into a rainbow of colors. But even the natural beauty within this precious gift could not lighten my heart. Not on this day. Not until Robin, my Robin, returned from the Crusades.

He looked so handsome, almost saintly in his beauty, wearing his white tabard with the red cross emblazoned on the
front. I had sewn the costly red cloth upon the white, bleached
linen. I had turned the edges neatly so they would not fray. I
had cried for weeks as I plied my needle preparing my lord,
my love, to leave for battle.

"I envy you," Henry said to his younger brother.

In the two years I had lived in this household I'd watched
Robin grow into his body and soul. He now stood half a head
taller than his father and a full head taller than his older
brother. His chest had filled out, and he swung a sword as
easily as a table knife. His older brother did not shrink in size,
but he grew no more than he already had on the day I first
met them.

"You have the calling for the church, dear brother," Robin
said quietly so that their father could not hear them. But I
could. "You were not meant for battle, though."

They both hung their heads as they gripped each other's
shoulders. The love they held for each other flowed freely
between them.

I felt shut out of that moment that only men bonded by
blood and friendship could share.

"You'd best be off if you are to meet the Marshall's men in
York on time. The sun already climbs above yon knoll," Earl
Robert said, he strode down from the tower to stand before
his son. "Safe travels, boy. And return to us when the Holy
Land is once again free."

Was that a tear trembling on the lashes of the stern old

man? He clasped Robin in a hug, long and bony fingers clutching his surcoat fiercely. "If I were twenty years younger, I'd be riding off today, not you."

"And I'd gladly have your strong sword arm at my side." Robin gulped, his throat apple convulsing. "Don't be too hard on Henry. He's not made of the same stern stuff as you and I."

They broke free of each other and Robin turned his attention to me. Finally.

I clasped my hands at my breast, daring to look up from my feet and catch his gaze fully, boldly. "I cannot say I am glad you are leaving," I said.

"I know." He cocked a crooked grin at me. "You told me so, and threw a pewter pitcher at my head when I first broached the idea."

"I care not for the riches you might bring home. I care not for your absence while I grow old enough to marry you."

"Do you care that His Holiness has promised that my soul will be saved if I go?"

"To my mind, you do not need saving."

He shuffled his feet awkwardly as his father and brother turned away, giving us a brief illusion of privacy.

"Stay bold and firm, my love. Mind this castle and my family for me. Keep them safe from each other, as well as from those who would steal our lands and honors."

I nodded, unable to speak from the tears gathering behind my eyes.

Then he drew me close, gently, tenderly, tipping my chin up with a single gloved finger. "You are the bright light that will guide me home." He kissed me, covering my mouth with his. The lightest of touches in fond farewell.

But then a fierceness grabbed us both and we deepened our bond, pressing ourselves ever closer. His arms came around me, engulfing me until I could not tell where he ended and I began. I clamped my arms around him as well, holding him tightly.

And still we kissed. Still we clung together, promising so much, and yet dreading the future that could rip us apart forever.

"I will return, my love. Through fire and flood, I will trod to return to you."

And then he was gone.

Emptiness and loneliness chilled me to the bone before he'd passed through the castle gates.

***

"Father Tuck, are you feeling better now that the rain has stopped?" Hilde asked the old man. She didn't like the lack of color in his face, though the tinge of blue around his lips had gone away in the last couple of hours.

She fetched him a wooden cup full of broth from the stewpot.

"Nothing wrong with me that a bit of sunshine won't cure," he said, and flashed her a smile. Then he sipped at the hot broth. "Ah, better than a fine French wine. Needs a bit more salt, though."

"And where do you think we'll find salt?" Hilde stood back, feet braced and hands on hips. She, too, missed freely adding salt to every dish as she had at the convent. More times than not, salt was the only thing that could make Sister Marie Josef's cooking palatable.

"Have Nick bring some from the abbey kitchens."

Hilde wrestled a moment with the moral problem of *stealing* salt from the abbey. But Father Tuck and Nick both belonged to the abbey. Supposedly, the monks all lived in a communal society, where they shared everything. Therefore, for Nick to bring some precious salt to his friends wasn't stealing—especially if ordered to do so by his abbot, even if the abbot was in hiding . . .

Too complicated to think about right now. She needed to take some of that rich broth to Jane, check the new mother's dressings, and make certain she had clean, absorbent moss to swaddle the baby in.

Thankfully Alain slept deeply beneath the shelter of a different lean-to on the opposite side of the fire from Father Tuck. She needn't tend him for a bit.

A tingling vibration ran through the packed dirt of their campground and into her bare feet. Something strange and thrilling. What it was, was unknown and therefore dangerous. She had to know the source and figure out how to deal with it.

Alain shifted and moaned in his sleep.

"Did you feel that?" Father Tuck asked. His eyes grew wide with wonder.

Immediately, his face brightened, with a return of health and rosy color to his cheeks.

"Aye," Hilde said cautiously. "What was it?"

"Magic. Deep earth magic trying to break free. Will? Will Scarlett, where are you?" he called into the air.

Will emerged from the tree line along the path toward Ardenia's pond, plucking a stringed instrument Hilde had never seen before—sort of a wooden horseshoe, painted and inlaid with shells and a dozen fine strings. His step was jaunty and his voice firm. None of his normal hesitation and forget-fulness. "What do you need, Father Tuck?" He plucked three strings in a vibrant chord while he sang his question.

"Will, I need you to find Nick and tell him we have need of Elena's advice," Father Tuck replied. "Please."

Will stuffed his musical instrument back into his pack and shook himself in preparation for transforming.

"And tell him to bring some salt!" Hilde added as the first red feathers appeared beneath Will's arms.

Then he was a bird again, flitting through the treetops.

"Sometimes I wish I could fly," Hilde murmured. "'Twould be so much faster to pass messages to the far corners of the forest." She lifted her arms away from her body as she'd seen Will do just before his feathers sprang into view. For a brief moment the breeze played with the sleeves of her old nun's habit, giving her the illusion of becoming lighter than air.

Then the joyous sensation was gone, and her arms fell heavily back against her body.

When Will had escorted her through the forest to safety, he'd been . . . thoughtful and courteous and protective, al-most as if given a task he could concentrate on, all of his flighty scatteredness settled and the job anchored him.

Something to think about, after she made certain everyone among the Woodwose was where they should be and doing what they were supposed to do.

Cold embedded into stone penetrated Nick's knees, through the thick wool of his cowled robe. His bones ached as the chill crept up his thighs and down to his bare feet as he continued to kneel in obedience to Prefect Andrew.

The altar of the Lady Chapel stood before him. Atop it, rested the most precious object owned by the abbey: a knuckle-bone of St. Indract rescued from the fire at Glastonbury fifty years before.

"Nicholas Withybeck, swear upon this holy altar and our holy relic that when your duty to Abbot Mæson, now known as the itinerant monk Father Tuck, is completed, that you will return to Locksley Abbey for a minimum of one year before deciding if your life must be dedicated to God or to wandering freely among the lay people," Prefect Andrew said solemnly. He raised his hands to shoulder level, two fingers extended, the rest curled inward in the universal sign of benediction.

"I so swear," Nick said.

"Place your hands upon the reliquary and repeat your vow."

Nick rolled to his feet and stepped up to the dais where the altar rested. Two fat candles burned brightly upon the altar, relieving the day's gloom. A censer hung from a golden chain to his left. The heady incense robbed him of a sense of direction. His concentration centered on the box made of an exotic wood and inlaid with a golden cross on the lid.

When he squinted his eyes to keep his mind from drifting upward and outward, he saw ripples of power emanating from the box. This must truly be a holy relic he could trust to speed his prayers and his vows upward to heaven.

His breathing grew short and shallow in the dark closeness of the chapel.

His next actions held great import to himself as well as to the Woodwose and Father Tuck. And to Hilde.

"I, Nicholas Withybeck, orphan, raised by Locksley Abbey to a life in the church, do swear that my leaving the abbey precincts is temporary, for as long as I am needed as scribe and assistant to the itinerant monk Father Tuck, previously known as Abbott Mæson. When my service to Father Tuck has ended, I will return to Locksley Abbey for at least one year before making a decision about my future, before taking vows to the Church or living a life among the laity."

Nick's heart beat hard and loudly in his own ears. The air around him grew lighter, as if accepting his words, and his intent, and wafting them to the ears of St. Indract and thus to all the angels and to God.

He folded his hands within his sleeves and bowed to the altar and to Prefect Andrew.

"Then, by the authority vested in me by Abbott Mæson, before his involuntary exile, I grant you leave to depart these precincts and commend you to the service of Father Tuck of the Wildwood." Prefect Andrew raised his hands above his head in supplication, then lowered them in blessing upon Nick's head. "Go in peace, my son, and know that when you return to report to me important messages from Father Tuck, you will be welcomed and free to go back to him as needed."

Peace and warmth filled Nick's heart. His duty was clear. This was where he belonged when Father Tuck released him.

He backed away from the altar, taking care not to stumble as he stepped down from the dais. He bowed again before turning toward the doorway that would lead him to the cloister. Purpose filled every step.

A flicker of movement caught his attention. A large red bird, with a cocky crest perched on the ledge of the single window of the chapel behind the main church. It opened its beak and croaked a sound that sounded a lot like "Salt."

"I believe that messenger summons you to hasten to your new duties," Prefect Andrew whispered. He snuffed the candles, leaving only the vigil light and the incense burning.

Thirteen

uriosity won over Robin's normally cautious nature. He found a stout stick and began digging at the place where he'd rested and felt the magical connection.

Strangely, his fatigue dissipated with each thrust of his arm until he'd worked out all of his muscle aches and joint pains. His twisted gnome body felt . . . felt almost like his normal human self. For many long years he'd accepted low-level discomfort as part of being a gnome, living half his life with it. Now, as he stretched his arms and legs and achieved straightness of both, he knew that something had changed in him and around him. His vision was clearer, too.

"I wish Nick could bring Elena to me," he said quietly, hoping that Liam's keen ears did not hear his words.

If he did, he showed no signs of it. He kept his head bent while tending his fire beneath the limestone, singing to it to encourage it to burn at the right temperature.

Robin used the rhythm of Liam's tune to guide his strokes with the stick. Soon he had cleared a shallow hole about the length and width of his gnome body. Dislodged turf ringed his work, making a wind barrier.

"Now what?" he asked himself and the air, not expecting an answer. He'd felt no repeat of the magical vibration.

His body grew tired again. A different kind of weariness. He'd been a gnome too long and needed his tall body.

As quickly as he could, he expanded the hole to accommodate his other self. Then he climbed into his nesting place and covered himself with a deer hide blanket from his pack. His eyes grew heavy as his legs grew long and soon sleep claimed him.

Robin knew he was asleep and that he dreamed, a rare occurrence since his curse. He knew that his tall body rested in a crude dirt depression. And yet he drifted through bright clouds of magical power that pulsed in visible chains of blackened silver and dull red, like old blood.

He shivered in his sleep at the sense of decay that surrounded him. This was not the oblivion of death. He'd been close enough to the end of all things often enough to know the difference. This was something else. Something caught between life and death.

Marian! his mind and memory shouted.

She was close. His heart swelled at the thought of gazing on her sweet face once more. If he could not hold her in life, then he would hold her in his memory and. . . .

The dream changed. Movement within the chains. They twisted but did not rattle as metal restraints would. His dream world remained preternaturally silent.

With the swaying of the chains came a pale glow around the edges of his vision. He needed to press forward. The bit of brightness tugged at his heart. That vital organ beat rapidly, setting up a drum cadence inside his ears. Frantically, he pawed at the chains, pushing them away, stripping away the darkness like clearing away old tarnish from long-neglected silver plate.

A smooth circle of polished bronze appeared before him.

All he could see was the reflection of his ugly, distorted gnome face looking back at him and laughing at his foolishness.

He woke with a start to find rain dripping on his face and Liam staring down at him.

"Who are you?" Liam snarled and raised Robin's digging stick high, ready to bring it down upon his head.

Tuck stretched long and hard. His feet thrust out from the protective warmth of his deer hide blanket. He wiggled his toes within his soft buckskin boots—a luxury granted only to the old and infirm within his Order—and found his feet no more chilled outside than tucked under him. His hands retained their own warmth.

The time had come to venture out of his lean-to and explore the camp. He had responsibilities to the people who gathered here in this forgotten corner of Sherwood Forest.

The cloud cover thinned, and feeble sunlight broke through in places. One stray sunbeam landed on old Catryn who continued to cut into the stewpot whatever wild plants people placed beside her. For a brief moment Tuck caught a glimpse of the young woman she had been, long ago, when he himself had been young and without vows of poverty, obedience, and celibacy.

Bright memories eased the ache and stiffness in his joints.

Something about that brief ripple of magic he'd felt had renewed him.

He sought to take advantage of the blessing before it, too, faded, along with so much of his life.

Will circled above and spiraled down to land beside the fire. He grew to man-height in an eyeblink.

"Did you find Nick?" Tuck called to him.

"Yes. And I told him to bring salt."

"How much salt?" Tuck didn't trust the dolt's memory.

Will held up his hands and cupped an invisible object about the size of a sack that would hold a pound of the precious mineral.

"Good. When will he come?" Tuck prodded his messenger.

Will shrugged. "When he gets here."

"What does a man have to do to get a drink around here?" Alain a'Dale grumbled, rolling over beneath his own lean-to. He moaned and groaned with each tiny shift of his body. A bruise on his left cheek and eye had started to turn bright purple, and the cuts on his knuckles had begun to scab over.

"Food and drink come at the cost of work," Will replied for Tuck. He narrowed his eyes and cocked his head from side to side, examining the refugee bard from different angles.

"Can't do much but sing and play," Alain croaked. His

voice shifted from normal to scratchy dry in an instant. "Can't do much of either until I heal, and I can't heal without a draft of ale."

Will spread his arms in preparation for shifting. He scrunched up his face in anger. Then Hilde appeared across the clearing in the direction of Little John's dwelling. She carried the new babe in her arms, crooning softly to the tiny scrap of life who belted out a cry of bewilderment, not certain why she found herself uncomfortable, or maybe just needing to stretch her lungs. She swung her tiny fists at anything and everything.

A bardic harp appeared in Will's hands. He strummed a gentle and soothing chord and sang a few notes of a familiar lullaby. Hilde smiled at him in gratitude.

"She's fussy today, and Jane needs some sleep," Hilde whispered an explanation for why she carried the new infant.

Will strummed a few more notes and sang the next phrase of the song. Little John's and Jane's daughter settled and began sucking on her fist. Her unfocused eyes drooped and closed almost immediately.

Alain scowled, then got his knees under him. He had to breathe deeply three times to gain enough strength to stand. But he managed it with only a minor groan and wince of pain that required him to grab his rib cage with both hands to contain it.

"That's a beautiful instrument," Alain said. He walked stiffly, placing each foot carefully in front of the other as he made his way around the central cookfire to where Tuck and Will stood. "May I see it?" He held out a hand, as if expecting Will to hand over the harp.

Will shook his head. "In mortal hands it will crumble to dust." With that, he opened his pack and stuffed the harp inside. Instantly, the bulge within the painted and embossed leather flattened, the contents invisible to any but the most magical eye.

Alain squinted, staring at Will in puzzlement. "I lost my lute to the uncareful hands of one of the sheriff's men-at-arms. I perform much better with an instrument."

"We don't need another minstrel to lighten hearts during supper," Will replied.

The waves of jealousy coming from the two men almost knocked Tuck off his feet.

"Master bards, perhaps we need a competition between you. I'm certain neither of you is better than the other, but a little lighthearted rivalry will entertain the rest of us mightily," Tuck offered. "Shall we say three days? Time enough for you to heal, Alain a'Dale."

"I have no lute or harp or lyre, not even a hand drum to balance my voice," he grumbled.

"Something will turn up. It always does," Tuck replied.

"In the meantime, you can earn your supper by gathering moss from the rocks by Ardenia's pond," Hilde said, shifting the baby to a more comfortable position. The child remained asleep, Will's song still working its magic.

Alain grunted something and headed for the path that all the men took several times a day.

"But if you need to take a piss, make sure you do it downstream," Tuck reminded the young man. It was likely he'd never lived outside a city and knew nothing of the etiquette of rough living.

Derwyn paced the boundary of Sherwood Forest where the Royal Road entered the expanse of meadow. Deer grazed here as well as stray sheep and cows. No one could hunt the beasts except under royal warrant.

Most people could not legally enter the preserve. But if they passed under the cover of night, or they didn't care if the sheriff's men caught them, they could move between forest and village lands unhindered. Derwyn could not enter because his father had cursed him into exile from his native home. To his dryad-born eyes, the barrier appeared to him as a faint shimmer.

He poked at it with his finger and watched as the air rippled across the entire surface of the barrier. His fingertip tingled into a burn. Uncomfortable, but not painful. He tried placing his hand flat against a magic field designed to keep him out. Him and him alone, not any others that he knew of.

For the count of ten he endured the unseen flames on his palm. Then he had to jerk his hand away or risk permanent damage.

This time the ripple lasted longer and spread farther. He'd triggered an alarm.

Who responded to that signal would determine his next action.

He crossed his legs and sank to the ground beside a fire ring he'd laid when he first arrived. A few sharp strokes of flint against his iron knife sent sparks into the kindling. A little careful tending and soon he had a tidy little blaze to warm his hands and feet. Strange how before the curse he could not touch iron and he never felt the cold, in either his human or tree form.

Now he fondled the knife the sheriff had given him without pain. Touching the barrier was akin to how iron had affected him before his father banished him to the human world.

Less comforting was the chill seeping through his clothing to his skin. His thick, bark-like hide had thinned over the months, until it came close to the texture of a human. Little John had spent more time in his human body while reigning over the forest as the Green Man than in his tree. Derwyn guessed that the frequent changes had kept his skin smooth and supple.

Derwyn preferred his tree.

Now he had no access to his true self. That was the part of the curse that hurt the most.

He'd set into play the plot to bring down the reign of the Green Man and his protection of the human outlaws. That satisfied his mind but not his heart.

By the time his fire burned down to embers, he felt the vibrations in the earth of heavy steps striding across the meadow. None of the grazing sheep or cattle shied away from the intruder. But the deer lifted wary gazes and bounded away into the protection of the trees fifty long paces away.

Derwyn remained seated, hands open before the remnants of the fire.

"You can no longer come home," Llwyf said. He stood inches away from Derwyn's shoulder, astride the invisible barrier, looking down upon him.

"I know," Derwyn sighed. He allowed a hint of a sob to invade his words. "But I need to return to the sacred stones."

"Why?"

Derwyn chanced a glance upward to his younger brother.

"Because there I can repent and worship the old gods. The human churches do nothing to ease my soul."

"The human's God has retreated from their churches until King John and the Bishop of Rome sign a peace treaty."

Derwyn sighed heavily. "That will not happen soon. Both men are stubborn, and both feel they are right. Neither will compromise." Or so the sheriff had led him to believe, during many a long night of drinking and gaming after the rest of the castle populace had retired to their beds.

"You can take me to the sacred circle, my brother. If I can get there, I can break our father's curse, and resume my tree again."

"That is the first time you have ever called me brother." Llwyf turned as if to leave. "And Verne is in residence by the standing stones. There is no room for another fully grown tree in the sacred circle."

Derwyn continued to sit though he longed to rise up and smash his way through the barrier no matter how much damage he did to himself or to the magic that restrained him.

"How can I take you to the stones? I do not agree with Father that you had to be banished from Sherwood."

"Thank you for that, brother. You can stand astride the

barrier. While it is open to allow you passage, I can hold onto you and slip through. But I must be touching you until I am on the other side."

"What will happen once you are inside?" Llwyf looked all around him. "I have no awareness of the barrier."

"Because it was designed to keep only me out. Only I am aware of it. Perhaps our father can sense it because he is the creator of it. But it offers no hindrance to anyone else."

Llwyf took one step back.

Derwyn heard the magic snap back into place.

Llwyf continued to look around. "I know it is there because Father told me of it. But I still cannot see it, smell it, or feel it."

"Can you perhaps hear it? Just below the volume of a whisper. Just above the annoying hum of a troubled insect."

"I don't know." A frown tugged Llwyf's mouth down in concentration. But he took the one step forward that put him astride the barrier once more.

Before either of them could change their minds, Derwyn leaped to his feet, embraced his younger brother, then pushed them both back inside the boundaries of Sherwood Forest.

Fourteen

ill Scarlett jumped and startled. He pushed out red feathers before he landed.

Nick scuttled out of the way before Will's wings could flap and scratch his face.

What was that? Elena demanded. Her voice in the back of Nick's head was strident with alarm.

Then Will settled and resumed his mannish form.

"I didn't feel anything," Nick grumbled.

Something that shouldn't have entered the forest.

"How can you tell?" Nick asked. He looked around the familiar path for signs of movement, or something out of place, as Little John and Robin Goodfellow had taught him.

"How can you not sense it?" Will asked.

"Because I am not magic," Nick replied, more than a little annoyed at the birdman's lack of understanding.

"Oh."

Oh.

"We should enter camp from a different direction. In case we are being followed." Will stepped off the well-worn track and disappeared behind a giant tree.

"No!" Nick called. "I've been led astray within Sherwood Forest before. I'm not straying from the paths I know." Memories of the twisted tree that wanted to engulf him and feed off his life energy, and the trap Mamoch had dug below the tree sent shudders up and down his spine. Since that adventure, Henry, his best friend at the abbey, had refused to set foot outside the grounds of their home.

Scatter some salt across the path behind us, then, Elena advised. *Salt will stop anything with the essence of evil. Or at least distract a natural beast of prey.*

"I don't have a lot of salt with me. Hilde needs it. I can't waste it," Nick protested.

"I brought extra," Will said, retrieving a small pouch of the precious stuff from his pack. What couldn't he conjure from that pack that seemed much, much, larger inside than it looked from the outside? He grabbed a small handful and dribbled it through his fingers in a fat line across the path and extending a full foot on either side. He still had a handful to dump back into the pouch.

That should do it.

Nick shook his head. "I still don't see why you two are so upset."

"Someone who should not enter Sherwood Forest has come inside the barrier," Will said, striding ahead, a whistle on his lips.

"What barrier?" Nick grabbed him by the shoulder, exasperated by the half-knowledge he had gleaned.

"The one the Green Man set in place when he exiled his son." Will shook free of Nick's restraint and continued forward.

"Why didn't I know that?" Nick asked the air.

Because you had no need to know, Elena explained. *Until now.*

"Why do I need to know now?" He paused while the logic of the illogic of magic spun thought circles he had trouble deciphering. Sort of like trying to read Greek when he had no references to grab hold of.

"If Little John set up the magical barrier when he exiled Derwyn, to keep his son out, and no one else, then the alarm you two felt must mean that Derwyn has found a way to penetrate the barrier. No one would notice if I, or Hilde, or even the sheriff crossed the barrier we don't even know is there."

Precisely. Now hurry ahead and warn Father Tuck.

"Tuck has more forest blood in him than I do. He should have felt it."

"Not enough." Will replied. He spread his wings and flew ahead.

"I don't think I'll ever get used to watching people change back and forth between human and fae."

There are few enough of us left that most people will never watch one of the Wild Folk transform. It is an amazing privilege. Continue to be awed by the majesty of it.

Robin rolled toward Liam, shrinking into his gnome form instinctively. The hunchback had to step backward to maintain a good angle to swing his stick.

"Wha . . . What?" Liam protested, dropping his makeshift weapon to the side.

"I'm Robin Goodfellow!" Robin chortled, as if shape-changing were an everyday thing and the joke was on Liam. He jumped to his feet and began prancing around and around his companion, keeping him dizzy and confused.

"Robin Goodfellow?" Liam's eyes crossed trying to follow the gnome through a series of gyrations no human body should be capable of performing.

Robin paused to catch a breath. He noticed that Liam had moved far enough away from the fallen log to give him room to escape, if he still needed to.

"Surely, you've seen the Wild Folk out and about, since you spend so much time in the woods, felling and burning trees to make your charcoal? Depriving us of our homes!" Robin's anger made his voice rise to a screech.

"I don't know."

"You don't know, or you don't want to know?" Robin kicked the stick out of reach of both of them. He didn't want to succumb to the killing rage that had saved his life during too many battles as both a Crusader and a mercenary. Over the decades, he'd learned that life was too precious, to precarious, to deprive another unless faced with his own death.

He had to stay alive long enough to rescue Marian and, hopefully, break his curse to live beside her for a normal mortal span.

"I . . . I . . . the Church says that the Wild Folk do not exist, and if you do, you are the spawn of Satan and not God-fearing . . ."

"Contradictions. Either we exist, or we don't." Robin assessed his body. No, he could not go back to being a man yet. He'd slept too long in his big form. "Demons do not exist, so why does the Church maintain elaborate rituals for banishing them? The Wild Folk were here long before the Church of Rome came to England. Now the Church has deserted England, and we are free to come out of hiding, to live our lives as we were meant to."

"But just a little time ago, you were a man." Liam plunked down with his back against the stump, stretching his legs out as straight as he could; not very far with his twisted spine interfering with them.

"My curse." Robin turned his back on the charcoal burner. "Sometimes I am one, sometimes the other." He clenched his fists in frustration. He'd dreamed of Marian. He had an idea of how to find her. But he needed help. Little John and Nick came to mind. Neither was here to talk through the meaning of his dream.

"My hump is my curse," Liam said quietly.

"You earn a livelihood by burning my forest home into charcoal."

"Your . . . your home?"

"Do you think I can live in Nottingham or even a village as this?" Robin gestured the length of his short body and then pointed to his warted nose that curved to almost meet his chin. "Do you think God-fearing people would allow me to live if they saw me transform as you just did?"

"They will not allow me to live among them, and I do not transform."

"So I, like others of my kind, depend upon the forest to feed us, shelter us, and gives us places to hide from the sheriff's men. And you destroy it."

"I have no other way of earning a living."

"We of the forest cannot allow you to continue earning your living this way."

"So, you'll do what? Chase me away with your torches and clubs, just like everyone else. The old tales say you are better than that." Liam rolled and twisted and grunted to his feet. Then he winced in pain as he bent to retrieve his stick.

It looked much larger than Robin remembered using when he was big. More menacing, too.

He backed out of Liam's reach.

"We will do what we have to." Strong Liam might be. But Robin knew how slowly he moved. He could easily stay out of reach. He now faced the ruins of the old castle. His first home. Every year it lost more stones, showed a more ragged silhouette atop its motte, the hill within the bailey that made the tower rise high about its outer defensive walls.

If Robin of Locksley were ever to regain his ancestral lands, his honors, and his bride, he was running out of time.

"Why did you choose this place to build your kiln?" he asked.

Liam looked confused at the abrupt change of subject. "The sheriff's man, the one who put the idea into his head to apply for a charcoal license from the king, said I must clear this stretch first and I must burn in the kiln built atop this hill until the land cracked and the demons sprang forth."

Robin's body chilled, and his mind grew numb. "I need

the help of the Green Man," he whispered. "But there is no Green Man. Not until the autumnal equinox."

He gulped and drew in a deep breath.

"Do what you must, Liam. Clear the land from here to yon castle. Expose every crack and crevice in the rock formations. But no more. I will be back." Then he took off running, praying with every gasping breath that someone, anyone, from the Woodwose camp crossed his path before he ran out of strength enough to run all the way home.

Hilde dropped an apron load of wild onions and parsnips beside the washing bin. She'd gleaned her treasure from the clearing made when an old tree fell in a windstorm two winters ago. Amazing how the forest tried to fill the gaping wound in its landscape with fresh green stuff so quickly.

In shifting her gaze from keeping her harvest in place, toward the camp as a whole, she became aware of Little John carrying his tiny daughter around the central fire, bouncing and cooing to her.

"Where's Jane?" Hilde asked, instantly searching for the baby's mother.

"Asleep," John whispered. "Only time wee Fern here is quiet is if I walk her." He paused to smile and gaze in wonder at his human child.

The heartbeat he stopped moving, little Fern began to fuss and then wail at the top of her lungs.

Little John began walking and bouncing once more. Instantly the baby settled.

Hilde watched in awe as Fern's unfocused, blue eyes fixed upon her father. She smiled and then relaxed into sleep, totally trusting the big man to keep her warm, comfortable, and safe.

"I have seedlings aplenty in the forest," John said quietly, not risking his booming voice to wake her. "But this is my first human child, conceived in love, nurtured under the heart of my beloved. Isn't she wonderful?" More a proclamation than a question.

"Aye, she's beautiful. When did she nurse last?" Hilde brushed her hands clean of the dirt that clung to the vegetables she'd gleaned. Her heart itched to hold the baby close.

But she dared not wrest the infant from her father. Not only would Fern start to fuss again, but Little John would not take kindly of being deprived of his daughter for even an instant.

"About an hour ago. She fed well then slept a bit. Jane slept, too. But then Fern began to cry, and I took her so that her mother could rest." Little John sounded more like a natural father with no concerns but his wife and child. Gone was the forest giant or the Green Man who had to see to the safety and well-being of all that dwelt within his realm. He needed only his family now.

"How does Verne fare?" Hilde asked. Would the younger tree be as fine a Green Man as his father had been?

"Verne?" Little John looked up from his enchanted gaze upon his daughter. "Verne." His face cleared. "Yes, Verne. He stretches his awareness a bit more each day. Some of it puzzles him, and he has to pause in order to figure it all out, then he stretches again until he reaches something else that he cannot fathom. 'Tis a normal process." He returned his concentration to the baby.

"Puzzles?" She had to think back to some of Nick's tales of the forest beyond the usual trails and the areas frequented by the Woodwose. "You mean like the barkless tree that continues to live only by absorbing the lives of the people who fall within its traps?"

Will had said something about the old being moving around the depths of the woods where few dared tread, except the lost ones.

"Why is the evil one a puzzle?" John looked startled.

"Why did you allow it to live, to continue to menace us?"

"Oh, that. Yes. Verne asked the same question. I don't really know, except it has always been a part of the Wild Folk. We are incomplete without all of the wild ones. Even Mamoch and other predators are part of the fabric of life."

Hilde had to think about that. The Church held a similar view. Evil was all around. People had to work hard to escape it and could only stay free by following a righteous path.

For some, that path lay within the convents and abbeys, monasteries and priories, dedicated to a life of prayer and seclusion.

Except she knew from experience that evil lurked there, too. She'd run from the evil of Sister Marie Josef in the convent of Our Lady of Sorrows and found safety in the wild amongst the supposedly evil forest dwellers, human and fae alike.

Life was all about contradictions.

"Did you feel the magical disturbance that upset Father Tuck and Will Scarlett a short time ago?" she asked Little John, wondering how much, if any, magic he had left. Supposedly, he only transferred some of it to Verne at first, and the full loss of it would not happen until all four seasons had passed.

"I noticed a ripple in the land. It happens sometimes. I took little note of it." He stared down at Fern, the most important thing in his life now.

"So Father Tuck says. He sent Will to fetch Nick and Elena."

"Good. Elena will help sort it out." With that, he turned away from Hilde, still cradling and cooing to Fern.

Fifteen

"Father Tuck, I have permission from Prefect Andrew to stay away from the abbey for as long as you need my assistance," Nick said, kneeling before the aging priest.

"Does Father Blaine know about this?" Tuck asked. He looked down from his sitting rock that somehow resembled an abbot's throne.

Nick didn't dare speculate why the old man looked so much sprier and less careworn than he had for the past several weeks. Except that the sun shone through the leafy canopy, dappling the clearing with the brightness of hope for more good weather to come.

"I do not know if Prefect Andrew consulted Father Blaine. I asked permission and was granted leave to suspend my duties at the abbey until you release me." The unfinished manuscript of Brother Luke's herb lore seemed to sing to him across the miles separating him from the scriptorium.

But when he was within the walled enclosure of the abbey, he wanted nothing more than to be in the wildwood with his friends and the senior cleric, his great-grandsire and the only family he knew.

"Very well. I have need of you. I presume you brought parchment and ink and such?" Tuck shifted to his feet with only a little more trouble than a man half his age—whatever age that might be.

Nick patted his bulging sleeves to indicate he had all that was required from his scribe duties.

"We shall use the altar . . . I mean a flat rock I have found that is a small distance from here and more private. I have messages to send and letters to write. You have a finer and surer hand than I."

Nick grabbed his pack with his personal things and made to follow him.

Hilde stopped him with a firm hand on his upper arm. That hand slid almost naturally down to entwine her fingers with his.

He leaned toward her, suddenly focused only upon her and the intimacy of her firm touch. If he could ever think of a place as home, away from the abbey, it would be here. Now. With Hilde.

"Nick, did you bring salt?" she asked.

He jerked his attention away from how naturally she fit next to him. How he wanted to touch more of her than just her hand. To kiss her. To awaken . . .

"Will has a sack of salt in his pack," he replied, straightening away from her. "And I have some in mine." He used his now free hand to reach inside the cloth satchel, the hand that was as empty as his gut at the small distance she put between them. He handed her the pound of salt he'd removed from the abbey kitchen on his way out the door.

"Oh, thank you, Nick." She turned her grateful gaze up to him, brown eyes liquid with emotion. "And where is Will?" Suddenly, she was all practical and cool.

Nick took one step in the direction Tuck had taken. "I don't know. He took his bird form just outside of camp and flew . . . I think south, but I'm not certain. He circled three times before deciding on a direction."

"Will Scarlett will return when he remembers he has something for you," Tuck called from the tree line. "Especially if it's for you, Hilde," he muttered more quietly.

Nick wasn't certain he wanted to know for certain that was what Tuck said, or why.

"Come along, Nick. We have work to do." He continued his trek away from the center of camp.

"Oh, I brought this, too, for the minstrel." Hastily, Nick's fingers found another package in the crowded satchel. He handed the bundle wrapped in white linen rags to Hilde. "Bandages and balm for his wounds. Brother Daffyd sent them special for the patient."

"I'll heal faster with my lute in my hands," Alain a'Dale called from his lean-to across camp.

"Nick!" Tuck said with all the authority of an abbot to an erring postulant.

"Coming, sir."

Living with the Woodwose wasn't going to be all freedom and lying about doing only what he wanted.

Robin took his time walking back toward camp in his gnome form. He needed to think. When he grew tall, his fingers itched to hold a bow and shoot something. Anything, to unleash his frustration. If he put all his human energy into shooting, bringing game for the communal stewpot made as good an excuse as any; he didn't think about the passage of time without Marian. He didn't want to consider that the magical spell entombing her might break down since he'd killed the magician who cast it. He didn't want to know how much time he'd wasted.

He told himself that he couldn't do anything for Marian until he found her.

But had he truly looked for her?

For the first time in a long time, he stopped his churning thoughts long enough to remember what had happened that fateful day he'd returned to Locksley Castle, after ten years of wandering the Holy Land and Europe, first as a Crusader, and then as a mercenary.

Late summer and the cool breeze atop the natural crag where the castle perched had soothed his weather-roughened face like a healing balm. Inside the curtain wall he smelled smoke. Not the welcoming aromas coming from the kitchen fires, or even the sweet woodsmoke of a fire in the hearth to ward off the coming chill of nighttime.

No this was the acrid odor of a fire gone unchecked, scorching wooden flooring and dividing walls, of burned tapestries, and dead bodies.

The smell was old. The bailey was deserted.

He hastened forward, dismounting his tired horse at the base of the steps to the entrance of the great hall. As he ran, he fitted an arrow to his bowstring, preparing to defend . . .

An empty burned-out shell of a fortress, built to withstand siege and invasion. Even a trebuchet with a huge boulder for ammunition would have difficulty breeching the outer walls.

But something or someone had emptied the castle and its environs of people and livestock.

"Your villagers took exception to my residence," said an elderly man standing on the dais where the lord's chair had presided. Once he'd been tall and strong. Now his shoulders curled forward, and his head seemed too heavy for his neck. He wore robes that had once been of rich wool with velvet emblems of magical stars and pentagrams, lightning bolts and arcane squiggles. Now the vibrant colors had faded, and patches of lesser cloth appeared at elbows and hems. He carried a long, gnarled staff embellished with a dull rock crystal at the top.

He didn't need to announce his wizardly profession.

"Who are you, and why should I not kill you on the spot?" Robin demanded, taking aim.

But as he narrowed his focus to the region of the man's heart, the mage's robes rippled, and the man wavered in and out of view.

Robin blinked rapidly and shook his head. The man came back into focus. Then as he took aim again, he faded in and out of reality.

"Oh, you'll not kill me yet, my forgotten lordling."

"Where is my father, my brother, my stepmother, and all those who serve them?" Robin kept his bowstring taut and his arrow fixed.

"Dead or fled. I don't care which. Except I now claim this castle and its lands. The honors still elude me. I have to prove you dead as well before King Henry will release them to me."

"Why?"

"Because this land was to have been mine. I fought for Empress Mathilda in her war against King Stephan during the long years of anarchy. The barons had pledged to her father the first King Henry that they would accept her as queen, his only legitimate child. Then those same barons deserted her in favor of Stephan, a mere cousin. This earldom was to have been mine, but Stephan stole it from me. Then when Matilda's son, the second Henry, took the throne, he left the earldom with its original owners, your grandfather and his line." The old man coughed, betraying his age and weakness.

"I vowed to reclaim what should have been mine! I gathered an army and attacked the castle, but King Henry stopped me with his own army and condemnation among the barons. So I learned magic and poisoned your father. Your brother became earl for the span of three days before he, too, succumbed to my powers. I moved in, and then Lady Marian, your father's ward and heiress to many lands, refused my suit and King Henry denied my claim to her."

His back heaved as he coughed and gasped for air.

Robin decided to hear him out, to learn all he could before placing an arrow in his heart, even if he had to shoot a dozen times to find it.

"I placed a spell on your beloved Marian. She lies asleep in a hidden cavern, never aging, unknowing of the passage of time until I release her. But I will only do that when I can present you to her in the most hideous form possible so that she gives up all hope of you returning to her."

"When did the villagers revolt against you?"

"I don't remember." He dismissed the thought with a gesture. "Now for your curse." He began mumbling in a tongue reminiscent of Persia but not quite what Robin remembered of that language.

"Where is she?" he demanded, desperate to salvage something, anything, of his old life. "Where is Marian?"

The unnamed magician continued his litany, now waving his staff in a circle above his head and prancing in an odd pattern, as if following a maze only he could see, dancing to music only he could hear.

The scent of exotic incense rose around him.

Robin loosed three arrows in quick succession. The first found the magician's leg. He kept dancing, limping now and dripping blood upon the flagstones. The second arrow pierced his side. He slowed his movements and dropped his staff. But he continued chanting.

"One more time through and you will become the most hideous gnome this land has ever seen!"

The third arrow found the old man's heart. His staff dropped from lifeless fingers and broke into three pieces. The crystal atop it shattered and spread across the floor of the entire hall. Each shard picked up a bit of light and broke it into an arching rainbow. Then, in an eyeblink, they winked out. The crystal and all the magic it contained died at the same moment as the old magician.

And Robin shrank into his hideous form with hunched back, twisted knees, elongated nose, and rheumy eyes.

But the spell was incomplete. He only had to maintain his ugliness for half of each day.

He had no idea where to begin looking for Marian. All of Nottinghamshire was riddled with limestone caves, any one of which could be her magical bower.

Sixteen

erne!

Elena's scream near deafened Nick.

"Even I heard that," Father Tuck gasped, shaking his head to clear it.

Nick got his feet under him in one quick movement, heedless of the freshly sharpened quill and dish of ink tumbling off his rock desk. He managed one quick glance at Father Tuck for permission to leave.

"Go, go, go." The old man gestured him in the direction of the standing stones.

Nick grabbed his mentor by the forearm and yanked him to his feet. He knew from long experience that Tuck had more trouble rising than walking.

"I'll gather the others and follow. Now go," Tuck ordered. "Will? Will Scarlett?"

Nick heard the priest call into the air for their birdman friend.

He didn't waste any more time. Elena's demands for action weighed heavily in his sleeve and heavier in his heart.

"What can I do to help Verne?" Nick asked as his feet found the most direct path toward the standing stones at the heart of the forest.

What you must.

Nick didn't have enough breath to ask his next question. He pelted through the underbrush where the trail looped around a boulder with a bog on the other side, neatly leaped up, and took a longer leap forward. His sandals only slipped a little in the damp ground.

Then he was off again.

Twenty long strides brought the top of the tallest of the triad of stones into view. Another twenty and he burst into the clearing. He stopped short outside the boundary stones.

In front of the smaller altar stone, at the center of the space, Verne grew tall and firm, his leaves just unfurling into broad green platters, his bark straight and his lowest limbs curving upward in search of light. He seemed to have grown since the last time Nick had been here, now dominating the clearing.

But that didn't deter the dark figure of a man scuttling out of the forest with a long-bladed knife raised in attack. His other hand held a blazing torch.

Either weapon could weaken Verne to the point where he could not maintain his responsibility as the Green Man or would be destroyed.

Nick didn't pause to think. He ran across the grassy space to grab Derwyn around the knees and take him down.

The torch flew off to the side.

Derwyn rolled, taking Nick with him. He raised the knife.

Nick freed one hand and clamped it on Derwyn's wrist. They rolled again, Nick on the bottom, only the strength of his arm keeping Derwyn from plunging that vicious dagger into his heart.

His muscles trembled.

Darkness encroached on his vision, narrowing his focus to Derwyn's grimly determined face. Drool dripped from his eyeteeth and his nostrils flared.

Gathering his strength, Nick rammed his knee upward.

His foot tangled in his long clerical robes.

Still, he connected with Derwyn's soft parts enough to make him grunt and lose focus.

"You never learned that trick in yon abbey," Derwyn spat.

"No, I learned it in the village."

Blaidd leaped from the forest cover and sank his teeth in Derwyn's ankle. No growls. No warning. Only doing his job of capturing the man who endangered the fae.

But Derwyn had once been a dryad and Blaidd could not, would not, rip out his throat as he would a full human.

Just then Will Scarlett dove downward, wings spread wide. His thick beak, designed to crack hazelnuts and thick seeds, penetrated the soft skin of Derwyn's hand at the base of the thumb.

His grip on the knife slackened.

Robin stomped up and grabbed for the knife.

Derwyn firmed his grip and slashed downward.

Little John reached down and grasped his eldest son on the shoulder, pinching tightly on the nerve by the collar bone.

Derwyn slumped and the knife dropped, cutting across Nick's chest and through his long sleeve.

Elena's three-faced pitcher fell away.

Derwyn grabbed the silver treasure.

Instantly, Nick's belly cramped, his feet grew numb, and his mind lost focus. He'd given Elena to others in time of need. He'd released her to work her magic. She'd always come back to him, her chosen carrier.

But never, *never* had she been taken from him by force.

Help me!

Nick couldn't move. *I'm sorry.*

He heard a string of curses, much stomping of feet and fists slamming into bone.

And then—miraculously—Father Tuck placed the pitcher on Nick's chest and folded his hand around the home of the little goddess. "Now get up and let her direct you in helping Verne heal from the burn at the base of his trunk."

The silver of the pitcher warmed against Nick's hand, and his mind snapped from bewildering confusion into sharp and detailed focus.

"The burn balm in Brother Luke's herb lore," he said as he tried to figure out how to roll to his knees and then upward.

You need both hands, silly boy. Put me in your sleeve as you always do.

Nick fumbled toward his left sleeve, and found only empty air within.

Your other sleeve will do for now.

"Oh."

Derwyn had slashed the heavy fabric with his dagger. And the folds of wool across his chest.

"I think I'm going to need some mending thread," he said sadly. Patched and mended robes never held up as well as ones made of whole cloth.

He gained his feet and tucked loose bits of his robe beneath his belt, exposing an unseemly length of leg.

"The burn balm?" Little John asked anxiously. He pressed both hands to Verne's bark, close to the ground.

A bit of oak-brown skin appeared through the scorched patch of bark. Higher up, a hand grew out of one of the lower branches. Verne's leaves rattled as if dry and brittle in late autumn.

"No, no, no, do not become a man again." Little John sounded stern, like a domineering father reprimanding his son for a serious misdeed. "No! It is not yet time. You will break your grip on the forest magic. Let us help you. Stay!" He moved one hand higher to the exposed bit of foot and pushed.

"I need . . . I need . . ." Nick couldn't remember the ingredients, though he'd written them down for Brother Daffyd just a few days ago.

Mint, waxy sap from the succulent growing beside the poppies, Elena prompted him.

Nick's mind began working again. He rattled off a dozen different herbs. "I know it eases the pain of men suffering from minor burns. It wasn't enough for Brother Thom."

"Let's hope that Verne's own sap can bind the soothing herbs together as I doubt any of us can get into the abbey gardens and back before Verne rips away all of his bark and his magic," Robin said as he shrank to his gnome form and bounded to the verge just beyond the boundary stones. He broke the leaves from a number of plants with his horny fingernails, kissing each one and murmuring a few words in the ancient language of the land that Nick did not understand. Then he handed each stem to Nick.

He stared at the plants from which Robin had harvested the herbs. None of them matched his list, and yet, as he took them from the gnarled fingers of Robin Goodfellow, they became precisely what he needed, both sweet smelling and acidic.

"Don't question magic," Father Tuck said from behind his left shoulder. "It is older and more potent than we are."

Hilde held a wad of moss atop Verne's wound until the gooey balm Nick had devised bonded with the plant into a firm bandage. "I hope that feels better," she whispered. She felt strange talking to a tree. But then she'd known Verne when he was a man. And she'd known Little John when he was a tree. And. . . .

And nothing about her life in Sherwood Forest felt right compared to the convent. But then Sister Marie Josef at Our Lady of Sorrows was not right in the head. She'd been so badly used by life and her family that the only way she could ease her mental anguish was to make the girls in her charge hurt more.

Fortunately, Hilde had only lived there a year before she found the courage to run away.

She'd found a new family here, different from her blood relatives, strange in her surroundings, and yet much the same. She foraged for food, cooked, cleaned, help birth a baby, and now she bandaged a wound. Why should magic and shape-changing creatures out of legend be so strange?

Verne let loose a sigh of relief. Hilde felt more than heard or saw the tension of pain leave him.

Slowly, she removed her hands from the bandage and sank back onto her heels. "You might have a scar on your bark, but you should heal clean and free of pain. The torch was only in contact with you for a few moments. Barely enough time to burn through your bark." Somehow, she knew that Verne heard her and returned to his year-long vigil of learning the forest.

"He'll be maimed. Deformed. He can't rule as the Green Man!" Derwyn shouted.

Little John had bound his hands and legs with rope made from sturdy vines that twisted back on themselves the more Derwyn struggled, and he sat on the other side of the altar stone from Verne.

Father Tuck sat on the altar, presiding over a makeshift trial of the malcontent.

A misty figure that Hilde remembered from the rescue of Jane from the Faery Mound drifted around and around the group of men who'd rescued Verne, including Nick. Both Will Scarlett and Robin, in their man forms, perched upon boundary stones, not far away. Nick wandered between the men and Elena in her misty essence.

Hilde busied herself gathering the remnants of the healing balm and extra moss into her apron. She didn't want to think about how Nick was bound to Elena. She could never compete with the goddess of crossroads, cemeteries, and sorcery.

In that moment, she knew that Nick would never love her as he loved the goddess and that no matter how deep their friendship, and even if they made love as their bodies seemed to demand, his mind and heart would always return to Elena.

Even Tuck, who had carried the goddess in his sleeve as a young man, followed Elena's movements with his eyes, letting her command his attention when he should be presiding over the decision of what to do with the criminal Derwyn.

Then Will Scarlett caught Hilde's gaze with his own. He smiled slightly and nodded to her.

Something bright blossomed in Hilde's mind.

"Thanks to young Nick, your brother will not be maimed or deformed," Little John said. He looked as if he wanted to kick his oldest son, but thought better of it and continued pacing. "We will have our Green Man come the next equinox."

"But what are we to do with Derwyn until then?" Father Tucked asked the group. "We tried exiling him, but he broke through the magical boundary. How are we to prevent him from harming the forest in other ways?"

He did not mention punishment.

At the convent, that had been Sister Marie Josef's first reaction to any misdeed, even if it was an infraction of rules that only she knew or acknowledged.

But that was not the way of the Wild Folk and the Woodwose. They'd all been punished at one time or another by the villagers, the city folk, the sheriff, and even the Church.

Hilde's own father had died under the hooves of the sheriff's horse because he was deaf and did not hear the nobles galloping on the road behind him.

"What is the worst thing that can happen to a man of the forest?" Hilde asked.

"Confinement," Nick echoed her thoughts.

"If we wall him up in a cave, we'll have to feed him, provide him with firewood and blankets. These are things we barely have enough of to care for ourselves," Tuck reminded them.

"Then return him to the sheriff. Let him confine him in his dungeon most foul," Robin said with a sneer, as if he had personal knowledge of the deep and dank cells beneath Castle Nottingham.

"Go ahead. The sheriff will reward me rather than imprison me. I have succeeded where none of his plots have to rid this forest of those who don't belong here, who break the law just by walking off the Royal Road."

"He's right," Tuck said. A sad frown set his entire face into shadow. "The charcoal burner works even now, under royal license to clear the trees. We cannot stop him, short of killing him, and the sheriff will send another and another to take his place."

"What does the charcoal burner want, more than a means to make a living?" Hilde asked. She didn't know where that thought came from.

Elena stood still for the first time since she'd emerged from the little silver pitcher Nick constantly fingered in his sleeve. *You have the right of it, my girl.* The goddess nodded to Hilde and smiled, then faded and streamed back into her home.

"He wants to no longer be rejected because of his hunchback. He wants to no longer be lonely," Robin whispered.

"As do we all," Hilde said. "He wants a home and a community. Can we offer him that?"

That might solve the problem of the charcoal burner. But nothing about Derwyn.

Seventeen

uck resisted the urge to pace the circle of standing stones, pausing before the center stone of the triad, the tallest, four or five times his height. The two on each side were smaller, one thrice his height, the other only twice as tall as an average man. They formed a semicircle with a flat altar stone at the center of the open space. No one knew how old they were or who had erected them, or why. But through the millennia they had become a place of worship and of judgment, their sanctity adding weight to all human actions that took place within their space.

He knew of old that he must present a figure of authority, and such august personages must show no sign of indecision to the gathering of the entire community of the Woodwose. As an abbot, he found passing judgment on a miscreant—no matter how heinous their crime—to be the most distasteful of all of his responsibilities.

At least as an abbot, he had over one thousand years of Church history and law to give him precedents and the weight of authority. In the community of monks within the abbey everyone had a voice. He did not have to heed those voices if logic fled in the face of fear and anger. But he did need to listen to them.

Here among the Woodwose and the Wild Folk, everyone also had the right to make known their opinion. Opinions only. They had elected him as the elder with the experience and the knowledge to preside and decide Derwyn's fate.

But they had all gathered here for this trial and judgment, even the newly-come Alain a'Dale. He was one of them now.

The sacredness of the standing stones made this place as important as the altar dais in a church.

As a symbol of his authority, Tuck had donned his stola, the last remnant of his priestly status. He fingered the colorful embroidery on the silk scarf draped around his neck. It had been made for him with the tree of life as well as the communion chalice depicted among the designs.

Nowhere did the scales of justice figure among the symbols of his calling.

The exiled son of the Green Man had attacked Little John's heir. It was the equivalent of an attempted assassination of young Prince Henry, the son and heir of King John in the outside world.

Their situations were similar. King John's hold on the throne was currently tenuous at best. Little John's reign over the forest was in transition to Verne who needed another half year before he could follow in his father's giant footsteps.

So, how did the community deal with Derwyn? How did he, Father Tuck, deal with sentencing the man?

His ruminating on the subject ceased as Little John and Robin of Locksley wrestled their prisoner—from wherever they had held him while the community gathered and prepared—into the circle and made him stand facing Father Tuck, the altar stone between them.

Derwyn stood tall and proud, showing no signs of remorse for his deeds. Having his hands bound behind his back only made it easier for him to straighten his shoulders and firm his spine. The dirt and bruising on his face could have come from his fight with young Nick. He'd certainly delivered severe blows to the boy's cheek and collarbone.

Tuck hated to think that Little John and Robin had beaten Derwyn while he was bound and helpless.

Life was brutal and often violent. But the Woodwose had chosen as a whole to curb those natural tendencies. They would not initiate violence, though they might return it with equal measure.

"How plead you, Derwyn, son of the Green Man?" Tuck asked, invoking the formality and thus the officialness of these proceedings.

"I say nothing. I have done no wrong."

"You say you are not guilty?" Tuck raised his eyebrows in surprise. "We have an injured party and witnesses. You broke the exile imposed upon you last autumn. Your presence here alone makes you guilty of breaking one of our laws."

"Your laws? You made me a man and thus subject to the laws of king and sheriff. By their laws, I did nothing wrong."

"You tried to destroy a tree within the Royal Forest. You entered the Royal Forest without a license," Nick said. His voice was neutral, betraying no emotion. "By the laws of king and shire you should lose a hand, at least."

Derwyn blanched.

Little John looked as if he would vomit.

Tuck looked closely at each face of the Woodwose. They had all suffered from the harsh laws of the kingdom and Nottinghamshire. Some had lost hands, or had their noses slit. Most had lost loved ones who had been convicted of poaching when they tried only to stave off starvation. All of them had lost their homes and livelihoods.

None of them looked askance at the punishment demanded by law. Three men drew their knives, each blade a different length and keenness. They were ready to carry out the punishment.

Only the Wild Folk, the fae who belonged to the forest more than the world of men and laws and property took on the posture and grimace of deep discomfort.

Tuck had to do something and quickly before others took away his authority and meted out punishment on their own.

"If you wish to be judged by the laws of king and shire, then you will be surrendered to that authority. Nick and Llwyf shall take you to the gates of Nottingham, where you will be stripped, bound hand and foot, and left to be found at dawn. And a placard shall be devised and hung around your neck with your crime of poaching emblazoned on it."

Humiliating, to say the least, and something the sheriff

could not ignore, no matter how much he favored Derwyn at the moment.

"So be it!" Tuck announced loudly. His words echoed among the standing stones, gaining strength and volume with each reverberation so that all heard.

And none questioned his judgment.

False dawn lightened a few of the nighttime shadows, giving them shape. A glimmer of gold softened the silhouette of the tall walls around Nottingham, the rampart appearing as a jagged line above them. Soon, the sheriff's men would throw open the city gates to market day traffic in and out. Already, the sound of creaking cartwheels and the plod of oxen hoofs on the dirt road announced the coming of farmers from the outlying villages.

Derwyn ground his teeth in resentment as his brother Llwyf—*his brother*—tied his ankles to his bound hands while he knelt before the gates. The boy, Nick, took great care to suspend a bark placard proclaiming him a poacher around his neck so that it hung straight and even. Every time Derwyn twisted his neck to relieve the itchiness of the clinging and twining vine rope, Nick stopped and changed the position of the square of bark. He'd taken as much care to pen the letters neatly, using his near endless supply of things secreted in the sleeves of his clerical robe.

"No sense in leaving those fine clothes for the sheriff to

give to another favorite," Llwyf said, pointing to the pile of brown doublet and hose that had recently adorned Derwyn. "And your robes are in tatters—no thanks to him." He kicked Derwyn in the backside to show his contempt.

Nick's dark eyes widened and his mouth turned up in joy. "I've never worn lay clothes before. Only postulant robes as befitting an abbey boy."

"Take 'em," Llwyf said. "The boots will be a bit big for you, but not for long. You've grown a lot this last year. Got some more growing to do still."

"This is not the end of our dispute," Derwyn said, trying again to find a less uncomfortable, less humiliating position with all of his private parts exposed to view.

The guards would not be able to read the placard, but they would take it to Sir Philip Marc, the sheriff, or one of his clerics. Before the sun had risen fully above the horizon, the entire city would know why he'd been deposited here, like a bit of pottery broken beyond repair and cast into the midden.

Sir Philip would have to address the accusation.

Derwyn chewed on possible arguments in his own defense.

As the boy gathered the clothes in his arms, he said, "I expect we'll hear from you again. But not soon, and not before we have the chance to strengthen the magic that forbids you Sherwood." He fingered something in his near bottomless sleeve. "This time we'll have help."

He disappeared into the shadows thrown by the city walls just as Derwyn heard movement and then the groan of the gates opening.

He lifted his chin and glared at the sergeant-at-arms who peered outward before fully opening the heavy portal. He had nothing to be ashamed of. He'd done nothing wrong.

"Will?" Robin Goodfellow called to his friend as he paced the Woodwose camp. The place was becoming too open, too visible to outsiders as they gathered more and more wood for their cooking and hearth fires, and trampled ground cover. Now that Derwyn had been judged and humiliated, Robin feared that he would unleash the sheriff and his men on this camp. He feared the charcoal burner would fell too much timber, reaching beyond the newer growth surrounding Locksley Castle.

Will flew erratic circles around Nick's head, raucously teasing him about his fine new clothes.

"Save your monkish robes to use as a blanket," Hilde clucked over Nick, pleating the extra fabric in the new doublet to fit his skinny frame. Nick twisted out of her grasp, trying to hoist the hose up where it sagged around his knees and ankles. Though growing upward by the day, his body didn't have time to fill out to fit clothes cut for a much larger man.

The abbey boy would never have the girth of a dryad. He had too much of a stag's leanness from the Huntsman's blood to ever put on layers of fat.

"Makes me long for the less cumbersome shift, skirt, and bodice of the other women." Hilde sighed, and picked at her own heavy woolen nun's robes.

"Will!" Robin demanded the attention of the noisy bird. "Have you checked on Liam?"

"Who?" Will dropped to the ground and grew upward into a man as he shed his feathers. His attention remained on Hilde.

Ah! So that was Will's problem. He'd realized that their refugee from the convent was growing into womanhood. And now that Nick was officially Tuck's scribe, he'd be in camp long enough to rival Will for Hilde's affections.

An interesting drama, if Robin did not have other affairs demanding his attention.

"The charcoal burner. He has a name. Liam."

"If you give the man a name, he ceases to be just the enemy and becomes a person," Alain a'Dale said, coming up behind Robin. He'd started walking around a bit in the past two days. He held his arms as if cradling and plucking a lute or a harp. The bruises on his face had faded to ugly green shades. But his breathing remained short and sharp.

"I've spent time with Liam. He might become a friend in other circumstances." There. Robin said it. He cared about Liam's welfare.

"Then change the circumstances." Alain's words took on a lilt, as if he needed to compose a song around them. "When enemies become friends, you can find common ground and compromise. Mistress Hilde said that he's an outcast like the rest of us. All he truly wants is a home and community. We can give him that."

"Easier to think of him as the enemy every time he fells a tree." Will returned to Hilde's side, adding unhelpful tweaks to Nick's new clothes.

"When did Locksley Castle become part of Sherwood Forest?" Robin asked. Suddenly, that became very important to his future plans.

"After King Richard returned from the Crusades," Alain said. "He declared you dead and saw no reason to honor another man with your titles and lands. The castle was already in ruins, and your family treasures lost as well. It also extended the royal hunting preserve well beyond the traditional boundaries of Sherwood."

"How do you know what our late king was thinking?" Only ten years had passed since Richard Lionheart had died in France. He hadn't been much of a king in England, preferring war and his continental duchies to his damp and dank kingdom. But his barons loved him because he left them alone, leaving them to rule their estates without interference and to make war on each other in an endless dance of power and land changing hands after each battle.

Robin was almost grateful he hadn't been earl at the time and needed to pour all of his resources into maintaining an army of knights. The monies held by the Knights Templar in his name wouldn't last long if he had to make war defending his castle and lands.

"I was with King Richard at the time," Alain said, not engaging anyone's gaze.

"You must have been quite young," Robin surmised.

"Just a stripling, but he loved me as a son." Alain looked up and smiled at each of them in turn.

All within the camp grew still. Hilde, Will, and Nick ceased bickering. Even the normal forest sounds quieted so that the minstrel's words hung in the air a long time after Alain had ceased speaking.

"No wonder King John has issued warrants for your arrest."

"Aye. I can never be a rival for his crown since Richard never bothered marrying my mother. But if people know my heritage, the barons might pay heed to my satirical songs and band together against King John. Sir Philip Marc is John's man, owes him his titles and lands. They borrow money from each other all the time, so much that few can keep track of what is left owing to the other at any given time. My life is worth less than those debts of honor." He turned sharply and took the first path away from the camp.

"Much to think on," Robin mused. "Please, Will, check up on Liam. I need to know he fares well. And if you can direct him toward clearing the land around the ruined castle and not Sherwood proper, he'll heed the advice."

Will took one last longing glance at Hilde before changing back into a red bird and flitting off on his errand.

Eighteen

"hat am I looking for?" Nick asked. He lay prone, atop a small limestone cliff to the north of Locksley Castle and the knoll overlooking the dry ditch that once might have been called a motte.

"I thought Tuck trained you to be observant," Robin replied. He sprawled to Nick's right, in his tall form scanning the landscape with keen eyes. His right hand kept his bow close, with an arrow ready to nock.

Nick knew that the archer could be on his knees, or his feet, in a heartbeat and let the arrow fly in one more heartbeat.

"I cannot see the charcoal burner."

"Liam."

Nick swallowed deeply, remembering the conversation about giving an enemy a name to make him a real person in one's mind. "I cannot see Liam. But there is evidence that he has felled new growth along the ditch and hauled some of it to the top of the knoll. The girth of those trees is small, barely bigger than a branch of an older tree. I presume he will use them either for a shelter or the outer layer of the kiln."

"Good. If I am ever able to reclaim my honors from the king, I need that area cleared," Robin said. He rolled to his side to gain a new perspective on the knoll. "Do you see that long crevice on the north side of the knoll, where the rock shows through when the sun hits it?"

Nick had to twist his neck and squint to bring the white splotches along the slope into focus. "Aye. Barely a crease in the folds of the land. Down at the base and running upward about a yard, maybe a little more." The little hill looked too symmetrical to be natural. He wondered who had taken the time, and expended so much energy, to build and shape the mound. And why.

He paused to check more of the mound of dirt. "There's another to the west. I wonder if there is an opening at each of the cardinal points."

"We'll have to look at all of them."

"Do you want to enlist the char . . . Liam's help?"

"Not sure yet how much I trust him."

"Then I suggest you divert him, and let me investigate." The puzzle of the place intrigued him. "Has the knoll always been there?"

Good question, Elena confirmed. Her voice held an undertone of laughter. He patted the leather pouch that now contained her silver pitcher. It rested between his shirt and doublet.

He had no deep pockets in his new clothes. Gentlemen must carry a scrip on their belt for such things, or have a servant carry them for him. Nick had neither. So, finding a place for the little goddess had not been easy. Hilde had come up with the solution and the bit of tanned boar hide, as well as some strips to braid into a thong. But Nick had to cobble together the pouch. Not so different from mending a sandal.

Robin rolled back to his original prone position and eyed him askance. "The knoll has been there for as long as anyone can remember. I used to race my brother to the top and back down again. We followed older village boys the first time. We taught the game to younger boys. A time-honored tradition. Until recently."

"Did you ever explore the area around the mound?" Nick knew Elena would prod him to ask that question.

"Not much. The forest was already encroaching on the hill when I was a child. It grows too thick for even a ten-year-old to weave between the stems." He shifted his focus to the bailey of the old castle. "The place is more ruinous than I would expect after only sixty-odd years since it was abandoned. Fifty, since I returned from the Crusade, and it had only just started to crumble at the top of the battlements then."

"I read somewhere that a previous Sheriff of Nottingham removed some of the stones from the keep and outer walls for his own castle. Cheaper to haul already dressed stone from here to the city than to quarry and finish new."

"Of course you read about it in your precious scriptorium and library," Robin snorted. "You read everything."

"Do you come here often since . . . since . . ." There was no easy way to phrase his question.

"Since a jealous mage cursed me?"

"Yes."

"No, I haven't had the heart to view my empty home." He crouched briefly, scanning for signs of activity, like any good hunter or mercenary. He retrieved his bow and stashed the free arrow in his quiver. Then he rose to his feet. "I'm going to find Liam and take him up to the bailey to investigate the state of the buildings. It may take a while to persuade him to come with me since there aren't many trees up there for him to fell. Once you see us enter the gates, start looking for an entrance to the knoll." He strode off toward the path down to the old ditch without another word.

Robin pushed aside a patch of concealing shrubbery. The old Robin, from his Crusader and mercenary days, cursed that the defenses of the castle, his home, had been weakened by the overgrowth. He'd been on both sides of battles for possession of strategic strongholds. He knew what to do.

He rattled the tall shrubbery and stomped noisily through the ferns. He wanted to attract Liam's attention.

Sure enough, he detected movement down in the ditch within moments. A slender, juvenile elm creaked and then fell, taking down a swath of similar trees as it crashed to the ground. Liam knew how to clear an area with minimal work.

Robin hoped that Nick noticed all this activity and had taken the opportunity to investigate the knoll. He dropped into his gnome form as quickly as he could, only moaning a little as his joints twisted and his form shrank even as his nose and chin grew to compensate. Liam had learned to trust Robin Goodfellow, where he still beheld Robin the Archer with suspicion.

Liam marched up the slope toward Robin, swinging his ax with too much energy for Robin's taste. He knew how to build speed and force of a weapon with each deliberate movement.

"You're back," Liam spat as he came abreast of Robin.

"Aye." Robin played at peering through bent branches toward the pile of dressed stones that used to be tall ramparts.

"Why?" Liam stilled his ax, finally resting the head on the ground and leaning heavily on the handle as he would a cane.

"This was my home. I want to reclaim it."

Liam laughed heartily; it was the first time Robin had heard him do that. His body relaxed, and his fists unknotted. "Not worth the effort," he finally choked out. "King and sheriff aren't likely to let one such as you have the honor." He shook his head and turned to go back the way he'd come.

"Aren't you curious about what is left?" Robin asked. "Don't you want to know if it can be restored?"

"Best leave this place to the ghosts," Liam said. All traces of mirth left his voice and his posture.

"One of those ghosts might be me," Robin whispered, wondering if the insane mage had robbed him of part of himself and left it to wander aimlessly through empty rooms and along broken ramparts.

Sometimes he thought that a truth he did not want to ac‐ knowledge. That was why he'd returned here so rarely over the decades. He was afraid to meet himself.

But what if bringing that missing piece of his soul back into himself was part of the way to break his curse?

"Best you be gone from here before nightfall," Liam said. "Yon knoll is the only place in these parts that's safe from the angry spirits that haunt this demesne. The sheriff told me so when he gave me license to burn charcoal in Sherwood Forest."

"The sheriff?" Robin turned and looked at the knoll with new insight. Sir Philip Marc never did anything with a single motive.

Nick was right in suggesting it was too regular in shape. The forces of nature didn't usually erupt and slide with such perfect symmetry. He'd seen some hills in the Holy Land, and on the continent that people revered because their ancestors had . . . worshipped or lived there. Some had built villages atop them.

His multi-great grandfather had left the knoll alone when he chose this higher crag to build his castle.

Was the knoll, perhaps, haunted instead of the castle?

Robin had felt a strange frisson of magic when he carved out a sleeping place atop it. And while he'd slept there, he'd dreamed of the day the mad mage had cursed him in more vivid detail than he had in the fifty odd years since that day.

New fear near choked him. Nick was exploring the mound for an entrance that might have been used by a vengeful magician.

"It's Sunday, Robin. We should be at Mass," I remembered protesting quietly. Or did I dream again? Had I argued against his grabbing my hand, leading me out the postern gate to a shadowed pathway down the castle promontory? Or had I suggested we run away for the day and he protested?

No matter. We had run away and confessed our sin that evening to the family priest.

We'd confessed to the sin of skipping morning Mass, not to what we'd done on that hot and lazy summer day more than a year after I'd come to Locksley.

I rubbed at the crystal and settled my mind into one of the happiest days of my life.

Robin didn't stop running—or laughing—until we reached the base of the knoll west of the castle. We'd waved to the guards at the drawbridge and jumped from the far end onto dry land, the roadway baked in the late summer heat leaving only ruts and footprints from the last rain, more than a month ago.

I remembered that last rain in late July because it had been the first day of my moonblood. I had become a woman much earlier than the women of the castle thought proper. It should have been a day of celebration among the women of the castle. But I was only eleven and needed another full year before the Church would sanction my betrothal to Henry of Locksley.

The ladies shared with me the ritual cleansings and bind-
ings, admonishing me the while to keep this secret. If the lord
knew I had become a woman, he'd push for me to marry
Henry forthwith. My chaperones and female companions be-
lieved me too young to endure the trials of the marriage bed.
Too young or not, the time of carefree and childish games had
come to an end and the age for me to marry fast approached.

We slowed to a sedate walk as we climbed the spiral path to
the top of the knoll. Little more than a sheep track, we could
not walk side by side, and I stumbled often over the uneven
footing.

About halfway to the top, Robin paused. Beside the path
lay a tumble of small boulders; a tiny spring bubbled from their
midst. In the wet season a creek ran down the side of the hill in
a curving path, seeking the easiest route to the bottom where
it joined and helped freshen the motte. But now, at the end of
the summer, it merely moistened the nearby ground. A cluster
of tiny violets sprouted in the lee of the biggest rock.

Robin bent and plucked a single flower, tucking it into the
top of my left plait. "Would that I could give you a full crown
of flowers fit for a bride."

I blushed and tried to look away in embarrassment, but his
gaze held mine.

"Robin, we can't. I . . . I'm betrothed to your brother."

"Not formally. Or officially. 'Tis only an understanding.
You are still too young and . . . and Henry has no interest in
marriage." *Or women.*

He left the last unsaid. But we both knew it to be true.

"Some men love the Church more than any woman," I

quoted Lady Suzanna, wife of a knight in the earl's retinue. That was the explanation she'd given me when the studious heir to the title and lands had been found naked on a pallet behind the scullery with one of the squires.

"Father still won't accept that Henry will not step into his role as heir and forget his childhood dream of becoming a priest and scholar. Until they can reach an accord, your betrothal and marriage remain an ideal," Robin said. He dropped my hand and scuffed at the ground, his back to me.

I started up the hill on my own. Soon, I heard the tromp of his boots on the path behind me.

"If Henry takes vows, he will no longer be the heir to the earldom. You will be," I reminded us both. Such things had happened before, more so in the old days, before the Conqueror brought Norman inheritance laws to England.

"That probably won't happen until my father dies and can no longer block Henry from the Church," Robin said. As we neared the top of the hill, and the path gave way to open ground, he took my hand again and led me to a small copse where we could sit on a fallen tree and stare back at the castle.

"On that day, I promise to marry you, my beloved Marian." He lifted my hand to his lips and kissed it.

I swallowed my awe and tried to remember what I should say at this momentous moment.

"Your father is hale and hearty," I said quietly. "He is likely to live many more years."

"I know." He pulled me close against his side, keeping his arm tight around my shoulders. "I spoke to him last night about Henry."

"And?"

"He still insisted that Henry was his heir and that my destiny should be in the Church. He is a most stubborn man."

"And what about me? He holds my lands and dowry in wardship. My life is his to command."

"He insists that you will marry Henry and your dower shall be merged with that of Locksley."

"Even if Henry and I recite our vows, it will not be a true marriage. He is not likely to get an heir on me."

Robin released me abruptly and stood, pacing back and forth the full length of the tree.

"It is the dowry that motivates my father. He can see only extending his power so that he may better defend Locksley from other greedy barons or the king's taxes."

I sat in silence, watching him. We both needed time to think through all of the options, not that we had many.

"If I had enough wealth, I could buy the dowry from Father." He stopped pacing directly in front of me. His eyes glistened with a bit of hope.

"And where do you hope to find such treasure?"

He shrugged. "The Holy Land. I've heard of a new Crusade."

My heart stuttered and my breath caught. "If you survive."

That dreadful possibility hung heavily between us.

Then he flashed his crooked grin at me. "I'm strong and wily, proven in battle."

I glared at him.

"Granted, it was only a small skirmish of my mounted men against a few poorly armed outlaws. But I have wielded my sword in battle. I will return to you. And you will be grown up and ready to marry."

"I don't like the idea of you leaving me for *years*." I swallowed deeply, knowing I could share my secret with Robin, my friend and companion for over a year. "I am a woman already. Your father will seek my marriage before you return."

Robin whirled and faced me directly, mouth agape. He blinked rapidly as he did when thinking furiously. "A year or two only, to give my father and Henry time to come to an accord and give you time to finish growing up." He clasped my arms and drew me upward to claim a kiss.

I should have drawn back, protecting my maidenly virtue. Lady Suzanna had been most stern in her lecture about that.

But by the Virgin Mother and all the saints, I leaned in to be closer to him, let him enfold me in his strong arms, and returned his kiss.

He stroked my hair and explored my back with his strong and callused hands. I came up for air and rested my head against his chest, listening to his heart beat rapidly and surely. It would require more than a Saracen sword to take him from me.

"We must seal our bargain. Come." He took my hand once more and led me to another pile of rocks at the crest of the mound. "Sometimes there are special treasures to be found up here, left by the fairies or the ancients, or someone who thought that this hill is special."

He dropped to his knees and began pawing at the tiny bits of stone that had broken off the bigger boulders. "Aha! I thought I saw this the last time I was here. But I had no use for it then."

He rose with a small bit of rubble held up to the sunlight

between his thumb and first finger. The light seemed to narrow into a single shaft and struck the stone, sending arcing
rainbows in every direction.

"Oh," I gasped.

"You must keep this safe, for us, a token of our love. When
I come back, I'll have it polished and set into silver for you to
wear always."

"Oh," I said again and held my palm flat to receive the bit
of ordinary looking rock with chips broken away in places to
reveal the raw crystal within.

Gently, Robin—my Robin now—curled my fingers around
the gem. "Keep it safe, my love. This is my token of promise that
I will return to you with greater treasures to buy your dower
from my father and ensure my brother's safe passage into a life
within the Church."

Then he kissed me again and held me tightly. "Here in the
sight of God, I do plight thee my troth," he whispered. "With
this token I do thee wed."

Nineteen

"Give me a good reason I should keep you around, feed you, clothe you, *listen* to you?" Sir Philip Marc said as he paced his private apartment above and behind the hall of Nottingham Castle.

Derwyn stood solid on his braced feet, barefoot, but clothed in a rough linen shirt. He didn't quite understand the human need to cover their bodies except for protection against the cold and rain. At those times, Derwyn had taken his tree form and let his bark shelter him.

The enticing smell of roasting meat in the kitchens beside the undercroft made his stomach growl. He hadn't eaten in more than a day. A flagon of wine might help reduce the aches of the bruises on his face and gut as well.

Most of a day had passed since the guards had found him at dawn naked and shivering in front of the gates.

He couldn't transform into his tree for rest and to suck nourishment from the earth anymore. And so he was reduced to enduring hunger and thirst, wearing this coarsely woven shirt that the sheriff insisted he don. It hung to his knees. The men at arms, judging by their smirks and muffled laughter, seemed to find this as humiliating as standing naked before their lord.

"I have served you well," Derwyn replied to the pacing sheriff.

Thunder and lightning, the man was as restless as a tumbling brook, or a wind that couldn't decide which direction to go.

"Aye, you gave me the idea and the arguments to obtain a charcoal burning license from King John. But now you are caught poaching and trespassing within the Royal preserve, stripped, and dropped on my doorstep by the people I wish gone from the forest."

"I have damaged the next Green Man. When he assumes his role as King of the Wild Folk, he will be weak, unable to lead. They will all be vulnerable and unable to resist a full-out attack by you and your knights. Your iron swords and armor will destroy them all."

"Hmmm." Sir Philip continued pacing, but now he rubbed his chin through his recently trimmed beard. His finely woven robes rustled with each step. Not an unpleasant sound, still not as refreshing and restoring as wind in the tree canopy and water flowing over rocks and around bends.

"By my reckoning, I should launch my campaign just before the autumnal equinox, before the new Green Man emerges full of magic, but after the old Green Man has lost all of his powers." Another turn around the room. "How much of Sherwood will the charcoal burner have leveled by then?"

Derwyn shrugged. "If he's as good as reported, I reckon close to fifty acres."

"And what part of Sherwood feels the keenness of his ax?"

"I do not know for certain."

"Why not? You assured me you know every nook and cranny of the forest." Sir Philip whirled to face Derwyn directly, fingering the dagger at his hip. The weapon looked purely ornamental with bright red-and-green jewels in the pommel and along the scabbard and belt.

Derwyn had watched the sheriff shear through heavy bone to get to the meat of a roasted ox with that knife.

He dared not show fear by backing away, though his gut trembled, and his feet itched to run—as any wary forest denizen should.

"I no longer *feel* the forest as I once did. From what I overheard, I assume the charcoal burner is working in the environs of old Locksley Castle. That area was added to the royal preserve during King Richard's reign. Many of the Wild Folk do not consider it a true part of the forest. I do not remember ever being aware of what transpired there." He walked back through his earliest memories of exploring all of Sherwood and found only a dim recollection of seeing the castle ruins atop a hill in the distance. The air of the place had tasted bad, so he'd not returned.

If the charcoal burner cleared only that area, he'd bring no harm to the Wild Folk, or the Woodwose, for they never ventured close by.

But he'd not reveal that to the sheriff yet.

"Guards, have food sent up. And wine for me. Ale for my friend. Lots of it to slake his thirst."

And loosen my tongue. Derwyn decided he'd not drink much, no matter how dry his throat became.

"I cannot wait for autumn. King John arrives next week to King's Clipston. He feels the need to hunt. I have been invited to join him. The forest needs to be cleansed of the Woodwose and the Wild Folk before then. You will find them and lead the men who will burn them out."

Fire! Derwyn shuddered and recoiled in abject fear. "I . . . if you set fire to the wood, you will deprive the king of wild game to hunt." He had no other argument against the dire use of flame to cleanse a forest that wasn't tainted with killing beetles or fungus.

"I need to destroy the pestilence of outlaws and the Wild Folk who aid them. The king must find no poachers in his forest when he hunts. Poachers who pay no tax and eat the bounty of the *king's* forest. You, Derwyn of Sherwood, will throw the first torch. And I don't care if your dryad of a mother is caught in the flames or not. You will burn them all out."

"Absolutely besotted," Hilde said, staring in utter amazement as Little John escorted his wife and baby to the central hearth.

"Have you never seen a man in love before?" Tuck asked, coming up beside her. He walked with surer steps these last few days, as if he gained strength and vitality from the sun, the land, and the people around him.

"I have seen men in lust before, but never this complete

devotion. It's as if his soul is incomplete without Jane and the baby."

"'Tis a rare thing, to be sure. He gave up his position and his powers to be with her. Can you imagine a king abdicating everything for the woman he loves?"

Hilde snorted at such an absurd notion.

"My father just took the women he wanted and kept his power and his kingdom," Alain a'Dale said. "But then, he loved war more than he did women, and rarely buried his need as most men do." He laughed harshly. Tonight, he was less steady on his feet than Tuck, and had to rest atop an old stump, having hobbled only a few yards from his lean-to. But then he'd been up and about more today than yesterday or the day before.

"Do you need more willow bark tea?" Hilde asked.

"Good stout ale would be better." Alain looked up at her with a winsome smile. That expression might work on other women. Not on Hilde.

She moved behind Tuck and spoke softly. "I'm worried about Nick. He went off with Robin this morning and neither has returned."

"I sent Will with a message for them around noon," the old man replied as he perched on the other side of the stump from Alain. As soon as he was seated, he lifted his face to the skies and whistled. Their red bird friend usually came to that summons.

"Will doesn't always remember the message. He'll stop and gorge on a patch of elderberries until his mind starts working again." She marched off in a huff to help Jane, but Little John had already settled her and the sleeping infant on a boulder that he'd already covered in bracken for her comfort.

"Nick has managed to slip in and out of trouble more often than I can count," Tuck said. "Give him some time."

"You mean he's managed to talk himself into and out of trouble too often. Fate may be catching up to him."

"Elena will tell me if Nick needs rescuing."

"What about Robin?"

Tuck scratched his chin beneath a wispy beard in contemplation. Was he listening to the little goddess Nick carried in a pouch near his heart? A goddess who would always be more important to him than any living person.

Then Tuck looked her square in the eye. "If Robin and Nick do not return tonight, in the morning we'll send out a search party," he said. "There is too much at stake with the charcoal burner for them both to be gone this long."

"And I am going with you," Hilde said to herself. She'd had enough of being left behind to manage the camp.

Twenty

ick braced his knees in the turf on the north face of the mound about one third of the way to the top. He pulled at the weak shoots of small shrubs. Nothing except grass truly wanted to take root in the thin soil. His efforts exposed a long line of white rock, the same stuff that made up the caves beneath Nottingham. It felt cool and moist beneath his fingers. But he found only a few cracks, barely wide enough to get his fingers into, let alone form an opening to the interior.

He checked the sky as the shadows and bright spots shifted. The sun had crept much higher than he thought, and wispy clouds flitted from the west to east. Rain would build and follow those clouds after sunset. He wanted to be back at camp and snug in his shelter before then.

Carefully, using imperfections in the rocks as handholds, he dropped back to ground level and wove his way through thick brush toward the east flank. The turf-covered slopes of the hill convinced him that this was not a structure nature had crafted on a whim, like the craggy hill yonder where the castle crumbled.

This side had been hidden from observation when he and Robin had studied the mound. More white rock showed near the base than the other side. On a whim, Nick placed his left hand flat against a vertical ridge of stone. It seemed to pulse, like a heart beating, cold and clammy in texture that in a human would give evidence of illness.

Move to your left, Elena said. She'd been silent since he climbed down the cliff in midmorning. Had she been sleeping? Or holding her breath in anticipation?

"What am I looking for?" He touched the pouch beneath his tunic. The once fine brown wool trimmed in velvet and leather was now stained with grass and mud. Oh, well. It was still whole, and he had no need to impress the Woodwose or the villagers with the extravagance the sheriff had given Derwyn. Best if it appeared well worn and a bit threadbare, as befitted his station as an outcast from the abbey.

You will know it when you see it.

"Another puzzle I must work through by myself."

Elena presented him challenges all the time. Nick presumed that Tuck had learned to do the same from his time as Elena's host.

Nick placed both hands flat on the turf and sidestepped around the base. His skin started to crawl with goose bumps. "I'm moving deasil!" He protested the eerie feeling engulfing him.

His breathing grew heavy and labored.

A sharp jab to his chest from Elena kept him moving when every instinct told him to run.

You are moving correctly, along the path of the sun. The spells encasing the mound are unnatural. The mage wove them widdershins.

"I don't like this, Elena."

Then his hand pushed through the solid-looking grass and dirt into a dark void.

"Found it." He knew for certain that Elena had directed him here.

Do not enter alone. You need to bring the others with you before you enter the domain of a vengeful mage.

"Just a quick peek, to know for certain what this is. I'll keep one foot outside."

NOOooooo!

He stepped into blackness with no penetration of sunlight from where he'd just been.

Robin Goodfellow walked backward as he and Liam descended the castle motte toward the protective ditch and bank. He could accomplish this feat over the rough ground only because he maintained his preternatural form. From this perspective he noted where the natural craggy peak gave way to the level bailey. The outer defensive walls and ramparts rose from there.

He knew that the earls of Locksley had governed this region for centuries, long before William the Conqueror had invaded England. The conqueror had reinstated the ancient title and helped build the castle, replacing the old wooden structure on the same promontory.

Decisively, he turned to view the knoll, its smooth slopes more akin to the artificial motte than the crag.

Why? Why had men gone to the tremendous effort to build a hill when there was a natural one barely half a league away?

From here the mound looked symmetrical, round, and even.

"Someone has been mucking about with *my* hill!" Liam swayed and wobbled down to the ditch using his ax as a crutch.

"Where? What do you see?" he demanded, as he himself staggered downward, keeping his gaze roving around the slopes. Occasional splotches of white showed through the green turf. Limestone, the same stuff that riddled the under-pinnings of Nottingham.

He wished he had the deep knowledge of the past the other Wild Folk were born with.

Part of him wanted to run back to camp and ask Little John what he knew about that mound.

But he couldn't leave without Nick. Now where was that boy?

Tuck tapped his foot in time to Alain a'Dale's raucous tune about how King John's latest mistress pleased him so well he offered her a boon. Her only request was to spend one night in the arms of her husband. King John's response was lost beneath the loud guffaws from the audience of Woodwose and

Wild Folk alike gathered together of an evening around the central fire.

Sweet woodsmoke filled Tuck's senses and bound the memory of this joyful time to his soul. The monks at the abbey sang, or chanted rather, with great love for the Lord God. But they rarely sang for pure joy, for freedom from the hard grind of ritual and obedience, for a love of life and their fellows.

His only regret in this moment was that Nick was not here to share it. And Hilde did not join in the fun because she stood at the tree line, staring into the shadows, her arms wrapped around herself as if chilled. She missed Nick as did Tuck.

He was also keenly aware that Will Scarlett and Robin were missing as well.

Not knowing what to do about the dilemma, Tuck rose from his stump and walked softly toward the flat boulder he let Nick use as a writing desk. Tonight he would recite the office of the day for Vespers, light a stub of a candle, and a pinch of incense, to waft his prayer to the heavens that his great-grandson would return to them safely.

Nick's curiosity and sense of adventure would be his downfall someday. Tuck truly hoped it would not be today. He had enough forest blood left in him to sense these things. But not to use the lore and the magic of his forebears to aid him.

Carefully, Tuck retrieved the remnants of his priesthood from a hollow in a nearby tree. He set out the candle, the incense, a few drops of wine, and a crust of old bread. Then he kissed the cross embroidered at the crux of his plain linen stola and draped it about his neck. With a deep breath for stability, he knelt before his makeshift altar, hands folded and head bowed.

He felt as much as heard Hilde join him. She'd only spent a year at Our Lady of Sorrows convent, but she'd grown up in a pious family and knew the comfort to be found in Church ritual.

Together, they recited the Mass and partook of the simple Communion.

Tuck recited the final benediction and lifted his face to the night sky. "He will be all right."

"How can you know?"

"Elena has not called me to take her back to her home in the crypt of the abbey church."

"I have not questioned how you, a priest, and an abbot, can have such deep faith and yet cavort with the fae folk the Church tells us do not exist," she said, still kneeling, as if reluctant to leave the small bubble of security invoked by ritual. "Since coming here, I've been too busy to question it all, and yet I helped battle Queen Mab of the Faeries to rescue Jane. I've been carried leagues of distance on the shoulders of the Green Man. I watch Will Scarlett and Robin Goodfellow change forms often and openly . . . Will I be condemned to hell for . . . this blasphemy?"

"I would hardly call my life among the Wild Folk cavorting," Tuck laughed.

"You know what I mean. You accept these people as normal and real . . . an everyday part of life."

"Because they are. The Wild Folk have dwelled in the

forests and fields of this world for longer than the Church. They have always been a part of my life, even after I found my faith and my calling. I do not have to agree with the dictates of bishops and popes and philosophers to believe. I accept that we are all God's creatures, and no matter what name we give to Him, he hears all of our prayers."

"He may hear our prayers, but he doesn't always listen." Now anger colored her words as she rose from her knees and brushed leaf litter from her robe with more vehemence than necessary.

"He listens. But sometimes his answer is to figure out the answer ourselves and take action, rather than sit around and wait for rescue or bounty or the safety of a loved one."

"Then I will be off toward Locksley Castle and the charcoal burner's abode at first light. If God won't rescue Nick, then I will." She turned abruptly back toward the main camp where Alain still regaled his audience with tales and songs.

A crashing in the canopy signaled Will Scarlett's return. He dropped from branch to branch clumsily, his wings thrashing wildly, not able to gather enough air to ease his landing. He lay panting in a crumpled heap of feathers and flesh, half man and half bird.

Twenty-One

ick held up his hand. All he saw was bright flashes behind his eyes.

He'd done this before, the first time he entered the crypt beneath the abbey church. After that first time, he'd always gone prepared with flint and iron and a small torch. Most of the time he'd left light making tools just inside the door so that he didn't have to inch his way to the bottom of the damp and slippery staircase by feel alone.

Since he'd found Elena behind a loose brick in the ancient altar (or she had found him, he wasn't certain), he'd had no need to hide in the deepest, darkest, most forgotten part of the abbey.

Now he was in an unknown place with no light and no idea where he'd entered, let alone where he should go. His mind flitted from one idea to the next without settling anywhere.

A deep breathy growl filled the space around him. He hesitated to call it a chamber with no sense of the shape or size of the place.

The growl grew louder; the breathing took on the rhythm of his racing heart.

Cold sweat broke out along his spine and down his chest.

"Elena, I could use some advice."

Silence.

Could she hear him? Cautiously, he touched the place beneath his tunic where she lay hidden in the leather pouch.

Coldness. Inert.

The muffling cloud of darkness seemed to engulf his companion in a blanket of nothingness.

She might as well be back in the niche behind the loose brick of the ancient altar in the crypt.

"I have to think." His words sounded flat, no echo, no sense of space around him.

He, too, felt wrapped in a suffocating blanket.

Except . . . was that breathy growl coming from his own throat? It came no closer. The hair on his arms didn't prickle in warning.

He couldn't tell if the sounds menaced him or not.

"I need to get out of here." He stretched his arms to their full length at his sides. Openness. No obstacles.

"If I stepped in facing forward, then the exit must be that way." He reached behind him. His fingers brushed only cold air.

Slowly he turned what felt like a half circle. Then he reached forward and to his sides.

The chamber had swallowed the entrance.

"Elena, I could really use some help here."

The only thing he heard was his own heart beating wildly in panic.

Hilde ran to Will and knelt beside him. Cautiously, seeking damage, she ran her hands along his wings/arms. Then she touched his torso in the region of his heart. Everywhere her fingers brushed, the feathers faded as the skin beneath became warmer, more muscled, more manlike. Frantically, she brought his legs back to normal.

His bright tunic and hose seemed to be missing, but his crest became his cocked hat with the jaunty red feather, and his soft felt boots clung to his clawed feet. She pulled off the coverings and massaged his claws into normal feet with toes, even if his nails stayed thick and horny.

But the thick beak remained across his nose and mouth. Strong enough to clip small branches from trees, she dared not get her fingers close to it. She didn't know if his bird instincts prevailed, or if his human mind had returned.

"Will?" she spoke clearly, seeking to awaken his mind.

He mumbled something around the beak.

"Will, you need to lose the beak before you can speak," she said, as if coaxing a child to put down a sharp kitchen knife.

He mumbled something again. Then his eyes opened, clear and aware. He brought his hands up to feel the beak. He squeaked/chirped in surprise. Then closed his eyes again and screwed up his face in concentration.

Slowly, the beak lost shape and his nose and mouth emerged—with the help of some judicious prodding from his fingers. Those nails also needed trimming.

"Can you sit up, boy?" Tuck asked from behind Hilde. He pulled some big maple leaves free of a low-hanging branch and dropped them to cover Will's nether regions.

Hilde swallowed a giggle at the old man's blushing modesty.

Living cheek by jowl among the Woodwose, Hilde had become used to adverting her eyes when nudity was impossible to avoid. She'd bathed both men and women with cool water when fever ran rampant through them last winter in the cave.

"I'll fetch help," Tuck said and hastened away from the open space around his altar.

"I . . . I think I can sit," Will said, his words still sliding one into the other.

"Let me help you." Hilde got an arm beneath his well-muscled back and helped him heave upward until he sat, legs sprawled in front of him like an ungainly colt.

"What happened?" Little John asked as he came thundering through the woods from the direction of camp.

Will looked around in confusion. His eyes darted in every direction seeking escape or a place to hide.

"You're safe here," Hilde soothed, keeping her hand on his lower back and stroking his shoulder with the other. "You have nothing to fear from Little John."

"We won't hurt you, Will. We want only to help." Little John's voice lost volume and took on gentler tones.

"Tell us what happened," Hilde said, letting her hands work small gentle circles on Will's skin. She felt the slightly enlarged pores and coarse hairs that could sprout into feathers at a moment's notice.

"I . . . can't remember. I found Robin Goodfellow with Liam. But . . . what else was I looking for? What message did I need to pass to . . . him?"

A burning, aching itch began in Robin's ankles and traveled rapidly upward to the top of his head and outward to his fingertips. Damnation! He'd been short for too long. And he needed the fae qualities of his gnomish body to sense where Nick had gone.

His knees collapsed, and he fell to the ground halfway through the ditch ringing the castle crag.

"What ails you?" Liam asked, pausing before climbing upward to the level pasture and the mound.

"My curse," Robin gasped, curling his body into a ball. The aches became stabbing pains. He tried to draw in a deep breath to help ease his transition. One slow rise and fall of his chest. Then another. He counted the length of each inhalation.

Gradually, his legs elongated, and his fingers untwisted. Then his spine straightened, and his chest filled out. Breathing grew easier as his chin and nose returned to normal proportions. He couldn't do anything about the sensation of a hundred spiders crawling over his scalp as his hair sprouted. His beard took a little longer to emerge.

"I wish I could do that," Liam said. His spine seemed more crooked than usual.

"No, you don't," Robin replied, shaking off the last of the pain. "It's easier if I choose when and where I change. If I've held one form or the other too long, the change is worse. Let me help you out of this ditch." He climbed partway to the top, only twice a normal man's height, with the ease of long legs and feet appropriate in size to the rest of him. Then he paused and reached back a hand for Liam.

With the charcoal burner's fingers clasped around his, Robin hoisted his companion up level with himself, then climbed the rest of the way and repeated the process.

The west slope of the mound lay ahead of him, blocking his view of the higher ground to the north. It took a few moments for him to find the white streaks of rock he'd pointed out to Nick earlier.

How long had they been separated? He couldn't remember. "Nothing for it. I have to circle yon hill to find Nick's tracks."

"I need to finish my kiln," Liam muttered. "If I don't have a hundredweight of charcoal by the next full moon, I won't get paid."

"I doubt you'll get paid even if you produce two hundredweight. Sir Philip Marc is not noted for honoring his bargains where money is concerned. He collects rather than pays."

"I'll see the color of his pennies before I turn over my black silver." Liam swung his ax so the blade rested behind his shoulder. Robin had seen him wield it with the agility of a trained warrior. With its long handle, he could easily fend off a mounted knight.

"Do what you must." Robin dismissed him as he trudged around the bottom of the knoll. Liam followed, pausing to fell the overgrowth as he progressed in a deasil path.

Robin grunted his acceptance that Liam took down only the trees that had sprung up in the fifty years of neglect since his father and brother had fallen to the spells of the magician. A castle needed a clear line of sight all around it for defense. The trees offered too many hiding places for enemies.

The north slope offered only a smooth turf surface. No slashes of white or gray rocks. A little further in his circuit Robin found traces of footprints, smaller than his own, but not by much. Nick had been here!

The boy had walked a careful path, weaving in and out of the saplings. Was that a crushed frond amongst the ground cover? Robin doubted any but a trained hunter could track Nick's passage. He'd learned much while living amongst the Woodwose.

The air grew thick and humid as Robin rounded the hill to the east side. Harder to breathe. He felt almost as if he had to swim forward. Something—or someone—did not want him here.

Liam was now far behind him.

He had to face the menace of this hill alone.

As Nick had.

His sense of urgency pushed him forward. Every step of the way he checked the ground for signs of Nick's steps and the hill for signs of an opening.

The footprints stopped.

The mound remained blank and closed.

Twenty-Two

"t's awfully dark in here," Nick said, as much to test the sound quality of the underground chamber as to convince himself he was still alive.

His words echoed again and again, telling him nothing about the size or shape of the room.

"Are you still with me, Elena?" This time he thought his words spread out more, like the space was large, pulling sounds away from him.

Silence.

But . . . did the area above his heart grow warmer and throb?

He grabbed the little leather pouch from beneath his tunic. His palm tingled where he cupped Elena's container. The random starbursts before his eyes steadied into a faint outline of his fingers.

Carefully, he loosened the drawstring around the top of the pouch and pulled Elena's silver cup free. Each of the three figures standing back-to-back to form a tiny pitcher in the center carried a lamp. All three of those lamps glowed with a supernatural blue/white light.

"Can you talk to me now, Elena?" Nick asked, gaze fixed on the nearest face of the little goddess.

The three lamps grew dark for a heartbeat, then brightened again, twice.

"Does that mean no?"

The lights winked out again then on again, holding steady.

"I take that to mean one blink for yes, and two for no."

Another extinguishing and re-emergence of light.

"Agreed. Now what?"

No answer.

"Oh. It wasn't a yes or no kind of question."

One blink.

"Then we keep this simple. Is there a way out?"

One blink.

"And I have to find it on my own."

Another blink that lasted two heartbeats. In his memory Nick almost heard her chuckle "Silly boy."

She called Little John and Father Tuck "silly boy," too, so he wasn't insulted. Indeed, he felt a warm flush of affection.

Slowly, shuffling his feet to maintain contact with the floor and not move forward or back even a tiny bit, he turned a circle in place, holding Elena's lamp high.

He couldn't see much beyond his own little circle. But then the lamps flared brighter when he thought he'd turned a full circle.

Biting his lip in trepidation, he took one step forward. The lamps brightened again. "I'll keep walking in this direction then."

The lamp blinked once.

One step. Then two more.

He caught an impression of a stone wall in front of him. He reached out with tentative fingertips and met numerous flat stones piled tightly on top of each other without mortar. Regularly shaped stones making a pattern. A manmade wall.

He let his fingers explore some more and found a large flat slab etched with designs.

"Is this part of the undercroft of the castle?" He didn't think so, given the distance to the castle crag and . . . those large flat slabs.

Two blinks of the lamp, and another impression of a chuckle.

"You know I have to ask," he told his companion. "Eliminate possibilities before drawing a conclusion. One of the first lessons in logic."

Elena blinked again.

Nick stepped closer to the wall, then turned to his right, one hand still pressed against the stones tracing a design in a circle—no a spiral. Three of them clutched together. He took one step to the right to follow a long wavy line. With his fingers.

Two blinks.

"But that direction is deasil to me. If I go left, I'll go widdershins . . ."

The light held steady. He had to think this through on his own.

"I believe that whoever constructed this place used magic.

Magic is contrary to my belief that the path of the sun is always correct."

A pause and then Elena blinked once.

"So, this one time, I need to walk opposite the direction of the sun."

Another blink and a sense of an impatient sigh. Elena was rarely impatient, but she punctuated with a sigh when he seemed especially dense.

He shifted to his left. That put his right shoulder to the wall. He switched hands to hold Elena so he could keep one hand on the wall. Eventually, he must find an exit.

One step after another. Out of long habit he counted them. Twelve, then fifteen. And twenty . . . his fingers met a new column of the skinny bricks piled together tightly without mortar. Just beyond the column, which turned out to be an arch, his fingers met a vacancy. He held his lamp closer to peer to his right.

Elena's benign light could not penetrate the gloom.

Tuck watched Alain a'Dale saunter around the central cooking fire, making jokes, tweaking noses, and making acorns appear from behind children's ears. Muted laughter followed him as he did his minstrel best to lighten the heavy atmosphere of dread.

No one wanted to think about Will Scarlett's injuries and memory loss—worse than his usual inability to hold two thoughts together for more than a few moments—nor of Nick's unknown whereabouts.

Finally, fully a man and properly clothed, Will drew a small harp out of his magical pack. A gasp, followed by silence, rippled around the rough circle. Will looked at the instrument and then up at Alain. "Can you play this?"

"Aye." Alain's fingers clenched and straightened rhythmically, an unconscious stretch anticipating playing such a fine instrument, and a withdrawal in . . . dread at playing a magical instrument belonging to someone else.

"Sing something bright." Will handed the harp to eager fingers.

Alain tested the weight and balance, sitting and resting it in his lap. He hummed a note and plucked a string that matched him perfectly.

"It is always in tune," Will confirmed.

"Saves a lot of time, that." Alain drew forth a fluttering chord that sounded like the flourish of a bird's wings. Then he plucked single notes to form an almost familiar simple melody.

> *There came strolling one day*
> *A tall lad*
> *Strong of faith*
> *And clever of will*

They all knew he sang of Nick, the scholarly boy from the abbey, full of mischief, and adventure. A trickster who got himself into and out of trouble with quick wits and an agile tongue.

The tension in the shoulders and the faces of the gathered

Woodwose eased. Of course, Nick would come through whatever pit he'd fallen into. He'd done it before.

There was a special magic in Alain's music, a true bard who used lyrics and melody to bring people back to joy, to invoke laughter, and make them remember what needed to be remembered, whether good or ill.

Around the edges of the firelight, the Wild Folk gathered. Herne the Huntsman, Ardenia the water sprite, and Blaidd, the pack leader of all wolves. Behind them crept the less powerful folk: dryads, trolls, brownies, and night flyers. They came to listen. Will Scarlett was one of them, but even his fine tenor could not match Alain a'Dale's compelling voice that shifted in tone and range to match the character of his song.

The fearful mood lifted, Alain switched his tune to speculation about Nick confronting Sir Philip Marc, the sheriff of Nottingham, also a wily and tricky player. Who would win that duel of wits? No one knew.

The moon soared across the heavens, and still Alain sang. Then, finally, as clouds drifted in and the stars shifted through their nightly wheel, the troubadour faltered, and his breathing became labored. They'd all forgotten that only a few days ago he'd been badly beaten.

"Thank you for the blessing of this harp," Alain said graciously as he held out the instrument to Will.

"Keep it, my brother. I cannot match you in song. The harp deserves one such as you." Will passed a hand over the harp and touched it briefly in affectionate farewell. The harp was now Alain's. Then the bird man struggled to his feet and made his way to a nest on the ground near Tuck's lean-to.

"To bed, for all of us," Tuck said. "Tomorrow we must search for our missing lad."

Herne stepped forth with an outstretched hand to help his elderly cousin to his feet and then to his own rude shelter. "We will help," he said before disappearing into the darkness, a silent shadow.

Derwyn watched the dawn emerge from behind the stone cross that marked the junction of three roads. The widest and best maintained Royal Road had two high centers and two ruts on either side of each. On Market Day in Nottingham, or other important events, the way would be crowded with carts filled with livestock, pack animals loaded with wide panniers, and families carrying their goods on their backs. Traffic would pass in both directions, or sometimes jam up because some impatient noble or merchant would try to pass a slower or bemired vehicle and encounter an equally impatient, important personage headed in the opposite direction.

As a young sapling of a man, Derwyn had found the antics of humans infinitely entertaining. Now, just the thought of all the noise and smells churned in his empty stomach and near blinded him with head pain.

When the sun's rays shone through the open space between the cross and its joining circle, he whirled about to catch that same first light shimmering against the magic shield keeping him out of Sherwood. Perhaps the superstition of religion would grant him a few clues about how to re-enter his home.

A rainbow of colors glistened where he had broken through the barrier a few days ago. His father's magic repaired itself. But to the south the sunlight didn't bounce off the wall as strongly there.

He moved a few steps off the green island surrounding the cross to see better.

The sun rose another bit above the horizon. He couldn't see the wall at all. When he placed his hand flat where the barrier should be, magic tingled all along his arm with prickles of fire. Not enough to deter him from pushing harder until the magic gave like a thick layer of newly fallen leaves on the ground.

What was different about this segment of the forest?

He had to think back to his youth. King Richard had enforested the lands all around Locksley Castle. The last earl and his heir had died, and the next heir did not return from an earlier Crusade for at least ten years. Little John had already been the Green Man at the time. Derwyn remembered that he'd had to work hard to bring Locksley under his influence.

Logically, then, Verne would spread his awareness and his authority over the area naturally, because it was considered part of Sherwood while he was locked in his tree during the transition of power.

But until Verne emerged, this area was vulnerable. No one would think to defend this border against intruders.

Derwyn marched a little farther to the south, testing the barrier every few steps.

There! At the southernmost point before the lands curved west again at the base of a ridge—a natural border—the magic barrier defining Sherwood and altered to keep Derwyn out, weakened to the point of nonexistence.

Broad meadows spread out across the land. Once it had been plowed fields and pasturage, divided by sprawling hedgerows that even a pig could not penetrate. Now the only crop seemed to be leafy weeds, good grazing for forest animals but no longer available for humans and their livestock.

The place needed a tree to shelter and nourish small game. Derwyn needed to stand guard.

He stepped through the wall without hindrance.

His toes itched to dig into the turf and grow roots again.

Throwing caution to the wind, he let his natural urge to become a tree take over. In glorious amazement, he watched his fingers elongate into twigs while his arms became branches and leaves sprouted through his skin.

Derwyn of Sherwood lifted his head and howled in defiance and delight. Sir Philip Marc and his men would have to look elsewhere for a guide to the outlaw camp.

Twenty-Three

obin Goodfellow waited on the east side of the mound for dawn to brighten the forest. Just past the equinox, the sunrise sent a shaft of light directly at the spot where he'd lost track of Nick. With the magic inherent in this body, he peered more closely at the trailing vines and scrubby turf at his eye level.

Something different from everyday grasses and weeds and covering vines . . . something very old caressed his vision.

He dug his gnarled fingers in, pulling away a few inches of dirt and tangled roots. The horny nail on his pointing finger broke raggedly, exposing the quick. He kept going, grabbing and pulling and digging.

Then, as the sun rose, he spotted white limestone facing a series of overlapping rocks, like slender bricks laid out in a tight pattern. Made by men? None of the probing rays of sun-light penetrated.

Except there . . . a narrow gap that might be the outline of a gateway.

Might. He couldn't be sure. His magical sight was too young, too incomplete to tell him more. But he had a sense deep in his bones that whatever he uncovered was old—very, very old.

The ground beneath his feet trembled, then rocked. He had to grab the greenery he'd been tearing away from the mound to remain upright.

A great hunk came away in his hands, so violently that he fell backward. His spine slammed into the ground knocking the wind from him.

Sharp pain stabbed his lungs. He gasped for air, but his ribs wouldn't move.

The ripple of magic coursed through the ground again, jolt-ing air back into him. Along with it came the primal scream of . . . of a man. No. No human throat could make that sound. Some wild creature of the forest.

"What? What is happening?" he asked the air. He needed to investigate.

The trembling in the ground faded.

Robin sat up slowly. He couldn't feel the disturbance in the air anymore. He needed to find the source of that scream.

But the last bit of green he'd ripped away from the hillside exposed a gaping hole as wide as his hand with his twisted fingers spread as wide as he could and about as long as his arm.

"Nick! Nick are you in there?"

Robin jumped to the opening, pulling away more plants and trying to squeeze in only to find his head stuck in the gap.

"I hate walking while it's still dark." Will Scarlett sighed and plodded on, barely lifting his feet.

"Then why not transform into a bird and fly ahead to scout for us!" Hilde replied, more than a bit annoyed at his frequent complaints.

False dawn offered hints of a sunny day with broken clouds as the eastern horizon gradually brightened. She and Will and Tuck and Little John had been walking this broken and convoluted trail for . . . for far too long.

Herne and Blaidd and some of the other Wild Folk stayed abreast of them, hidden by the greenery.

"If I allow my bird to dictate my form, I'd still be back at camp, in full feathers with my head tucked beneath my wing," Will replied on a jaw-cracking yawn.

Before Hilde could snap back at him, he spoke again. "This is for Nick. We have to find him before . . ." His voice trailed off as he searched the sky for answers.

"Before what?" Tuck asked anxiously, coming up to walk directly behind Will. The path wasn't wide enough for them to walk side by side, but the trees were thin here, the undergrowth dense and tangled.

Will shook his head. "I can't remember."

"You have trouble remembering many things," Little John said gently.

"This is different," Will protested. A single ray of light shot above the horizon as sun began its daily climb. The growing light brought brightness and alertness to the bird man that had been missing a moment ago.

"Take us back to what you do remember," Tuck urged.

"But keep walking while you do it," Hilde prodded Little John forward before he turned and paused. "We need to find Nick. He's in trouble. You know it and I know it."

"You don't know that," Tuck protested.

"He's Nick. If he's not where he's supposed to be, back at camp, then he's in trouble. He finds trouble even when he's not looking for it." She lengthened her stride, determined to find her friend.

Until now, they'd used John's deep knowledge of the land and a tiny candle flame to guide them toward Locksley Castle. Hilde had stumbled often over protruding tree roots and holes left by persistent puddles. With the rising sun, she could see more and more of the path and its obstacles, so she pushed ahead faster than the men.

"I remember flying to the castle ruins and perching atop the old keep. The tower roof is still intact. Most of the out-buildings are crumbling—too quickly to be normal. There's bad air around that place. I couldn't stay long, pressure in my chest." Will clutched at his heart and gasped for breath. His face turned pale even as his jaunty cap sprouted feathers.

"Easy now. Breathe deeply. You are out in the open now," Little John said in soothing tones as he clasped Will's shoulder.

The black crest feathers retreated back into a cloth cap.

Will's chest heaved as he drew in a lung full of air. "From

the top rampart of the tower, I spotted Robin Goodfellow and the man with the bent back."

"Liam, the charcoal burner?" Tuck prompted him.

Will nodded.

Hilde walked faster. She didn't like what Will had experienced at the castle. Nick had a penchant for cramped dark places. The crumbling castle would entice him to explore, bad air or not.

Cold sweat filmed her face and her heart began beating faster, pounding at her rib cage as if needing to escape.

"What did you see after you spotted Robin and his companion?" Tuck continued to push Will to remember.

"There's a knoll west of the castle crag," Will said. He hung his head. "Then nothing. A blackness until I returned home."

"The knoll?" Little John shook his head. "I should know that place, and yet I don't. King Richard enforested Locksley Castle as part of Sherwood after I inherited my responsibilities as Green Man. My knowledge and awareness of that demesne is not as deeply ingrained in me as the rest of my lands." He stopped walking, placing both hands on the sides of his head as if that would help him think.

"We don't have time for this." Hilde stalked forward, thrusting overhanging plants aside in her haste.

Herne appeared before her. He lowered his magnificent rack of antlers and gestured toward his back. *Climb aboard.*

Hilde heard him think his invitation to her.

"Thank you, my lord." She bowed slightly, grasped the tip of one horn, and hoisted herself atop his back. Then she leaned forward and wrapped her arms about his thick neck.

He barely waited for her to entwine her fingers in his fur before bounding forward in mighty leaps that covered the ground much faster than she could think.

Behind them, the men stumbled to keep up until Herne stopped abruptly at the edge of a sharp cliff. White rock plunged downward. Hilde gasped at the danger of any one of them tumbling over the edge.

Herne dropped his head so that she could see the valley below. To their right, castle ruins stood out on the top of a ragged promontory. "Locksley Castle," she whispered. "Robin's home."

"There," Tuck gasped, trying to catch his breath. He pointed directly below them. A small knoll, no more than three man-lengths in height, stood out among the overgrown fields and rolling meadows of the estate.

"It's a knoll." Hilde wanted to argue there was nothing special about one hill among many when the castle dominated the landscape.

"It is too regular in shape," Little John said. "There is something about this place I should remember." He frowned and shook his head.

"Don't think about it. It will come to you," Tuck advised, slapping the big man's shoulder.

Little John shaded his eyes with one hand and looked into the far distance. "There's a tree on the southern border that wasn't there the last time I came here."

"What?" Tuck asked, also straining to the limits of his age-weakened eyes.

"I'll go look." Will said, growing feathers and dropping to bird size in the blink of an eye. He took two running steps forward to the cliff edge with his wings spread wide. He dropped a bit, then caught an updraft and soared out along the broad valley.

Herne ended the discussion by stepping carefully to the left where a faint trail led downward, doubling back on itself several times.

Looking back, Hilde spotted a similar path. "Is this a processional way?" she asked.

"Looks like it," Little John answered her. "Same twists on both sides. Ends in nearly the same place."

"But where does it go?" Hilde kept looking for something different—or out of place.

The burial chamber, Herne told her.

Elena's lanterns blinked on and off in a ragged pattern.

The air within the deep darkness moaned.

Chills ran up and down Nick's spine.

Another moan came, sounding as if it originated in another world and another time.

Nick didn't know how long he stared at the light and dark, trying to decipher what Elena was trying to tell him. He thought she was agitated. Afraid.

If the goddess of crossroads, cemeteries, and sorcery was frightened, he should be, too. "I will explore that passage another time, when I have a torch, rope, and friends."

The flashing light calmed down, but continued a confusing signal.

The ghostly groans faded into the distance.

He held Elena's pitcher up to find the lintel on the opposite side of the passage. Once again, he found stacked flat stones to define the doorway and then more flat slabs inscribed with spirals and waves, slashes and pits.

"Is this some kind of language? Like Greek?"

Elena resumed her steady flow of light.

Another puzzle he'd have to decode on his own, at another time.

He continued his path, sensing a curvature to the walls. His hands and feet grew cold. How big was this chamber?

More important: how long had he been in here?

A steady drumming sound penetrated his awareness. Steady, like water drops hitting a pond. But there was no water in here. The stones remained dry to the touch, just . . . cold.

"Nick!" a voice came from just ahead. Flat, not echoey. Distant, yet close.

He walked a little faster.

"Nick!" A different voice this time. Higher pitched, more feminine.

"Hilde!" he called back, hastening his stride.

A confused murmur of many voices followed.

"Hilde!"

"Nick, where are you?"

"Here, I'm in here!" He reached a section of the flat stones piled into a column. Cautiously, he ran his fingers along the surface until he found the top lintel, then downward again, defining a doorway.

Elena sighed in relief and winked out.

The darkness became gray. Nick thrust his arm through the doorway.

Work-roughened hands clasped his wrist and pulled.

He followed the direction of the yank and stumbled out of the mound, into the real world.

Bright sunlight dazzled his eyes. He had to blink rapidly before finding the outline of three, maybe five, people. Like shadows but more solid.

"Nick, are you hurt? Where have you been?"

Questions from several people all at the same time. People he should know.

"Nick, what is wrong?"

"I . . . I don't remember."

Twenty-Four

"ick!" Tuck reached up to touch the boy's forehead, checking for signs of fever.

Cool, though Nick's eyes looked slightly glazed and unfocused.

"Who?" Nick turned his attention toward his great-grandfather. Then his countenance brightened, and the murkiness in his gaze cleared. "Tuck. You're Tuck and she's Hilde and that's Little John and Robin of Locksley, and . . . and you must be Liam." He nodded to the hunchback lurking behind them all. "Is Will here?"

"Off," Hilde said waving a hand vaguely toward the south. "Nick, what happened to you?" she repeated Tuck's question.

Nick looked at his left hand where he clutched the little silver pitcher of the three-faced goddess, Elena. The metal looked tarnished, minus the inner glow he always associated with her when she was outside her hidden niche behind the altar in the crypt of Locksley Abbey.

The pitcher had looked just as flat the day Tuck had returned her to the niche the night before he took his final vows to become a monk and a priest.

She'd gone dormant until another student at the abbey needed her.

Slowly, Tuck withdrew the leather pouch on a thong from within the folds of Nick's tunic—the fabric looked none the worse for wear from his adventures—and folded Nick's right hand around the pouch. Absently, the boy slid the pitcher inside and let it drop. The braided thong kept it from falling to the ground, its precious burden forgotten by her carrier.

Tuck's heart ached for both Nick and Elena. A tear formed at the corner of his eye and trickled down the outside of his nose. She'd have to go back into the crypt for renewal.

Which must mean that sometime during the night underground, Nick had decided not to pursue a life in the Church.

Another regretful tear fell. He had such high hopes that Nick would rise through the ranks and replace him as abbot, and also become the Pope's liaison to the senior clergy of England, a quiet leader barely acknowledged by royal or noble powers. Let the bishops and archbishops shout and argue politics. Tuck, and eventually Nick, needed to do the daily, hands-on work of ministering to the people of England. All of them, even the outlawed and the Wild Folk.

So, which of them, Nick or Tuck, would return Elena to the crypt?

Neither of them could openly return to the abbey and expect to leave again, something Tuck was not willing to risk.

***

"What aren't you telling me, Nick?" Hilde demanded.

Nick shook his head, trying to clear the buzzing sound that persisted at his nape. He batted at his ears. But he felt no midges or other flying insects.

"I . . . I don't know what you are asking. I . . . ." This time he stuck his little finger into his ear and pushed until he heard a pop and some of the stuffiness vanished. He repeated the process on his other ear.

Finally, he felt alert and could take in the group as a whole rather than individual faces. "Did you all come here to find me?"

"Yes, Nick. Now tell us what happened," Tuck sounded very much the authoritative abbot.

"Robin and I scouted the area from up there." Nick had to turn all the way around to discover where things were. Finally, he found the cliff face and pointed toward the top. "Then he went to the castle, and I . . . I . . . I don't remember."

***

"We need to get him back to camp," Hilde said. She looked for the path where they'd come down the hill. It was no longer visible from where they stood on the east side of the knoll. But she could just pick out the other path upward on the west side. Not even the path at her feet at the base of the mound appeared to her questing gaze. She looked to Robin, who was in his archer form. He stood with Little John a few long strides away from the hill, scanning the far horizon to the south.

"Robin, how do we get out of here?" she called to him. Unease crept upward from her toes to the base of her spine. She shuffled her feet trying for a more comfortable stance.

There wasn't one.

"The same way you got here." Robin shrugged and returned to his consultation with John.

Tuck tugged on her sleeve and pointed around the mound. "We must continue to walk deasil," he said quietly. "I do not like this place. There is strange magic here. Not the ancient, gentle magic inherent to the forest and its creatures. This is . . . alien. More akin to anger and insanity than nurturing." Without hesitation, he continued walking around the knoll.

Nick followed him as he was wont to do at all times.

Hilde had no choice but to set out in their wake. Little John and Robin would find their own way back to camp in due time.

As they rounded the curve of the path to stand between the knoll and the wide ditch at the base of the castle crag, she could clearly see the western path leading up the cliff in a series of sharp turns. She plodded along, noting how the trail brightened even in shadow. As she rounded the next curve, the cliff came into view. From this angle the eastern as well as the western path was obvious.

She shook her head, not understanding the magic involved. For the first time she thought that maybe life in the convent was easier. Grinding hard work, the random attacks of Sister

Marie Josef with her wicked rod, were certainly difficult. But she understood the purpose and the Bible as a guide.

Magic carried no logic that she could fathom. Will changed from man to bird on a whim. He magically pulled musical instruments from his pack. Robin changed from tall and handsome man to ugly gnome frequently, bringing his two personalities to the fore as he needed. Little John used to spend half his life as a tree. . . .

Now Nick, her best friend, had disappeared inside a hill for half a day and an entire night, but couldn't remember how or why, or what happened to him in that eerie darkness.

Best if she didn't question it, just accept it as a part of her new life away from the convent.

She could use the long walk back to camp as time to plan ahead the tasks of gathering food to feed twenty people.

❦❦❦

Robin stared into the fire rather than watch Alain a'Dale stroll through the Woodwose camp, laughing and joking and telling tall tales to the gathered outlaws and fae companions. The minstrel had exchanged the lute for a hand drum from Will's pack. The cadence he set up never altered from one step to another, one song to the next story.

Slap, slap, slap, flat palm against tightly stretched animal hide.

Robin found himself counting each step and slap that never varied. Nick bobbed his head in the same rhythm. The white heart of the fire burned steadily, drawing Robin's gaze no matter how hard he tried to look at something else.

He recognized that Alain wove some kind of spell. In his gnome form he was more vulnerable to this kind of magic than when tall.

Even Little John and Will Scarlett seemed lulled into . . .

A reed flute blended into the spell adding a sweet cadence. Robin's eyes grew heavy.

Then Alain added to the whole the rasp of two fresh branches rubbing together. Annoying. So annoying that Robin could not block the sound from his consciousness. Just enough to keep him awake, and yet he found himself waiting for the next buzz rather than trying to banish it.

"You left Robin and walked down the cliff side," Alain chanted, keeping his voice low and his words in time with the rasp and the barely heard flute.

Robin went back to that same moment when he headed toward the castle ruins to find Liam, expecting Nick to be safe, as Robin and his brother had always been safe when playing near the mound as children; when he'd taken Marian to the top and plighted his troth to her.

"I stopped to explore some patches of white stone," Nick replied in the same chanting rhythm.

"What did you find?" Tuck asked, keeping his voice low and in time with the spell that Alain set up.

Robin thought about what he had found: Liam, castle ruins, more ruinous than they should be after only fifty or even sixty years.

Illusion, some logical portion of his mind whispered.

Everything he remembered and suspected about his curse seemed based upon illusion.

"I pulled away weeds and vines and found only tiny cracks in the rock face," Nick continued.

"And then what?" Tuck prodded.

Robin relived his own day with Liam as Nick recited bit by bit how he'd come to disappear into the mound.

Where was Liam now? He'd been hovering a small distance behind the group when they pulled Nick out of the mound. He probably stayed behind to finish building his kiln and his shelter. He smelled rain on the wind, so Liam most likely would work on his shelter.

"And what did you do when you came to the void?" Tuck continued to coax the story from Nick.

The boy remained silent for a long time.

Robin thought of voids, remembered his encounter with the insane magician . . . encountered a void beneath the castle. . . .

And remembered nothing more until he woke up the next morning cursed to spend half his life as Robin Goodfellow the prancing gnome, with no idea how to find Marian.

A rhyme, no, the beginning of a ballad, suddenly tickled the back of his mind.

> *Sleep, my lady, through the years*
> *Sleep through your lover's tears.*

What was the rest of it? Robin knew the beginning of the

song held importance. He couldn't fathom how right now. Not until he returned to the mound and slept in his little hollow that had disturbed old magic. That was the key. He must sleep and dream there before he explored the void in the castle.

"I stared into nothing for a long time," Nick mumbled. "Then I moved past the void as Elena instructed, still wishing I'd had time and resources to explore. I need to go back and explore. . . ."

I, too, need to go back and explore, Robin decided. *Do I dare risk my friends when I do? Nick plans to take companions as well as ropes and torches and bladed weapons.*

Twenty-Five

tiny bit of warmth penetrated Nick's shirt to settle in his heart.

Elena was no longer inert, just in need of rest.

At the same moment, something flashed in his mind.

"Inside the void, there was a momentary light," he said, not certain if he actually spoke or if he only thought about the almost memory.

"What kind of light?" Robin asked, straightening as he hopped up and began to grow big again—his usual response to a threat.

"There and gone before I became fully aware of it." Nick rubbed the back of his neck, feeling the cords stand out with tension.

Hilde took over, gently massaging tight muscles. "Examine the flash in your memory. Was it like the sun peeking out from clouds?"

Nick shook his head. Her touch distracted him, and he couldn't focus on the dim memory.

He shook off her hand and stood, shook his shoulders and began pacing, opposite the path Robin took around the central fire. The archer walked deasil, as they had around the mound. Nick walked widdershins, as he had within the mound; as Elena had directed him.

A flash of light, here and gone. "It looked more like dawn light coming through the stained-glass window in the Lady Chapel. Hints of blue in the red-gold, headed toward blinding white but not completing the transition."

That. Yes that. Nick felt lighter, freer, ready to emerge from the long darkness that had folded around his mind inside the mound.

Robin ceased his pacing abruptly. He whirled to face Nick, hope warring with anger on his features. "Inside the mound, not in the castle cellars?"

Nick had to shrug. "I can't tell how big the chamber is, or how far back the void goes." He bent and rubbed his legs. "Maybe the floor dipped some and I climbed back up to exit the place. I honestly can't say."

"We have to go back. Now. The insane magician has entombed Marian there!"

"When I began withdrawing my awareness of the forest to give it to Verne, I noticed a void that shouldn't be there. But there was so much happening I just now remembered it,"

Little John said. He held his sleeping baby while Jane drowsed on his shoulder.

"We can't wait any longer. We have to go back!" Robin screamed, contrary to all camp rules that demanded hushed tones so as not to betray their location.

"It's too late," Tuck said. He had to stand and place a firm hand on Robin's shoulder.

Nick remembered the strength of those grips all too well from his days in the abbey before King John exiled the senior clergy. Abbot Mæson, now known by his childhood nickname while masquerading as a wandering mendicant monk, could convey comfort, affirmation, or reprimand in that single gesture.

Robin bristled. So, the grip had been a reprimand.

"We can't see in the dark. Nor can we transport ourselves in the blink of an eye," Tuck continued in a soothing voice.

Nick found himself nodding in agreement.

"You have to wait until dawn. One more night will not make a difference. She's been sleeping for nigh on sixty years, boy."

Nick felt the shift in Robin's mood as soon as he saw the tall man begin to shrink back to gnome-size, think better of the action, and regain his height and breadth. "The magic has been breached. The mound penetrated. The spell has begun to break down."

All of the Woodwose stilled in realization that a major change had come upon them all.

"Do you remember the spell?" Old Catryn lisped through

her broken and rotted teeth. "Can't reverse the spell until you can recite it backward."

Robin collapsed in on himself, holding his head in his hands.

"Maybe Alain can force the memory out of you the same way he did me," Nick suggested, adding his own heavy hand to his friend's shoulder.

Robin looked up. "Alain?"

"Worth a try," the minstrel said.

Hunting dogs belled in the near distance. They'd found their prey.

A loud crash echoed through the woods. A big tree had fallen.

But there was no wind to bring it down.

Little John looked startled and worried.

Instinctively, Nick reached for Hilde's hand.

"*Raiders!*" The word circled the camp. "Run!"

Nick ran, dragging Hilde with him. Silently they climbed the nearest elm. He prayed that Llwyf rested within that tree and could shelter them.

The dogs loosed excited yips. A burning brand landed in the camp, right where Nick had been standing.

Hilde kilted up the skirts of her long and cumbersome nun's robe into her rope belt, and set her feet to climbing the large elm. "I need both hands!" she whispered.

Nick released her but stayed one branch above her rather than climbing upward to his own illusion of safety.

No time to think and wonder. Reach. Grab. One foot up. Another reach and grab, then the other foot up.

Tall, rough-furred dogs dashed into the clearing, circling the still burning brand, looking to their masters in puzzlement.

Hilde settled, close to Nick in the crook of a branch where it met the trunk. She trembled in fear and shock.

He put his arm around her shoulders.

Life among the Woodwose and Wild Folk had been so peaceful and uncomplicated these last nine moons. Why did it all have to change?

She hid her face in Nick's shoulder and let his warmth and strength invade her. But he was as frightened and shocked as she.

A dozen men stomped into the clearing, all wearing chain mail and helms, and carrying fearsome weapons. Their leader, identified by his bared sword, shouted to his men and pointed with his weapon. More torches appeared in the hands of soldiers. They set fire to the crude lean-tos and makeshift shelters that dotted the sparse trees around the clearing.

Thatch and dry-leafed branches exploded in flames and smoke. Fumes caught in Hilde's throat. Her breathing became labored; her chest ached. She tried desperately to suppress a cough that nagged at her throat.

Nick covered his face with his sleeve to muffle his own coughs.

Hilde did the same. But the need to expel the irritating smoke continued.

She held her breath, watching the armed and armored men milling about in indecision.

The dogs lay down beside the central cooking fire. They'd found their prey, all that was required of them. Now it was up to their masters to finish the job.

The leader searched the area, thrashing at the undergrowth with his sword. Two of his men joined him, using the long-pole halberds to reach farther away from the packed dirt of the camp area.

One of them stood directly beneath them, thrusting his weapon upward into the leafy covering. The tip of its blade brushed past Nick's foot, dangling below their seat.

He yanked it upward, upsetting his balance.

Hilde held onto his fine tunic with desperate fingers. Her breaths came short and shallow.

Nick dug his fingers into her thick robe at her waist and pulled her closer to his chest.

"I'm sorry," he mouthed and clamped his mouth on hers, in a long and desperate kiss.

Robin ran one hundred long strides into the masking shadows of the woods. With each step, he debated his need to stay big and shoot his ever-present flint-tipped arrows at the intruders. They were all bullies and thugs who enjoyed dealing out punishment and pain—the same as Sir Philip Marc, the ruthless French mercenary, King John's close friend and chief tax collector.

But if he shifted down, he had a better chance at remaining hidden from their sight.

All of father's training about the responsibilities of a lord for his people flooded his mind. A lord was nothing without his people. He needed to shoot each and every one of the raiders, in order to protect the Woodwose and the Wild Folk.

That would bring certain and swift retaliation from the sheriff.

If he died in this conflict, then who would protect Marian and release her from the magical spell that entombed her?

He stepped behind a yew tree, the source of his bow and arrows, and dropped into his gnome-like persona. The fae in him needed to laugh and prance and play hide and seek with the sheriff's men. He needed to sow confusion among them and torment the hunting dogs until they either snapped him up in their powerful jaws or left the scene for the safety of home.

And then he heard a different sound that sent chills up and down his twisted spine. A wolf growled from the edge of the clearing. Firelight gleamed from its long, wet fangs and turned his eyes red. *Blaidd*, the leader of all wolf packs, guardian of all those he considered part of his pack, elusive friend to Little John, the Green Man.

And enemy of those who threatened the Wild Folk.

Tuck drew up the hood of his simple tunic to hide his face and melted into the woodland with the instinctive stealth of his deer ancestors. He needed to bound away from the threats of the strange men and their fire.

The hunting dogs milled about. Trained to find prey, not take it down, they'd done their job and didn't know what to do now without direction.

As a man who had lived as a man and not a deer for all of his sixty-three years, he knew that movement and noise would attract attention from the men as well as the dogs. And his ancient limbs would no longer respond to his wishes with the strength and agility of his youth.

So he remained hidden, watching in horror as the Wood-wose and Wild Folk alike fled.

Inch by careful inch, he retreated, feeling his way with his feet while he kept his gaze on the sheriff's men. He forced himself not to look at smoldering thatch and blazing lean-tos. They could be rebuilt. The lives of his people could not.

Blaidd and his pack of ten ordinary wolves leaped as one, each taking down a single soldier. An arrow zinged through the darkness, catching the lead soldier in the gut. The flint arrowhead easily pierced the chain mail. The sergeant-at-arms clutched at the wound, mouth gaping and closing in pain. Wounded, but not mortally so. Robin must not have put all of his strength in pulling the bowstring.

Another arrow came from a different direction. Robin was on the move and less likely to be found. The last man standing collapsed, his thigh bleeding copiously around the shaft of yew that pierced him through.

Tuck dared breathe again. His feet bumped up against the flat rock he used as an altar, and his fingers found his prayer beads tucked inside his shirt. He'd instinctively sought his own sacred place for safety.

But then the hunting dogs rallied and harried the heels of the retreating Woodwose.

"Dogs, down," Robin commanded from somewhere closer to the road.

The animals obeyed their careful training and slunk back to their masters.

The wolves froze with their jaws surrounding some portion of their prey, but not penetrating vulnerable skin and veins.

Tuck eased back toward the central clearing, still clasping his prayer beads.

Blaidd shifted to his human form—something he rarely did—keeping a thick beard and shock of mottled gray-and-white hair on his head. He wore a leather shirt and kilt, token acknowledgment of societal norms.

"Cease," he barked to both wolf and dog.

Recognizing their true master, they all released their victims and slunk back to their respective sides of the central hearth.

"Thank you, Blaidd," Tuck said, bowing to the wolf lord, but keeping to the shadows so the raiders could not recognize him.

"You can stay here no longer," Blaidd said. "We will escort the intruders to the road." He bowed to Tuck and went to stand over the sergeant-at-arms. "Your wound is not dire. You may retreat in safety. Do not come this way again."

Then he dropped back into his lupine form and gathered his pack around him, a formidable barrier between the sheriff's men and the Woodwose.

"You trespass in the king's forest!" the sergeant hissed through clenched teeth.

"Tell your sheriff, and thus the king, that we do not accept his enforestation of our lands," Tuck replied. "These were long our home before *your* mortal kings decided to reserve this land for their own hunting pleasure. We do not accept royal authority here. There will be war soon. And an end to tyranny." His voice echoed and resounded with the finality of prophecy.

Then Tuck faded into the darkness, uncertain where his words came from and how they affected him and his people from now on. The weight of portent near suffocated Tuck; it felt as if each step was as heavy as if he dragged a millstone behind him.

Twenty-Six

omething is different about my dreams. The darkness fades; gray seeps into my chamber. I sense the coming of dawn. A dawn. How many have passed while I slept?

I rub the crystal again, seeking comfort. Much of the raw rock surrounding the clear bits has gone away. I have rubbed the stone so often it is nearly free of its natural covering.

The end of this long sleep and my dreams is coming. But I cannot wake yet. My eyelids are too heavy, and my heart beats too slowly. My Robin must come for me soon. I will not survive if he does not come before all the darkness is gone and I have only a deep, gray fog to swim through.

What is this terrible weight that keeps me in place and my mind drifting in and out of unnatural sleep?

I rub the crystal again and again, and still this new restlessness picks at me and pricks my mind.

There is something I must do. What?

Derwyn wiggled his rootlets, trying to extend them past the edges of his meadow. He'd lost his connections to all of Sherwood. But his brother Verne needed a full year to claim authority over all of the lands. Derwyn had only been working on this small piece of Sherwood for a full day and night.

"I know you're in there, Derwyn of Sherwood. Come out and talk to me like a man," Sir Philip Marc sneered.

Derwyn looked down, startled. His farthest branches retreated and threatened to become fingers.

He forced himself to stay a tree and ignore the Sheriff of Nottingham.

"You can't hide from me forever." Sir Philip stabbed his dagger into Derwyn's bark.

He barely felt the wound. Still, he rushed some sap to the split that barely penetrated to his outer wood. Much deeper and the iron in the blade would have permanently damaged him.

The sap worked and pushed the metal tip of the dagger outward.

Sir Philip yanked it free and stared at his fine weapon with its jeweled hilt and decorated scabbard.

"My raid on the Woodwose failed last night," Sir Philip said, grinding out each word between his clenched teeth.

"The spawn of Satan called upon a werewolf to chase off my men. Their bite wounds suppurate and burn. I'll have to pay a priest to exorcize the demons left behind."

Everyone knew that Sir Philip rarely paid for anything. Money flowed to him and stayed there. Even the king rarely received his share of taxes. He had to win them from his sheriff in games of chance.

"Why didn't you tell me that such evil entities existed?" He screamed at Derwyn. "My dogs slunk away from it. *My* dogs! The fiercest in the realm. If we'd known, my men could have armed themselves with crucifixes and holy water! I'd have hung crosses on the dogs' collars."

Derwyn chose not to enlighten the man. If Blaidd had chosen to show himself, then he must have felt threatened as well. The spirit of all wolves, who could walk as a man when he chose, preferred to remain in the shadow.

Carefully, Derwyn allowed his face to emerge from the trunk of his tree, keeping bark and moss close, as much for protection as intimidation.

"The Woodwose have a priest. He protected them. You'll not dislodge them while the holy man declares Sherwood Forest sacred. You must bring down the triad of standing stones and desecrate the graves within their circle before you can diminish the priest's authority."

Sir Philip blanched.

So, even he would not go so far as to desecrate graves.

Then Derwyn withdrew from the world again to concentrate on usurping the acres that had once belonged to the Earl of Locksley and keep his brother out. The time was coming when Robin the Archer must reclaim his title and his lands, removing them from Sherwood. Verne's authority as the Green Man would not reach here. Robin would have to respect Derwyn as his Green Man and no other.

"You have not seen the last of me, wooden man. I will free Sherwood of the pestilence of Woodwose and Wild Folk alike. And that includes you!" Sir Philip Marc returned to his restive horse, then directed his men to come forth with kindling and dried branches. He watched impatiently as they built a ring around Derwyn's feet.

The silent men retreated and brought out bows and arrows, the tips wrapped in tallow-soaked rags. A sergeant set up a smudge pot, a small iron cauldron containing a glowing ember. He brought it to flaming life with a bit of dried moss and twigs.

"You have a choice, Derwyn of Sherwood. You can help me rid the forest of trespassers and poachers and those who aid them, or you can burn."

Nick gathered up wooden spoons, a few pottery bowls, and three iron pots for cooking, stacking them neatly atop his ripped monk's robe, then tied them all into a neat bundle for easier carrying.

"That looks like the last of it," he said with a weary sigh.

He looked around the once vibrant camp of the displaced who had no other home.

"Hard to imagine living away from Ardenia's pond. She has

been a good friend to us," Tuck said, coming up behind Nick.
He had his own bundle of personal items. All in all, none of them
had much to carry: a few weapons and tools, perhaps a change
of personal linen, the big cauldron. All else was unnecessary for
survival in the wild. Shelters would be built elsewhere.

Next time, they'd spread out more, be less visible to outsiders, become scattered and less of a community.

"I don't want to leave my home," Jane wailed. She clutched
her baby close while clinging to the doorjamb formed of stout
oak branches bent and twined together.

"We have to, sweetheart," Little John said with great patience. "You heard Blaidd. The sheriff knows this place now.
He'll come again and again until he can capture or kill all of us."

Nick grieved with them. Other than the abbey, this was the
only home he knew. He felt more welcome and useful here
than the abbey. Until the interdict was lifted by Pope Innocent
III, the abbey had no real purpose.

After kissing Hilde last night, he'd begun to question his
need to return to the abbey ever. He wanted . . .

He wasn't certain what he truly wanted out of life anymore. Life in the abbey seemed a waste of talent and energy.
Life among the Woodwose and the Wild Folk filled him with
a sense of purpose and stirred his mind to find new and cre-
ative ways to protect these people.

Hilde.

She shouldered her own burden bundle as she directed
people to finish packing and start their journey to the new
home Robin and Will had found for them, a league westward
and farther from the Royal Road.

Hilde was the center of this community, and he needed to be with her, protect her, and love her.

Nick took a stand beside her left shoulder, determined to walk beside her the entire distance of this journey.

Derwyn thought as fast as his sap would allow. He felt as slow and sluggish as he would from first awakening from a long winter's sleep.

In this state, he could see no good outcome from remaining in his tree.

But he'd just reclaimed his heritage!

Now he knew his father's and his brother's weaknesses. The Locksley demesne was not meant to be part of Sherwood. As long as he stayed at this end of the enforested lands, he could be who and what he was meant to be.

Slowly, he shed his bark and shrank back to his human size, a full head taller than Sir Phillip, and he was reckoned a tall man.

Standing in the center of the fire ring in only his shirt, he captured Sir Philip's gaze with his own. "My ability to help you is limited."

Casually, as if he did it every day, he stepped over the pile of flammable brush. Then, in utter contempt, he lifted his shirt and peed into the smudge pot, drowning the fire. He often had to void when he first emerged from his tree, and had accumulated quite a lot.

The man-at-arms in charge of the fire jumped back from

his crouch, and fell on his backside. He spluttered and spat in disgust.

Other men stepped away and lowered their bows. The iron tips of their arrows would still hurt a man, but they no longer carried the extreme danger of fire.

"The Woodwose have moved their camp. They are stupid and did not leave the forest, just moved. They are still trespassers and poachers. You must find them for me." Sir Philip spat the words as if they tasted bad. His English was bad and his French accent so thick Derwyn was almost unable to understand him.

But he knew what the man wanted. He wanted to clear the forest before King John came to King's Clipston on the forest border, his hunting lodge that rivaled a palace in size and luxury. His Royal Highness would not deign to stay at Nottingham Castle unless he felt threatened and needed its fortifications.

Derwyn didn't like the castle either.

"If the Green Man chooses to hide his friends, I can do nothing." Derwyn decided that should be enough of an explanation. All he wanted was to find a new place to plant and replenish himself, someplace less exposed than the middle of a meadow meant for livestock grazing with no other trees about.

"You said, the new Green Man has only been in charge for half a year. He needs another two seasons . . ."

"The half-year mark has passed with the equinox. His magic grows by leaps and bounds every day." Derwyn had felt his brother pushing his awareness into the Locksley lands, the newest added to the forest, and farthest from the sacred standing stones. Derwyn had had a hard time making his roots appear just like any other tree and thus hide from his brother.

"You have to do it. You owe me!" the sheriff screamed.

His men eased farther away from him, obviously uncomfortable taking orders from a man who bordered on madness.

"I will do what I can. But I promise nothing." Derwyn stalked with league-eating strides northward, toward the mound where the charcoal burner had built his kiln. Even Sir Philip Marc would not trespass there for fear of disrupting the vital work of producing charcoal to heat his cold and dreary castle, satisfy the king, and sell at great profit to ordinary people for more than they could afford.

Hilde surveyed the new clearing Will and Robin had found for the Woodwose. A spring burbled from a rock formation to give them fresh water. There was an opening in the tree canopy for smoke. Little John and Llwyf already carried stones to mark the cooking hearth. Jane wandered with her baby among slender trees searching for a perfect spot for a new house.

"Not enough cover," old Catryn said, spitting from her nearly toothless gums upon the new fire ring, for luck and to mark it as her own.

"We're farther from the road than before, and closer to the sacred circle," Nick said. He had dropped Hilde's hand some distance back as they negotiated the narrow trail Herne led them along. Now he dropped his small bundle close to the cooking fire since most of what he carried was utensils.

"Not there," Hilde reprimanded him. "We need to keep the area clear until we finish."

"We need like items close to each other for more efficient use."

"Not if it means stepping on them and *breaking* them." She placed her hands on her hips and glared at him, not certain why she was suddenly angry at him. Anxiety gnawed at her while her belly felt bloated and clenched at the same time.

"Fine, then. I'll keep them with me while I put together a lean-to for Father Tuck and one close by for myself." He picked up his bundle and stalked off, quickly disappearing in the direction Tuck had taken to find his own place.

"We aren't finished yet, Nicholas!"

"Yes, we are!"

She turned her back on him only to find Will beside her with a good-sized stone in his hands. "Where do you want this?" he asked with a musical chirp at the end of his question.

Twenty-Seven

obin clutched his middle with crossed arms and bent double over them. The normal aches and pains of this body became intense, a fire in his joints and his gut.

He had kept his gnome form all evening so that when the time came for the hard work of finding Marian's bower, he could retain his tall body as long as possible.

The pain grabbed him again, and he groaned. But it did not begin within him. The magic of the land told him that. He doubted his tall form would notice. This dynamic ripping through his entire body came from somewhere else. Some-*one* else.

"Something is changing around Marian's bower. We have to free her now!" Robin demanded of Little John, even as he groaned again.

And then it was gone, as if he'd only dreamed of demons gnawing on him.

"We just moved and haven't settled in yet. I need to build

a new shelter for Jane and the babe," Little John protested. He tested the bend and resilience of a stand of reeds near the pool and stream that formed below the spring. "These should do nicely as a framework."

"Time is running out, John. I can *feel* the magic leaking away from her. The spell that keeps her asleep, unknowing, unaging, is fading. She and I endure the ravages of the decades creeping up on us."

"Don't you need to remember the spell precisely so you can recite it backward to break it?" Alain asked. He brought another armload of reeds for John to test.

"Then work your magic on me so that I *can* remember. Now. Tomorrow is the full moon. The night the mage entombed Marian and cursed me was the dark of the moon. We have to go to Locksley now so that all will be in place tomorrow when the moon rises." Robin paced impatiently around and around the cookfire that Catryn already had burning and a pot of stew coming to a simmer.

"You men going to find me some wild carrots, or do the women have to do everything?" the old woman said as she fished through her pack for her favorite knife, the perfect size for paring and slicing wild vegetables. "I've a hankering for sunflower seeds with the rabbit," she muttered.

"It's the wrong season for sunflowers!" all three men shouted back at her.

Hilde rushed in with a kind word and gentle hand for Catryn before the old woman could figure out what her deaf ears almost heard.

"Fine. The moon sets late tomorrow night," John said, peering upward through the tree canopy to check the phases of sun and moon and stars. "We leave at dawn with ropes and torches. You, me, and Will."

"I attend," Blaidd said. He dropped a brace of rabbits at Catryn's feet.

"Verne . . ."

"Past needing constant guard. You embark on path of fools. But necessary." Blaidd faded into the forest, his mottled gray fur soon disappearing from view.

"That is the most I've heard him say in conversation in decades," Robin gasped.

"Then it needs saying," John replied.

"You aren't going without me!" Nick and Hilde said together. They looked at each other in surprise, then smiled and ducked their heads.

"Marian may be disoriented and will need a woman when she wakes," Hilde said. "I need to be there."

"I've been in the mound before and know the beginning of the path," Nick added. "You can't leave me behind."

"And is Elena willing to abide with your plan?" John asked.

Robin peered into the underbrush for Tuck. He was the one who should have asked about the goddess of crossroads, cemeteries, and sorcery. If he needed help from anyone on this most important journey of his life, it would come from her.

"Elena sleeps," Nick said sadly. "I do not know when . . . or if . . . she will awaken to my thoughts again."

This mission is doomed, Robin thought.

"I have to try," he said firmly. "I cannot live with myself if I do not try my best to free Marian from her artificial tomb."

"We are with you." Little John rested a firm hand on Robin's shoulder. A friend when he needed one most.

"I do not like this," Tuck said, adjusting the knot of the rope made from twisted vines around his waist. They'd gathered and twisted the long plant fibers, then braided them into a single length to bind them all together. Hilde had tied it too tightly. He couldn't breathe properly. His heart raced with trepidation, and . . . and his feet hurt after the long trek to Locksley.

Hilde "humphed" and pulled on her own knot, then moved on to Little John, the last in line for this expedition.

"We agreed," Robin said. He stood tall, the quiver and bow resting firmly on his shoulder. "We stay roped together. No one goes off exploring on his own."

They all glared at Nick who shuffled anxiously at the head of the line.

Will fluttered down before the vague suggestion of an entrance into the mound and shifted to his full height before speaking. "The air is still bad by the castle. The lone tree in the south meadow has moved. I do not know where. The charcoal burner tends his kiln. I do not think he pays attention to us."

"How much of my woods has he felled?" Robin growled angrily.

"Only new growth from the ditch." Will took up the last of the long line of rope and tied it about his own waist with a loose slip knot that he could undo himself if needed.

"Tighter," Hilde insisted, taking hold of the loose end.

Will placed his hand over hers and shook his head. "If anyone needs to retreat quickly and summon help, it is I." He held Hilde's glance a moment too long.

Nick growled and looked away.

No wonder Nick and Will vied for her attentions, and her temper grew shorter and sharper. In the past few weeks, she'd become a woman. Ripe and nearly ready to mate.

Tuck merely raised his eyebrows, curious at how this affair would end. He wanted happiness for Nick, his great-grandson. On the other hand, he needed the boy's clerical skills to help in the coming political crises that could not be too far in the future.

"Let's go!" Nick proclaimed. He stuck his torch into the smudge pot to light it, then pushed aside the hanging turf and vines to squeeze through the narrow opening.

One by one, they followed him. Robin and Little John having the most trouble getting their broad chests between the lines of rocks. Tuck had no problem, nor did Hilde with her small but blossoming breasts.

The wolf pack that had shadowed them the entire morning remained scattered about, observing silently from sheltering shadows.

No time to think on the consequences. Nick had to hold his torch high to join with the others and see what awaited them in the chamber of the ancients.

"I do not like the air in here," Will echoed his own thoughts.

"'Tis magic that taints it, not poison. Old magic that took

its form within a rotten soul." Tuck crossed himself and fingered his prayer beads, murmuring prayers of protection.

Derwyn found a sheltered place on the west side of the mound.

Above him, on top of the mound, the charcoal burner hummed to himself, an old ditty about a barmaid leading a trail of young men through the greenwood.

He had a surprisingly charming voice.

Derwyn lulled himself into contentment as he dug his toes into the soft loam and stretched his arms out on either side.

The change did not come easily. He was closer to Sherwood proper where his father's and brother's authority still held firm. But this place should be as open to him as he'd found in the meadow.

He wasn't as desperate this time. Out in the meadow he'd replenished much of what he lacked in food and water and . . . peace of mind.

He tried again, seeing in his mind how tall his tree grew, how full his branches, and how deep his roots.

A void in the hill behind him made it easier for his roots to explore the space. He let them roam free as he reached up and welcomed the sun.

Nick lifted his torch high for a better view of the carvings on the walls. He had to keep moving forward to make room for the others. With all the extra bodies, and the better light, the chamber did not feel as vast as it did when he was alone, with only Elena's tiny light.

He touched the pouch through his shirt to see if she was still there. A bit of warmth brushed his skin above his heart. A smile spread through him from his toes upward. The little goddess was still alive, just not ready to come forth yet.

"What is all this?" Tuck whispered as he ran a fingertip around one of the spirals.

"Magic nonsense," Robin replied, shivering and keeping away from the walls.

"Very old magic, but clean," Little John announced. He was the next to last to enter.

Nick suddenly had trouble breathing, like all the extra people sucked the air out of the chamber.

"How can any magic be clean when it has been touched by the mage who cursed me?" Robin complained. In the flickering torchlight his form began to waver and fade. His gnomish, elongated chin and nose drifted above his normal face.

Was it the curse, or just time for him to shift?

"We need to move forward," Hilde reminded them. She looked around her, eyes wide.

Nick couldn't tell if her face was paler than normal. He felt pale and uncertain.

"This cavern is not natural," Will said. He looked up and all around, stretching his arms out wide to gather the full dimensions into his awareness. "Built by men to revere their dead while keeping them separate from life."

"This place is little different from the crypt where you

found Elena," Tuck said, prodding Nick forward with his free hand.

Nick took a deep breath and turned to walk around the room widdershins, as he had before. Elena seemed to warm a bit at his decision. His next step became more confident.

Robin's teeth began to chatter as they approached the void.

"Any ghosts that were here have faded into nothingness," Nick said, feeling the words in the back of his mind, the place where Elena spoke to him. But only a sensation of the proper words to say rather than a true prompt from her.

He could see the next corridor fully this time with six torches lighting the way. The frame of stacked stones took shape before his eyes, followed by a stretch of walls made from the big stone slabs like in the outer chamber. These, too, were carved with spirals, wiggling lines, and strange symbols. He needed to linger and decipher them, as he would a manuscript in an ancient language.

Tuck's bony finger poking him in the middle of his back kept him moving.

"I need to examine this place in detail. I need to puzzle out what the carvings mean."

"Later. We have an innocent victim of magic to rescue," Hilde said firmly. But she peered closely at the marks on the walls and touched the spirals with questing fingers.

Nick moved forward, feeling the tug of the rope around his waist. Not all of them were as eager to explore as he.

The corridor sloped downward, gradually at first; then as the strain on his knees increased, he looked back to see Little John above him, not just taller but higher.

"Steps would be easier," Tuck muttered.

Nick looked toward the sides of the path, a dip about three fingers wide to channel water. They fell in regular steps. But the main path remained smooth, beaten earth, no gravel. He shortened his steps and kept plodding forward, fingers trailing along the now featureless wall. He let his imagination draw faces in the spirals and waves and symbols, as he would when illuminating a manuscript back in the scriptorium of the abbey.

The pouch resting above his heart thumped once, hard enough to bring Nick's thoughts back to the task at hand.

A dark shadow crossed the passage. He stopped abruptly. Tuck had been moving slowly enough that he had no problem fetching up before he smashed into Nick's back.

The path stopped. Ahead lay a pit wider than the length of three men. Nick leaned over, thrusting his torch forward.

"I can't see the bottom," he said.

Twenty-Eight

ilde crowded forward, standing beside Nick and leaning over the blackness. Will pulled her back to keep her from plunging over the edge. He clamped his fists around her rope and stood firm.

His fingers had begun to form claws in his attempts to get a firmer grip on the twisted vines.

She looked from him to the far side of the gap, just visible as a paler shadow amongst a myriad of darker places in the uncertain light.

"I reckon we are beneath the ditch at the base of the castle hill," Robin muttered. He kept an eye on the ceiling.

Tuck buried his chin in his chest and fingered his prayer beads. Hilde caught an occasional word in Latin. Something about the abyss of their sins. She'd only spent a year in the convent and knew the Mass in Latin but not much else.

Will pulled harder on her robe, forcing her to back up two

steps. His cap had become a crest and a few feathers had sprouted from his arms and neck.

"Can you change here underground, Will?" she asked quietly.

"What are you thinking?" Little John asked. He leaned backward, a firm anchor for all of them roped together.

"If he can fly to the far side, he can take an end of the rope across and we can hold on to it to get across."

All the men stopped and thought about that. Only Tuck looked back the way they'd come with longing.

"I don't think we can go back," Robin said. "The slope looks too steep to climb, with no handholds. I think the builders intended this to be a one-way passage. The exit is up, in what became the castle cellars." He began pacing the width of the corridor, three long steps in each direction, barely enough room for two to stand side by side.

"We have plenty of rope," Little John said. "We spent the better part of the walk to Locksley twining pliable vines together and braiding them. Should be sturdy enough." He began unwinding the extra length from around his middle.

"I think I can do it. I'll take the end to the other side and find a place to brace myself. Then . . . Nick should follow me. His weight and strength combined with mine should be enough to get the rest of you across. Only one at a time."

"Let me give you some extra light over there," Robin said. He brought his right arm back, as if pulling a longbow and hurled his torch straight and true. It landed on the far ledge with a plop, nearly dowsing itself as it rolled. They all held their breath in dismay. And then the flame reasserted itself.

Will handed his torch to Robin, took three deep breaths,

spread his arms, and became a big red bird. He hopped backward, then took three running steps forward to gather enough
air beneath his wings to fly the short distance across. His tal-
ons gripped the stony pathway on the other side, and he strut-
ted until he dropped the vine from his beak and stepped on it
to keep it from falling back into the pit. A cock of his head
and he began preening his chest feathers.

"Oh, come now, Will. You can do that later," Hilde cried.

He turned a dark eye on her and continued to pull dust
and mites from his feathers.

At last, without warning he stretched his neck and once
more became a man. He flashed Hilde a glance to prove how
proud he was of himself for completing his task before grabbing
the end of the rope and tying it around his waist. Then he sat
and braced his feet against the wall of the continuing corridor
before beckoning Nick to follow him, hand over hand on the
rope across the gaping darkness.

"Me next," Robin said. He threw both Will's and Nick's
torches across. Nick scrambled to set them within the corridor
and out of the way, but still provide enough light to help them
cross the pit in safety.

By the time the archer settled his feet again, his arms were
shaking.

"What's wrong?" Hilde asked.

Robin shook his head and braced his own feet while holding the rope. "I've been tall too long. But I can hold out a bit
longer. Tuck next."

"I can't do it," the old man whispered. "I'm too old. This
place is too alien and the magic tainted. . . ."

"Do you want me to throw you across?" Little John replied. He sounded more amused than angry.

Hilde lost patience. She wanted to be back in daylight as much as any of them. But they had committed to finding Marian and freeing her from her curse.

"Please, sir," Nick pleaded. "We will need you at the end of this quest to help banish the rotten magic. Now, keep your end of the rope tied tightly. We can haul you up if you fall."

"And I'll break my nose against yon cliff, when I do."

"Not 'when' you fall," Hilde reassured him. "If you do. Now put your beads away so you have both hands to hold the rope. Then use your faith in us and in God to keep you strong if you falter."

Muttering something in Latin that Hilde could neither fully hear or interpret, Tuck obeyed. She made certain the knots at his waist were firm, then added her own slight weight to John's to keep the rope taut.

With a deep breath, Tuck stepped off the edge and began the long trek across. He had to pause in the middle as his arms shook and his hands slipped.

Hilde held her breath until he started moving again. Her chest felt ready to burst by the time Nick pulled his mentor to safety.

"Now you, little one," John prodded. He checked the firmness of her rope. "You'll do fine, my girl. Just remember that we all need you with your common sense and strength of will to finish this adventure safe and sound."

Holding the slight praise firmly in her heart, she followed the others across. The chain of prayers she remembered that followed her beads, came quickly to her lips as she made her way. Grab with her right hand, release the left and swing it ahead. Grab, release, grab.

And then Nick had her in his arms while they both laughed in relief. He kissed her cheek and passed her on to Tuck's custody a few steps into the corridor.

"It's going to take all of our strength and weight to bring John across," Robin said.

Hilde grabbed a length of vine, noticing how some of the strands had begun to fray.

John must have caught some of her trepidation. "I've still got enough of my tree to dig some roots and stretch." From one breath to the next, he grew taller and launched himself forward in a mighty leap.

His fingers scrabbled at the lip of the ledge. He lost touch and . . .

The men hauled furiously to pull him up before he fell more than a head length. By the time he cleared the ledge, he was back to his normal height.

"We're safe," Hilde said on a sigh.

"For now." Robin shrank shakily into his gnome form. "Marian will not recognize me now and remember me as her one true love. We'll both crumble to dust in moments."

Robin, in his short and twisted gnome body followed Nick doggedly. The path curved back on itself as it climbed. His elongated nose picked up traces of the men and women who had walked this track before. A long, long time ago.

And was that a faint whiff of violets? Marian had often crushed the petals of those shy little flowers and blended them with her soap.

Mostly, he smelled death, decay, body odor, and ghosts. Lots and lots of ghosts. But they had no interest in the living, only in returning again and again to this place of ritual to finish something they'd left undone. A cobweb brushed his face, catching on his chin. But when he batted it away, nothing was there, only that vague trace of violets. No spider ought to be in this gods-forsaken place to spin a trap for the unwary.

Who but fools such as he and his friends would dare venture into this place?

He hastened his steps.

Tiny roots had crept between the stone slabs on the walls and begun to break through the beaten earth passage. They must have climbed above the level of the ditch back into the mound itself.

Ahead of him, Nick had to duck beneath a lowering ceiling. Even Will's cap came perilously close to being knocked off. Little John had to bend double. Tuck and Hilde, and himself of course, had no problem.

Robin stubbed his toe as his big, hairy feet scuffled along. They'd reached more steps. Three of them dropped downward into . . . a chamber that opened beyond the ability of their torches to reach. A narrow path continued upward but narrowed to a mere crack only a few ells forward.

They took the steps to the vast chamber—probably directly above the entrance room. In the center of this room, on a slight dais, rested a bier. Atop it lay a beautiful maiden, her thick blonde braids reaching her waist, hands neatly folded across her flat belly. Between her fingers winked a polished crystal. Her eyes were closed in perpetual, dreamless sleep.

But a frown tugged her mouth down, and a crease marred her brow above her nose.

She looked like she was in pain.

The scent of fresh violets dominated the room, yet all the flowers surrounding her body were dry and desiccated.

He needed to rush forward and embrace her, wake her with a lover's kiss . . .

But it wouldn't be her first kiss. He'd exchanged a passionate and lingering farewell with her nigh on sixty years ago. She'd only aged a little, perhaps ten years, the time between that achingly poignant goodbye and the time of the mage's curse.

"This is too easy," he said.

"You do not belong here!" the charcoal burner screamed as he raised his ax.

Derwyn opened one eye and blinked rapidly to banish sleep.

The comfort of bark and twigs and leaves held him in place. He knew he was in danger, yet he could not move.

The iron ax blade bit deeply into his trunk, penetrating his skin and burning with pain that shot from his roots to his top branches.

He found the will to open a space in his bark for his mouth to scream in pain and outrage.

His bark fell away quickly then, his branches shrank back into himself, and his hands grew free. By instinct alone, he grabbed the handle of the weapon and pushed upward.

The hunchback refused to let go, even as his arms reached painfully backward above his head. He howled in pain.

Something snapped, like an elder tree losing a dead branch in a windstorm.

Derwyn continued to push with human arms, while his feet remained firmly rooted in the turf of the mound.

He bared his teeth in feral glee at his attacker's disablement.

And then he felt the gush of blood from his thigh. Not the soothing ooze of sap rushing to heal a gash.

No. This was his lifeblood, spurting forth and spraying them both.

The thick scent of melting copper filled his senses as strength drained from him.

He had to release the charcoal burner to clutch at his wound.

He toppled, feet scrabbling for balance that wasn't there.

The ground shook as his body hit, pulling a big chunk of the mound with him where his roots would not let go.

"What is this?" Nick gasped. The others plowed into him at his abrupt stopping three paces into the chamber.

All around the space—twice the size of the entry room—ledges overflowed with treasure: silver plate, golden goblets, finely jeweled weapons. Bronze tableware, liturgical vessels, and ornaments dominated the hoard.

The torchlight turned it all into a winking and glowing spectacle. The tiny crystal beneath Marian's hands paled in comparison.

He hardly noticed the precious human at the center caught between death and life by a magic spell.

"No wonder this entire region smells of rotten magic," Will said, wrinkling his nose.

Tuck crossed himself and dug out his prayer beads once again.

The sickly-sweet scent of decaying violets lessened.

Nick retrieved his own beads and began reciting the ritual prayers.

"What is the spell?" Hilde asked, nudging Robin forward, toward the bier.

"It's useless. I cannot become a man again so close to the center of the curse." He knelt at Marian's feet and dropped his head to his chest. A tear leaked from his already rheumy eyes.

The earth groaned in agony.

A bit of dirt dropped on his head from a crack between two stone slabs in the ceiling.

Nick's gaze went immediately to the walls, to see if this place had been decorated in the same style as the entry. He stared, gaping in awe at the richness of the symbols carved so close together, mixed with paintings of strange beasts, still brightly colored. His fingers itched to trace them all, record them, incorporate those spirals and snakes and arcane symbols into an illuminated manuscript. He saw here the connections of past and present, of how one belief system blended, grew, and changed into another. His ancient ancestors may have been pagan, but they were a part of the universe God had created. Their gods were now saints. Their prayers fit neatly into his beads. . . .

A deep thud outside set the chamber wall to rippling.

More dirt dribbled down, near choking him. "We have to hurry!"

"Marian has to recognize me as her true love upon awakening, or our curses become permanent and we both die," Robin whispered.

"What is the spell?" Hilde rushed forward and grabbed a bronze mirror that was still shining. Nick had barely noticed it among the rest of the treasures—the accumulation of a noble family over a thousand years.

"I . . . I can't remember the spell now. My mind is crumbling as surely as my body will."

A hard thud pounded against Nick's chest almost as loudly as the noise of collapse surrounding the chamber.

Then he realized that something else demanded his attention beyond the demise of the mound.

"Elena?" He drew forth the leather pouch and opened the drawstring.

"About time," Little John muttered. He stood with his back against the rippling wall, feet braced.

The trickle of dirt paused.

Silence rang in Nick's mind.

He studied the angle of the stones and the curve of the chamber for only a moment. He knew that if John stepped away for even a heartbeat, the entire mound would collapse killing them all.

He dashed to join the big man and do his slight bit to hold back the forces of nature.

Will and Tuck joined them, bracing themselves against the shifting floor.

A column of bright mist flowed out of his pouch. It spread across the room hovering over the supine figure on the bier and the ugly gnome at her feet. Slowly—oh, so slowly—the mist coalesced into the figure of a woman with graceful draperies drifting in a celestial wind that Nick could not feel.

"Elena," he whispered.

She turned to him and nodded briefly, then she placed ethereal hands upon Robin's head. She was the goddess of sorcery as well as crossroads and cemeteries. She should be right at home here.

He opened his mouth and emitted strange words that were neither Greek, nor Latin, but something harder, more bitter, and angrier.

The figure on the bier stirred. But it was only a contracting of muscles as if in great anguish.

"No!" Robin howled.

The crack in the ceiling opened wider. More dirt and small stones cascaded down on them.

Nick pressed his back harder against the wall, as did the other men.

"Now backward," Hilde coached. "You have to say the

words backward." With that pronouncement, she held up the bronze platter so that it held Robin's reflection angled so that when Marian woke, she would gaze first upon the mirror.

Elena placed her hands upon Robin's head again. Her mouth worked as if speaking, but Nick could hear no words.

Robin spoke again. Tears leaked from his eyes and he folded his hands before him, locked in a desperate prayer.

But the words . . . the words this time sounded right way around. Arabic perhaps. Something older than Nick's scant knowledge of the manuscripts protected by the abbey.

Tuck spoke his own prayers, familiar to Nick. He joined his mentor in beseeching justice for these two.

The earth groaned.

Another thudding crash threatened Nick's balance.

"We have to get out of here," John whispered. He looked up.

Nick followed his gaze and noticed a tiny line of sunlight. It stretched lengthwise, drawing a line along the floor toward the bier.

"We have to finish this before the light hits her," Hilde said, still holding the platter in place.

"Amen! *So be it!*" Robin shouted and stood, locking his gaze upon Marian's beautiful face.

She stirred and blinked.

"Look here!" Hilde demanded wiggling the platter so that Marian had to turn her head slightly to obey the commanding voice.

Reflected in the shiny metal was the true face of Robin of Locksley, the archer who protected those who could not protect themselves.

Marian opened her eyes wide and whispered, "Robin, my love."

The gnome grew tall, his nose and chin receded, his hair grew back, thick and dark auburn. But his eyes remained the same, warm and loving and fixed upon the face of the one he'd worked so hard to find.

The crack in the ceiling widened, dumping soil and turf and rocks down on their heads.

Twenty-Nine

uck put away his prayer beads and sought a way out of the cavern. Will took Hilde out into the passageway where more cracks in the mound appeared. He dropped her hand only long enough to pry away a thick slab of turf and pull her through.

Two less he had to worry about.

Little John hoisted Marian over his broad shoulder and followed them, Robin holding up her trailing veil and hem so that John did not trip over the fine gown.

More and more dirt and turf and twisted branches crashed around them, deafening and confusing.

That left Nick.

Falling debris brought a cloud of dirt and shafts of blinding sunlight. Tuck shielded his eyes to peer through the mess.

Something moved over against the wall. Nick ignored the

treasure on the ledge in favor of a slab of carved stone. He tried to lift the massive piece of the chamber interior.

"Leave it!" Tuck grabbed the boy's doublet and tried to drag him out in the wake of the others. He doubted his words could be heard over the din inside the chamber.

"We have to study this. It tells of tales and cultures from our past," Nick protested.

And then a wall of rocks and dirt crashed atop them.

Nick blinked his eyes. Sunlight caressed his face. He had trouble remembering where he was and why he could not move.

The last thing he'd heard was a thunderous crash all around him. And dirt getting in his eyes and face, clogging his throat and . . .

Now all was silent. Unnatural. Not even a bird sang in the tree he could just make out at the edge of his vision.

"Nick!" a voice called to him from a long distance away.

"Wh . . . what?" He had to spit out dirt to clear his mouth and nose.

"Easy, boy. Let me clear away some of this debris. Don't try to move just yet." Tuck.

Yes, Tuck. Nick always knew the old man would find a way to take care of him, as he had when Nick was just a toddler and Tuck a wandering priest based at the abbey.

Tuck, a comforting presence at his side, who taught him the wonders of reading old manuscripts written in foreign tongues and guided his hand as he learned to draw wonderous embellishments around capital letters.

Tuck, his great-grandsire, who loved him as no one else could because they were blood family.

He had to get out of this mess and help Tuck move away from the treacherous landscape.

"I think I can move my hand," Nick said trying to wiggle his fingers without much success. Hot, burning, pain sliced upward from his fingertips to his shoulder. He screamed.

And then he felt an emptiness beside him even as the weight of the debris piled on top of him lessened.

A scrabbling sound.

A muffled growl.

In panic, Nick managed to twist his neck just enough to find himself staring into the golden eyes of a wolf.

"Blaidd?"

An affirming grunt and then big paws dug more dirt away from him.

A second and a third wolf joined the guardian of the forest hunters.

"Don't move, boy. We have to make sure you haven't injured your spine," Tuck said, trying to sound soothing and coming across as a studious scholar examining a logic puzzle.

More weight came off Nick's chest. Chills coursed upward as more and more of him was exposed to the early spring air.

Hands brushed at him, then paused.

Tuck sat back on his heels. "Elena?" He stared at the area of Nick's shirt where the leather pouch should be.

"Elena!" Nick tried to sit up, but a long wolf snout pushed him back in place.

Here. The pouch gained substance. *You will be safe now. I must rest.*

The wolves finished clearing Nick from the fallen wall and ceiling. Blaidd nudged Nick's hands and feet until he could move them without pain, just stiffness and, "Oh, ow, Christ on a crutch, that hurts!"

The burning robbed him of breath. Darkness crowded his vision from the sides. He felt backward. The strong and stolid body of a wolf kept him half-upright.

"Looks like you've broken your right arm. I can't fix it here. We need to get you back to the abbey. But how?" Nick rose from his crouch and studied the broken walls and ceiling.

Blaidd released another grunt and pushed Nick to roll to his left side.

He did so, cradling the injured arm close to his chest.

Strong wolf jaws snapped closed on his shirt at his nape. Another beast grabbed his belt and the tops of his hose and lifted. Nick whimpered through the pain of moving his arm. Together, the wolves carried him out of the mound to the open slope where Little John and Will awaited them.

"We'll take him from here," Little John said, lifting Nick up to cradle him like a baby. "Thank you." He bowed slightly to the wolves.

"I . . . I can walk," Nick protested. He tried to straighten his back and legs but met with the resistance of his gigantic friend's hands and arms holding him in place.

"Not yet, my boy. Not until the footing is more stable," Tuck admonished him. As if to emphasize his point, rocks and scree tumbled out from beneath his feet and rolled down and down and down to the base of the mound.

Nick settled until they reached level ground where Little John set him beside a small fire that Robin had built to help warm Marian after her decades of sleep in the cold cavern. She looked confused and worn. Her fingers compulsively rubbed the crystal she had held all through her long coma while her shoulders and thighs trembled.

One of the wolves sauntered up from the long meadow with a dead rabbit in its mouth.

"I'll deal with this, Hilde. You see if you can set Nick's arm," Tuck said. He took his knife from his pack and began butchering the animal, making sure the wolf got his share of the offal. He made quick work of preparing the rabbit for a spit over the fire.

Hilde knelt beside Nick.

His mind brightened.

"Does this hurt?" she asked, touching his forearm delicately.

Fire raced upward, and his fingers grew numb. He lost track of up and down as darkness crowded against his vision.

"You can never do anything halfway, can you, Nick? You've broken it in two places, and the bone is trying to poke through your skin."

"It will heal properly, though, won't it? I'll be able to work in the scriptorium again?"

"Probably. If you don't do anything stupid and try to do too much too soon," Tuck said. "I've been patching up boys for too long. Maybe it's time to retire."

"But . . ."

Hilde gestured to Will who appeared with two long, straight sticks. He measured them against the length of Nick's arm, then broke them to match.

"This is going to hurt," Hilde warned.

"Bite this," Robin said sticking another small branch between his lips.

Nick clamped his teeth together around the wood. He knew what was coming. He'd watched Brother Daffyd set bones too many times in the infirmary. It was never easy or painless. *I wish I had some poppy juice.*

Little John grabbed his feet.

And Hilde yanked his arm straight.

Fiery pain raced upward from his arm to his mind and he knew only blackness except for the halo of light that surrounded Hilde's sweet face.

Robin wrapped Nick's old woolen robe about Marian's shivering shoulders, then eased her head against his chest. She clutched the warm blanket close to her throat. "This is all so confusing."

He added his arm to the blanket for warmth. "For me, too. I'm not sure I know how to live in only one body again." He needed to pace in order to settle in his mind the changes that had taken place mere hours ago. But it felt *right* to hold Marian close.

"I kept this." She held the crystal up to the light. "I dreamed. My mind threatened to fly away to another realm. To be with the angels. But I felt this bit of stone, this gift from you, and I rubbed it. Every time it brought me back to this world because I knew you would rescue me though it would take ten lifetimes."

"Only two." Robin closed his eyes and kissed her temple. He'd been tall for hours and still did not feel the need to shrink. Maybe, just maybe, they had truly broken the curse.

"When I gave you that stone, it was raw rock with just hints of crystal winking through it. I intended to have a jeweler polish it and set it into silver for you."

"I rubbed it a lot during those two lifetimes."

They both chuckled at the shared memory of her rubbing the stone on that bright sunny day of pure joy. She'd rubbed it anxiously on the day he left as a crusading warrior. His promises to return for her had been delayed, not empty. But he felt empty inside as if he'd broken them.

"We need to look to the future now, not regret the past and the lost years," she said. "While I dreamed, I knew that you killed the mage. I knew that time passed, that King Henry died and passed his crown to Richard the Lionhearted. I knew that he added Locksley to the Royal Forest. But I did not know that Richard had died and his brother succeeded him. Will you be able to reclaim your lands and honors?"

"Unknown. I will have to petition King John and find someone to verify that I am descended from the last earl. It depends upon his mood and what favors I can grant him. I have a great deal of money deposited with the Templars that King John can use in his endless wars to regain his lost provinces in France."

"The money you earned to buy back my dowry?"

He nodded. "But I have to convince the Templars that I have a right to that money after sixty years." He looked deep into the forest for answers that did not yet exist. "I do not feel right asking you to marry me when I have nothing to give you, no way to provide for you." He dropped his arm from her shoulders.

"You and your friends have managed to keep body and soul together for a long time. I have no need of castles and servants and fine clothes." She plucked at her flimsy and useless gown that she'd been entombed with—a bridal gown of sorts. "At this moment, I'd give up hope of regaining your titles for a bite of rabbit and a sturdy shift and kirtle."

"The question will be, what does King John need besides money at the time you make your request?" Little John added. He kept frowning and searching the area around their campfire for something. "Sir Philip Marc won't like having another lord in the neighborhood."

Blaidd appeared out of the shadows, another brace of rabbits in his mouth. He nudged Little John with his snout and pawed at his legs.

"What do you need, friend? Have I thanked you enough for saving my young friend Nick and providing us with supper?"

Blaidd replied by digging his muzzle under John's arm, urging him to rise.

"You know this would be easier if you transformed into a man and just told me what you need," John said getting to his feet.

Robin rose, too, not liking the urgency in the wolf's gestures.

Marian shook her head. "Magic I can accept. The Wild Folk are still new to me."

"Get used to them," Hilde said. "The first time I watched John grow into a tree, and Robin become a gnome, let alone Will sprout feathers, I nearly fainted." She nodded toward Will, who perched on a low hanging branch, head tucked beneath his wing.

Blaidd trotted toward the sagging pile of rubble that had been a sacred barrow mound that morning. John and Robin followed, but only after he made sure that Tuck kept Nick from joining them. The boy was just too curious and adventurous for his own good.

"I can no longer see in the dark," Robin whispered to John. "That must mean I am truly a mere mortal man again."

John shrugged, his silhouette barely visible more than a few steps beyond the fire.

Blaidd led them around the base of the mound until Robin felt like he faced due west. At least that part of his fae form hadn't faded entirely yet. He still *felt* the position of the moon and the cardinal directions.

In the last rays of the setting sun, he saw five wolves sitting upright in a half circle around . . . something crumpled on the ground.

Robin crept forward, afraid of what he would find. In all of the excitement he hadn't spared a thought for his friend Liam the charcoal burner. He hadn't even wondered what had happened to the unused kiln and rude shelter that had been on top of the mound until . . . something brought about its collapse.

But now . . . now he caught the glint of dying sunlight on the iron blade of Liam's ax—his most prized possession, indeed his only possession.

Little John stopped short, a large barrier between Robin and the . . . lump. "Ah, no. I never wanted this for you, my son," he sobbed as he fell to his knees.

Robin crept around the big man until only a wolf stood between him and the thing Blaidd had brought them to see.

"This should help." Tuck approached them with a blazing torch. Nick and Hilde and Marian came with him, also bearing fiery brands.

Robin took the light from his friend and peered more closely.

The positions of the bodies told their own story. Liam must have tried to chop down Derwyn, a tree that did not belong in his narrow world of timber to be felled and reduced to charcoal. The ax cut too deeply. Derwyn became a man again, mostly, and bled to death, but not before he broke Liam's back in self-defense. His feet remained roots, buried in the mound, the source of the hill's collapse.

And now the two men lay together in death.

Tuck pulled out his beads and began reciting the litany to accompany their passing. Nick set down his torch and joined him in prayer, having trouble manipulating his beads with only one hand. Hilde helped him.

The pouch slung around Nick's neck glowed as Elena flowed forth, adding her own light to the scene. *Bury them here and mark their graves. They are at peace now, having moved on from the world that had no place for them. Let this barrow be forever a sacred place where you and your descendants may find solace in time of trouble.*

"Amen," Robin said. The others echoed him.

Marian placed a gentle hand on his arm. "We will teach our children to respect others no matter how the rest of the world treats them as outcasts."

"For we are all outcasts in one way or another," Robin echoed.

"We are free to choose our future as few are in these troubled times. I hope that others can learn from us," young Nick said, with head bowed, beads clasped in his hand, and Hilde supporting him. Standing close and yet distanced from him.